The world of boxing. Traditionally a sport for men, Katherine Sinclair wants to become the best at something her adopted father taught her from a very young age.

She grows up in a small town, wanting to branch out and discover new worlds. She marries at eighteen, births twins and discovers she cannot be a good mother or a wife because she feels imprisoned and suffocated in her roles as a woman.

She escapes to Chicago, where she attempts to become a female boxer. What ensues is illness, challenge and, ultimately, confrontation with the kind of woman she should be and the kind she hopes to become.

A Woman's Ring

By Rea Frey

Copyright © 2004 by Rea Frey

All rights reserved. No part of this publication may be reproduced in any form or by any means, electronic or mechanical, including photocopy, recording, or any information storage and retrieval system, without permission, in writing, from the publisher.

All characters are fictional. Any resemblance to persons living or dead is coincidental and quite unintentional.

ISBN 0-9755739-5-0
First Printing 2004
Cover art and design by Anne M. Clarkson
Author's Photo by Uchida Photography

Published by:
Dare 2 Dream Publishing
A Division of Limitless Corporation
Lexington, South Carolina 29073
Find us on the World Wide Web
http://www.limitlessd2d.net

Printed in the United States of America and the UK by

Lightning Source, Inc.

Acknowledgements

  This book could not have been written without Antonia Logue. Her persistence and constant inspiration helped me find not only the story but the drive to finish it. Words cannot express my gratitude. Thanks go to everyone at the Fiction Writing department for your support and allowance for us writers to harness our creativity inside and out of the classroom. Thanks to Tim Lotesto for the hard work in editing the manuscript and the many screaming sessions over commas. My thanks also to everyone at Dare 2 Dream Publishing who took a chance on my work, and provided the loveliest of atmospheres. Most of all, I want to thank my family and husband, without whom I would have no one to share my joy with – my happiness.

  For my mother, Emily, who has guided me along the path of excellence and has been the best friend anyone could ever ask for. For my father, Randy, who taught me the glory of words at such a young age and has nurtured me throughout the years to accept challenges. To my brother, Jereme, who shares the same creative mind and gives unending support, always. And to my husband, Jeff, who has endured many sleepless nights, many frantic episodes and who is always there to give me a hug when I need one. I love you all so deeply. You are the reason I write.

For my parents,
Emily and Randy.
You are the reason I write.

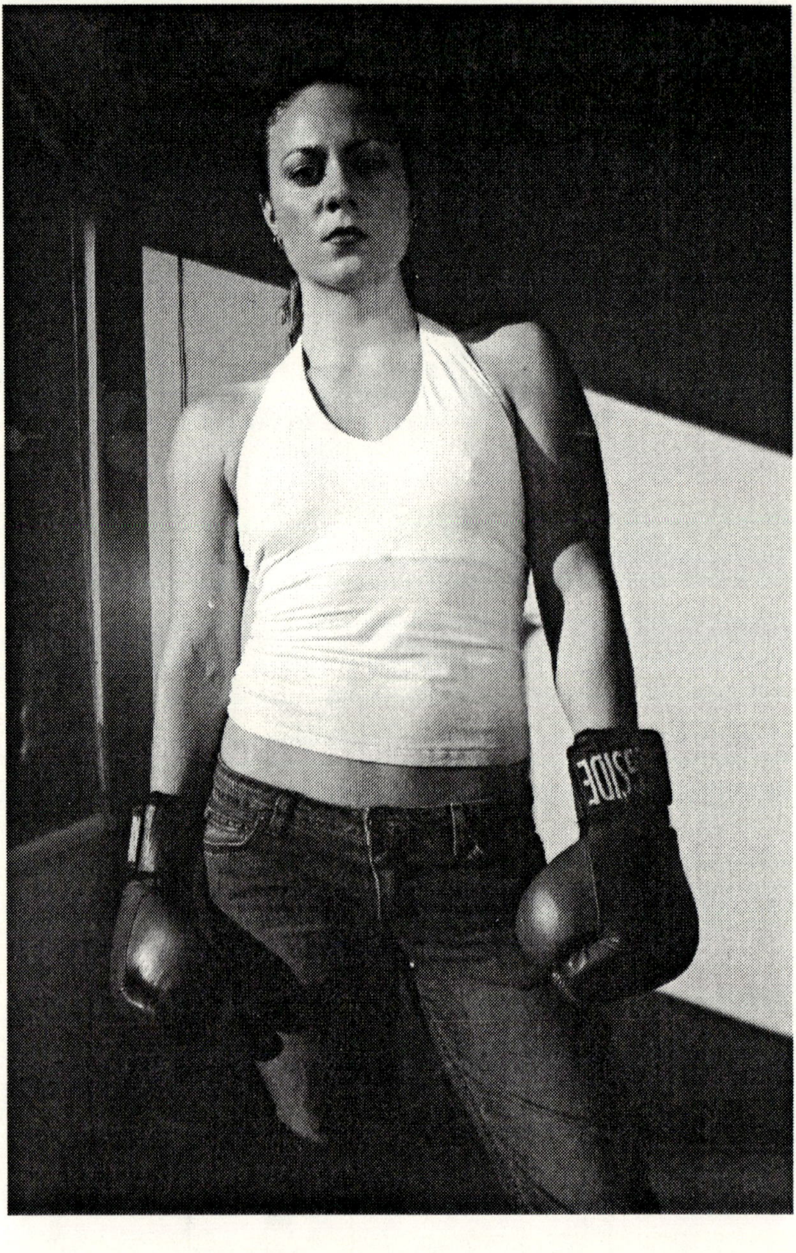

A Woman's Ring

Prologue

The first time she fit on the gloves, her past was abandoned. Only the warm material of the red existed, the worn grit on the inside. Her fingers curled into fists, thumbs descending in their own separate caves. She slapped the gloves together, a motion she'd watched boxers do on television with her father, a motion she'd watched fighters do on the street with their bare fists – the place she'd birthed that great dream of becoming one of them.

Walking home from school as a child, Katherine had clutched her workbooks to her chest, running over the chapters she would later be quizzed on. Two men stood in the street, fists balled, one with a beard coming off his chin in three distinctive points, the other clean and young, a mother's son. There was much animated conversation, drops of spit spraying like small human fountains up into the sky as Katherine ducked beneath the beads, hiding behind a bush in Mrs. McClintock's front yard.

"That's right, keep talking, just keep talking, Freddie!" The bearded man began to bounce as he spat. In that moment, Katherine's own feet ached to rock from heel to toe, to dance around the pavement as he did, the younger man bringing his fists to his face, jabbing at textbook angles. The older man deflected the punches, knowing the experience, the telegraphing that came from overeager fighters, their punches in slow motion, big looping shots that took blind men to miss. Then jumping in to crack the poor boy's skull with his hard, gnarled fists, teaching him the lessons of fighting.

Katherine panted at the impact, the crunch of nose and teeth and the colorful spray that began to transfer from inside the body to out. The two men flailed, beating out their problems as a small crowd gathered around to yell and clap. Some trying to break the two apart, yet they were inseparable, knowing what others could not know; that every jab was a release to something that had been building inside them; their fists mouths, their arms brains, just thinking and talking, thinking and talking, licking each other's bodies but never giving in to anything.

That curiosity found Katherine even behind the bushes, made her want to take all the pent up antagonism of her own life and mark it across faces and stomachs for the world to see.

The first time she experienced the sweet aroma of her own gloves in Chicago, the scent of sweat and competition burning the insides of her mind, a drug that froze her brain with the urgent power – she trusted only the gloves, the feeling, the sudden ache to hit things. The ruby ropes and smooth, wide canvas, the boxing gloves, focus mitts, and Thai pads that huddled inside tall, gray cages of the gym, ten heavy bags wrapped in sleek black leather, coiled to the ceiling and floor for accurate punching power and simulated speed. Windows allowed passersby to watch the boxing classes that Ethan taught four nights per week. Eagerly pressing their noses to the glass, cigarettes dangling from pairs of lips, they'd motion to their friends to watch the people practicing boxing drills, sparring, or hitting the bags round after three-minute round.

The moment her fists first made contact with the mitts, a pinnacle of momentum – the moment she first fit the headgear over her face, she was a warrior but a poet, the cheek protectors bent back like two flexed thumbs, the mouth guard taut beneath her lips, the feet secure in wrestling shoes, sparring first with Ethan, her trainer, bouncing around the canvas as if she knew what to do. She was not a wife or mother in that ring, not a small town girl from Ohio. She was an equal with the men, the strength of her body twisting into the shape of a man, the power of a woman, dancing metrically across the canvas.

She jabbed, she slipped, she took soft punches, and threw harder ones. The buzz in her head from a fist closed her eyes,

A Woman's Ring

opened them, made them tear. The guys hung on the ropes like slaves, the chains they clung to, prompting her to hit, Katherine watching with wide eyes safeguarded by leather, the power inside her trapped then released in small increments as she stumbled toward Ethan, delivering punch after punch with fingers and not fists, landing, missing, no matter, the beat of it all an eclipse of worlds as she danced there, riveted beyond riveting, sheer ordained action.

But now, where the hospital's walls flashed white, then gray, the machines on either side of the long, reedy bed breathed intenerately. Their bags of loose fluid moved as her lungs moved, in and out, hesitant. Her arms, muscled from countless hours of punching, spread at right angles beside her, needles in each arm, bags attached like wings of excess skin, flapping.

"Katherine, we're going to give you something to help you relax," a nurse said, a petite, cheerful woman with warm brown eyes like Frankie's eyes. She waited for that shot like she waited for death – plotting ways to avoid the inevitable.

Around the room, there were no warm bodies, though she imagined them there. On the small bench that sat opposite the bed, she envisioned her adopted mother's face, ragged from age, her lips in a downward sloping curve. Her father would be there, patting Katherine's knee with his faultless hands, whispering how his young girl was faced with such heavy burdens. His laugh would be the only distraction, that laugh that could heal poor, helpless fools. Brandon would kiss her forehead, removing the tears with the strong, able tips of his fingers, a touch that would, in that moment, be all that she needed to get through.

Who would have known from one headache, one doctor's visit, that the escape she thought she'd found in boxing would confine her to a hospital room? The pain an indicator of a stealthily hidden mass, wrapped in the soft tissue of her brain. An intra-arachnoid cyst, a degree of compression. The procedure -- a necessary craniotomy to the left parietal lobe. The words made little sense, yet somehow destroyed everything.

She exhaled, turning over the words in her head. Katherine wanted to kick and scream, to knock at the glasses that rested uneasily on Dr. Hopkin's shiny face. He'd abandoned sympathy and regarded her with undue sternness, clicking his pen against the MRI scans to point at the golf-ball sized cyst that rose from beneath her skull like the beginnings of a child pressing against a woman's womb. His mouth, tight and professional, revealed the risks, the potential threats to an otherwise healthy young woman. The membranes of her brain had split and filled with excess fluid. She was damaged.

"We'll want to excise it immediately," he'd told her, pushing his glasses further up the shaft of his nose. "Due to the bridging of the veins and the stress it's causing your brain, we feel it's imperative that we operate if you want to have an active life."

Katherine sat, watching the doctor's mustache twitch, his glasses slide, the hands gesturing wildly; hands that would soon cut her open, the fingers taunting her life with their accuracy.

Katherine could hardly ask the question, could hardly ask him what the difference was between this and a tumor? Perched in the doctor's stiff chair, foot tapping nervously against the tile, questions ran rampantly. Could she die from some random mistake, from some unplanned explosion, from some slip of his gloved fingers?

"Katherine," he said, crossing his legs, "you'll be just fine. The nature of tumors is malignant – cancerous. Cysts are benign."

As if this made everything better, Katherine nodded, floating from word to word, from phrase to full daunting sentence.

"Cysts," he continued, "are masses that can be completely fine on their own or more serious, like yours." He pointed back to the MRI scans she'd just taken yesterday, her body crammed into that endless white coffin, enduring the jackhammering of the pictures, the minimal space to breathe.

"You see this?" Dr. Hopkins pointed to the area of Katherine's brain that appeared darker, raised like a giant stone. "This is the parietal lobe of your brain – where the cyst is located. Your ability to write, speak and recognize things lies in this area -- your motor strip. You have a very aggravated vein sitting on top of this mass, ready to explode if you so much as sneeze the wrong way. That's the reason for the immediacy of the surgery." Dr. Hopkins sniffed, turned back to look at her. "I must tell you that your cyst is located in a very rare part of the brain, Katherine. Less than five percent of all cases of arachnoids are in the parietal lobe."

"So what does that mean?" The words were cold leaving her mouth, her body scaled by numbness and dread.

Dr. Hopkins smiled, his mustache shifting upwards. "It just means we never know what will happen until we get in there and take a look. And," he glanced back at the scans one last time, "we're going to go with excision instead of shunting as I mentioned before. Shunting in this instance could rupture the bridging veins and we don't want that to occur. The left side of your brain," he continued, holding up one cupped hand to represent the left hemisphere, "is supposed to be rounded like this. Your brain, due to years of compression, is more like this." The doctor flattened out his left hand at a sharp angle. "Your skull cap is incredibly fragile and your brain is under a great deal of stress. But," he leaned forward, folding his hands in his lap, "we'll do the best we can, Katherine. Don't you worry. We know what we're doing."

"Right," Katherine mumbled, shaking the doctor's hand as he stood, his shoulders rigid beneath the white fabric of his coat, lips pulling up and out in some sort of awkward expression – a smile maybe. She walked back to the reception area and filled out her paperwork. Would this mean the end of her boxing career? Would she now become sedentary and lethargic? Would her brain function normally after this operation? As she filled out her name, her new insurance forms, her new address, her eyes filled with tears. She had something in her brain. Something foreign that could explode at any given moment, without warning. Killing her. Like *that*.

Two days later, Katherine admitted herself to the Neurosurgeon's ward at Northwestern hospital, changing into a lightweight gown that tied in the front, exposing inches of her ribcage, flashes of pale, unseen skin, her nipples hard beneath the blue fabric, the washed out scars from her children evident near her hips and bellybutton. Where were Lily and Frankie now? In Ohio? With Andrew? With Brandon's mother, Mrs. Baskin, where she left them?

Before the nurse came back with the drug, Katherine brought one heavy arm toward her head, felt the freshly shaved skull, her hand rubbing across the blunted needles of hair. The sobs wracked her body before she could cradle them, smothering her inside the despondency of the hospital room.

The nurse finally entered, smiling warmly as Katherine wept, piercing her arm with yet another shot to make her dream. The cool liquid slid into Katherine's veins, the blood parting for the stream of drug that would allow her to skip the scenes to come: a blade carving against her head, sliding from ear to hairline, the parting of her scalp, the peeling of that virgin pink flesh back from the skull, the bone, thin as an eggshell, removed, her forehead held down by two giant clamps that would have to be drilled there, the cutting away of that great mass that sat, detonated, intricately weaved in and out of large, pulsating veins, the removal in clumps, the sighs of pressure as the flat side of her brain plumped slightly, giving shape to what was compressed for years, the putting back of a thin, eroded skull, four metal plates and sixteen screws hugging the top of it, forty-two staples closing the wound, fresh blood trickling over her ear, old blood clotting against her eyebrows, the making of a patient, the survival of a woman.

"Sleep now, Katherine."

Two nurses wheeled her into a hallway, pushing the bed through double doors that led into a large, stainless steel operating room. The cool draft blew up her thin cotton gown, exposing the gooseflesh on her arms and ankles. There was a giggle, a movement of her finger, a toe. Her only thoughts were of boxing, of childhood and how she'd come to be this woman in this moment. And then sleep, washing over her consciousness, one fierce, consummate wave, drowning.

Part I

Rea Frey

A Woman's Ring

Chapter One

Life was that thing you had when someone loved you. Life was a family portrait, a place called home, a smile on the lips of a stranger when they looked at you. Was this life, Katherine often asked years later, that adoption had given her? Two people taking her in, Katherine swaddled in a yellow jumper and slip-on shoes, her hair knotted in dark brown ringlets that had one pink bow stuck on the crown of her head?

Bruce had studied the ticking fingers and toes of his newly adopted child, pushed his warm face into her pale clothed belly, until he realized what it was to finally love someone more than you loved life or money or even your wife – that woman you'd once looked at and thought, "*This* is what love is."

Ruth stood next to him impatiently, carrying the grudge of women who were incapable of conceiving, who looked into the face of her fading husband, wondering when things went wrong, when her shroud of aloofness had pushed him toward a dingy hotel room with a girl named Sue. Where he'd wrapped his arms around slender shoulders and wept into the neck of a woman who was warm in places that Ruth couldn't be. He'd returned home with a faint flush to his cheeks, carried the slight residue of a sweet perfume on his hands and mouth. Ruth had looked at him and simply known, opened her mouth to scream, to attack, but only closed it again, feeling nothing in that moment beyond a minor aching.

Once, she thought, he would have been down on his knees begging for her forgiveness. She would have dipped her head and sighed, a deep, resonating breath that would have assured him that mistakes happen, that she still loved him. He would have groveled, scraping his knees against the carpet until small burns pushed against the kneecaps of his trousers. Ruth would let his arms encircle her waist and feel herself giving in. It would be easy because they had desire and commitment, those promises that married couples shared in the beginning years.

But she'd lost it through time, as women often did, reaching for something never to be touched with steady fingers. Marriage had outgrown her, just as time had outgrown her, leaving her dented in spirit, indifferent to everything.

Time would pass quickly, they both knew. As Bruce shifted Katherine in the able lines of his forearms, he traced her long face and soft fingers, wondering why they had waited so long to start a family. At fifty-five, he saw little evidence of youth left in his own face, little agility left in his stiff, aching limbs. He knew Ruth would have more ageless days, more emotions to work through. What if she never taught Katherine about being a strong woman, about the values of family? He stared back down at his new little girl, letting all his mistakes fade as he watched life pump in and out of her lungs. He gently carried Katherine to her room and laid her softly in her new bed, tucking the covers tight around her chin. How had this child not been adopted before now? All this time without a mother or father, only the sterile white walls and long, empty corridors of the orphanage as her company.

Bruce slipped quietly from the room, faltering as he considered facing Ruth in their bedroom. He changed directions and walked back toward the front hallway. He knew she wouldn't feel like talking, would turn gruffly from him when he entered the bedroom, shutting herself off in the bathroom. He would sigh and sit on the edge of the bed, overwhelmed with the urge to cry but not releasing it. No, he would not have that on this day. Even if Ruth's love had become conditional – even if her emotions were a dour reminder of what housewives could become when lost in the flow of monotonous ways – he would not let her wreck this occasion.

A Woman's Ring

Bruce moved to the kitchen, preparing a snack for when Katherine awoke. He sliced a piece of bread, mashed up a banana. He caught his reflection in the window and heard a rustle from one of the bedrooms. How had he become so old?

He knew Katherine would soon be grown and off to bigger things. She would have friends and dates and a life without him. But first he would teach her what it meant to have a goal, to be rocked in the night when a dire dream awoke her, to be read to – to engage in the power of communication. There would be summertime picnics and frilly dresses and then sports and elementary school. While most girls took ballet or gymnastics, Katherine would examine a sport virtually unknown to little girls. She would open the door that millions of athletes from all walks of life had discovered: that multifarious world of boxing.

It was Bruce's one dream as a child. He had memories of his own father nailing up a heavy bag and telling his son to swing big, to work hard. Bruce had prized himself as an aspiring fighter. He ate, slept and trained for the sport that would never open its arms to welcome him. There were too many obstacles, not enough heart to endure.

For Katherine, it would begin with the Foreman-Ali fight, shown in restored perfection. He would cuddle her on the couch, tossing kernels of popcorn in the air that would occasionally miss his mouth and dot the carpet, sending his wife into a frenzy. Just as the fights did. Gatti-Norris. Hagler-Hearns. Holyfield-Bowe. Tua-Ruiz. Mercer-McGee. Trinidad-Blocker. The past and present. The fierce and strong.

The television would be wired with chiseled fighters and aged judges, the purses reaching excessive levels for thirty-six minutes of fame. These were the bouts anticipated for weeks, where on normal nights Katherine's father would drag from room to room, restless. In those minutes of munching popcorn and ringing bells, Katherine could measure the relaxation in his bones, as if each bulb and joint were smiling. He would come so alive then, patting his wife's knee on the sofa if she happened to stop long enough to scoff at the beastly ways of boxers, ignoring her derogatory remarks about this sport, his beloved.

"You see that?" Bruce would wag his finger at the screen. "*That* takes work – that takes discipline. Amazing what those people can do with gloves," he'd mumble, resting his face in his palms. "Amazing what those people can do."

Katherine would watch, inspired, wondering if this was what boxing did to people – stirred up the stimulation that work days never brought, that wives of twenty years or children that weren't really yours couldn't provide. Only boxing – where a beer complemented a knockout and the sound of your voice yelling to jab and destroy, to hook and cover, was the next best thing to the slow awakening of alcohol in your veins.

Katherine would soon adore it. The way she would be able to tell the exact moment when a fight broke loose, that nanosecond of movement, the separation of a champion from a contender. She would gauge the traveling of their bodies and notice how offense was not the way to win, but defense – the intricacies of protecting – the men slipping and covering unremittingly. Oftentimes, Bruce would get so carried away with his daughter's reaction that he could read the fight without even watching it – because on Katherine's small, curious face it was mounting and unfolding in perfectly timed rounds. Eye-popping for jabs. Her blinks for crosses. A smile for a giant right overhand. The squeezing of her fist if someone went down.

He knew in a few short years he'd pack her up and take her on a plane to Vegas for her first live fight – he'd teach her every logistic of the game and then introduce her to the raw action of it, the boldness. That's what aroused people. The sheer courtship of boxing – the rude contenders, the humble ones. The kind of rounds where you knew a man could die but somehow hung on while the other threw flurried, boulder punches at his head.

"That's determination, Katherine. A battle of wills."

Katherine never said a word – just nodded and watched with her voice held back by the sound of gloves, the exhalation of breath, landed punches and power shots. It became a sort of addiction, knowing that boxing did something to people. That it somehow created a universal experience where the whole world would pay good money to see bloodshed, as if in those twelve rounds the skills would reveal the stories behind each of them.

A Woman's Ring

Stepping into the ring was valor, and that was the kind of thing that earned respect. And respect was what she craved, respect for something she'd have to work for and earn, just as she was beginning to respect each intricate matching.

"Why weren't you ever a boxer, Daddy?" Katherine would one day ask this question, and Bruce, tight-lipped and ashamed, would open his mouth to answer, groping for some well-versed lie.

"Never had time," he'd mutter, trying to swallow the past that always crept up on him in sleepless nights and lulls at the office. Katherine's interest would always resurrect it, bringing him back to the reason behind his failure.

He'd married Ruth at only twenty-three, still wanting to fight, but promising her that he never would. She assumed no respectable man would do such a thing – especially her husband. Why couldn't she support him the way other women had? He'd demanded to at least *watch* the fights – fulfilling his fantasies through television and occasional trips, through curvaceous women who would not tell him no, would not say he had five minutes for love-making before jumping in the shower to wash all traces of him from their skin, as Ruth did. There was booze and cheating and hoarding his little girl to himself – all distractions to abate the wounds of failure.

Not that Ruth even wanted Katherine. She was ignored, despite her big, vivid eyes and fire for life, despite her loving nature. Katherine learned that fathers loved and mothers grieved – that was the way it was, and no amount of wishing would make things change.

Ruth had not carried the weight of a child in her belly, had not felt the tiny elbows and fists ramming against her flesh, the special bond between unborn infant and expectant mother. It was all she'd ever wanted, and when she couldn't have it, when they'd exhausted every possible drug and cure, she'd simply given up the desire to become a mother or nurturer, leaving the job to only one of them.

When Bruce died in his sleep before her eighth birthday, Katherine experienced the rigid, deadening pain of losing a father. Bundled in her room, inside a closet, or under her bed, she would rock and scream for a parent that would never again sweep her into his arms for protection.

She needed something to take the pain of grief and loss and remind her of their happiest times together. When they would talk boxing and play in the shadows of the living room on summer afternoons. Eating banana splits at the local café. Playing flashlight tag in their abundant backyard. He would have given her the world and she would have taken it – "because you deserve it," he would always tell her, smoothing her wild brown hair off her forehead. "I want you to find someone who makes you happy. You should have dreams you can hold tight to no matter what happens – if you marry young or get a good job, put those dreams first or you'll be in an office one day regretting everything you've ever done and – "

His voice would always fade, but Katherine understood. Never let go. Never let go of the dream.

At his funeral, she rubbed her fingers over his ashen skin, his body situated there in the deep cherry wood of his coffin. She kissed the thin lips she'd adored since she could remember. She turned, heading for her mother, and Ruth, taking one look at Katherine, rejected her – the dismayed seven year old who sobbed with her eyes wide open and her hands reaching for a relative. Ruth wanted all reminders of her husband extinguished, and Katherine could feel it with every painful year that followed – as if her mother blamed her for being adopted, for stopping her father's breathing in the middle of the night, for owning all his affection. Without effort, Ruth was slowly pushing her toward the brink of rebellion. Toward boys and freedom and that urge for boxing.

Katherine wanted to seek ways to reinvent him – make her body do all the things she'd studied since childhood through hours of fights and slow motion movements, where the secrets of victories were held. She had to rise above her womanhood, sink into a world predominantly for men -- where the challenge would be proving that this fire burned to her very core, where her father had instilled it with those great champions of boxing.

A Woman's Ring

Chapter Two

Death left noises. The bittersweet cackle of a classic laugh, the smooth voice of a father, the pressure of fingers tapping on a desk – that even thump-thump – or the way Bruce had sucked his teeth when graced with a smile, making those small wheezing noises. Those were the sounds she remembered.

The day he died, his eyes had twinkled like two wet, spinning buttons when he looked down at her, and his mouth had stretched for his ears. He was beautiful in his manner, in his soft looks and wording.

At work, Bruce had slipped two tickets into his jacket pocket before shutting off the lights to his office, eager to give Katherine an early birthday present. He'd purchased tickets to Vegas to see Arturo Gatti in two weeks time. On his way home, he stopped at the only local bar, Jilly's, and downed his usual scotch, softening the edge for when he faced Ruth – when he witnessed her pasty hands folded together in her lap, knitting or doing crossword puzzles on the sofa, or just sitting there, the pressure of her fingers turning her knuckles a startling blonde.

At home, he popped a piece of gum in his mouth and made his way inside. "I'm home, Sunshine."

Katherine bounded from her room, her hair in pigtails with two red ribbons tied loosely at the ends.

"Guess what I did today, Daddy!"

"What, Pumpkin?" He kissed her on the head and crouched to face her. "Did you solve world hunger? Become the first female President? Cure cancer?"

"Nooo, silly," she swatted his hands that were poking at her ribs. "Brandon and I *sparred* today! Right outside with the gloves you got us and everything. I was Whitaker and you would have been so proud at how low I ducked, Daddy. I caught him with a good one in the eye and my arms are so sore! It's hard work learning to fight, huh?"

Her words bit at his heart, reminding him of his own childhood, when the whole world had been available, and of his honeymoon, when that world had shrunk to nothing concrete. He and Ruth had been cuddled in bed after a long day at the beach, Ruth just barely a woman then – so young but willing – and he'd trusted her enough to open up and confide his dreams of fighting professionally. How he wanted to travel the world and make money for both of them so they'd never have to worry about anything. He could still remember the way her slim body had tightened in his arms, the way she'd turned to look at him with a harsh look on her face aged past her years – a look that seemed to remain long after they discovered they could not conceive their own child, long after they adopted Katherine. The hard lines of unsatisfied wives.

"Boxing is for men that come from the *streets*, Bruce – men that can't do well in other things. They fight because they're not intelligent and *you* are not one of those people."

Her words stung, made his desires dim as he realized in that moment that he had in fact married the wrong woman. But he knew he would not divorce her and she would not ask for one – it was one of the things he'd been taught by his own father. "Have to live with your mistakes, son."

So, here was his little girl, a baby he'd begged for after they realized a pregnancy wasn't possible – and only after Ruth had resigned to life did he get his wish, his Katherine. Now *she* was producing the same dream, only this time it would be harder because she was in a nothing town with little money and would be a minority in the sport. Regardless, he would let her imagine, discovering all the things he'd never see.

"I bet you'll be a great boxer someday, Katie. First woman in the Olympics?"

A Woman's Ring

She nodded passionately and hugged his leg. "And you can be my coach."

He reached down to pick her up, smothering her against his jacket so she wouldn't see the tears in his eyes. "I got you something, Pumpkin. An early birthday surprise."

She wiggled in his arms, jumping back down to the floor, clapping excitedly. "Gimme, gimme, gimme!"

He pulled out the tickets, handed them to her and watched her face light up, watched her jeweled eyes narrow with curiosity. "Are these –"

"They're tickets to see a real live fight, baby. We're gonna go see –"

"You're going to see *what*, exactly?" Ruth stood in the hallway, emerging from the bedroom fully clothed, a purse in her hand.

"Where are you going, Ruth?"

"I'm going to stay with Claire for a few days. I'm…I need some time, Bruce –"

Bruce didn't try to fight, just nodded his head and let go a tired sigh. Claire had been her escape for years – when things were stagnant, when she became suffocated in a world that could actually offer everything if she would only open her eyes.

"Come on, Katie, let me take you out for an early birthday dinner."

Katherine turned, looking up at her mother with the tiniest flicker of hope. "You wanna come with us, Mommy?"

Her mother pushed past both of them, answering her daughter with a jingle of car keys and slamming of the front door.

Bruce and Katherine stood perfectly still until Bruce broke the mood by scooping Katherine up in his arms. "I guess your Mommy wasn't hungry, was she? Come on, let's you and me go get some ice cream!"

And with his kind words, her worry dissipated, leaving in its wake the same relaxed, trusting girl. "Ice cream before dinner, Daddy?"

"Shh, we won't tell anyone, will we?"

And together, they went off to dinner, hand in hand, the trip to Vegas on both their minds. Over ice cream and hamburgers, her father would share his dreams and failures, but Katherine would not judge him – would not judge him for all the wrongs in his life, all the unaccomplished goals. Her love was simple and constant – a daughter's wordless commitment to her dad.

And it would be that night, after he tucked her in and read her a story, after he flipped off her light and inhaled that sweet scent of his precious child, that he would retire to his vacant bed and pass away in his sleep, one tired soul unable to love his little girl enough for the entire family.

Chapter Three

Brandon became her only hope – the boy she clung to in recess by the swing set, resting her head on his shoulder, the sobs threatening to wrack her body in long, wearisome convulsions. He stood patiently while the other children climbed monkey bars, flew down the slide and trampled back up, did flips in the grass, and played patty cake games. At the age of eight and for many years after, she would become his responsibility.

Together they grieved, Brandon's arms wrapped firmly around her, his mother cooking meals and reminiscing about Bruce and what a great man he'd been, how charming, how selfless – while Katherine hung on to every word, wiping at her reflective eyes. Brandon attempted to mold her into that same lively child, though at times he could see the hardened edge of sorrow in her green eyes – a permanent, softly building anger for her mother and the immense need to escape this town.

"I just miss him so much. He was my best friend."

"I can be your best friend now, Katherine. I promise." He put his hand on hers and smiled. "I know I'm not as great as your dad, but will you be my best friend anyway?"

Katherine would nod her head and drop it against her bent knees in the schoolyard. Later, it would be in their tree house, in Thelma's coffee shop, and then over cigarettes when they were old enough to buy them. There was no friend better than Brandon – no boy who could make her smile in spite of circumstance while keeping up her passion for boxing. The sport seemed the only link to remembering her father. It wasn't like flipping through pictures, or smelling his cologne on an Urbana passerby – walking into her parent's room and seeing a sock or tie still draped over the bedpost as though Bruce would be back any second – thinking he might jump out of the closet with a funny grin and say, "Surprise – I'm here!"

It was only boxing. Whenever fights came on, Katherine went to Brandon's. Bringing the tickets her father had given her before her eighth birthday so many years ago, holding tight to them until the grease from popcorn or other snacks would seep into the paper, staining the tickets an oily yellow. For years, she did this – clutched the tickets, looking over her shoulder at Brandon when something exciting happened, as if her friend could take the place of such an amazing man.

"I miss you, Daddy," she'd mumble – in school, at home, in the shower. Her mother had stopped talking to her, would leave Katherine for days at a time and come home reeking of alcohol and cheap perfume. The house became sinister without her father, with its utter stillness and layers of dust over all the tables and bookshelves. Katherine truly realized that her mother had stopped caring not only for Bruce and Katherine, but for herself as well. She stopped dressing in silk blouses and slacks, stopped eating, stopped cleaning, stopped working, and became a casing of the woman she used to be. She slept all day when she was home and stayed up in the living room when Katherine went to bed.

Sometimes, when Katherine woke for a glass of water, stumbling blindly toward the kitchen, she'd find her mother sitting stiffly on the couch, hands folded in her lap, staring blankly at the wall. She would even come into Katherine's room some nights, hover near her bed, emitting slow, shallow breaths until Katherine woke and bucked at the sight of her sick mother staring down at her.

Katherine began to lock her door and wish for departure. A way to venture into the unknown – a desire to prove her dreams to her deceased father, to make something of herself like they'd both always imagined.

A Woman's Ring

Chapter Four

She was seven when they took their first and only family vacation. They'd gone to Florida, to a beach whose name Katherine couldn't quite remember. She did remember the ride, all arranged in her father's Toyota, singing softly to the radio, playing the ABC game with road signs, and watching Ruth pop two pills and snore quietly in the rare silences of the passing hours.

Katherine had the entire backseat to herself; wore her big sunglasses and floppy straw hat all the way there. Her father would catch her eye in the mirror, whisper, "I love you, Pumpkin," before returning his concentration to the road.

When the highway gave way to tiny towns and big palm trees, Katherine knew they were getting close. Towns with only one gas station, sagging grocery stores, and a bridge that mounted high over bright green waters. They ventured into the Destin strip where bungee jumping ads, roller coasters, miniature golf courses, and stucco roofed condos filled grassy areas, managing to reveal only small whispers of the ocean through all the manmade houses and sandy lots.

Katherine bounced on her seat, stirring her mother, who rolled grumpily toward the window, eyes still clamped shut. She was missing the beauty of the water, the smell of the ocean. Katherine rolled down her window, sniffing the salty air which was so unlike Ohio's.

"Daddy, this is Heaven!" She looked at her father, who was stealing as many glances as she was, running yellow lights and inching closer to people's bumpers.

"Isn't it something? I can't believe we haven't come until now. We'll make it our new tradition, Katie. Every summer, okay?"

Katherine couldn't contain her excitement. She squeezed her hands together, dying to shout that they'd finally made it, but knew it would wake her mother and then she'd get yelled at. Her jaws hurt from so much smiling. Those glimpses of the water were startling, the roar of the ocean, the subtle crash, the constancy of it all.

Half an hour later, fighting through traffic and the festivities surrounding the 4th of July, they finally pulled into the realty office to get their key. Bruce parked the car and left Katherine with her mother, who still slept soundly in the front seat.

It was unsettling to be alone with her. Katherine rested her head on the back of the driver's seat, studying her mother's peaceful face. She was pretty, but plain. Dark hair always fastened back in a bun, brown eyes, pale arms and spider legs. Once she would have been beautiful, before the bitterness crept in. Katherine sighed, blowing a few stray hairs off her mother's forehead, which awoke her. Ruth's eyes fluttered open, and for an instant the two locked gazes. For one fraction of a moment Katherine saw the tug of a smile begin to slope her mother's lips, then no trace as Ruth gruffly realized she had been in a car for what felt like a day, and was now awake thanks to this child. She jerked up, adjusting her bun.

"Katherine Ann Sinclair, do not stare at people while they are sleeping. I swear you don't have any manners in one bone of your tiny body."

Katherine slumped back against the seat, brought her Raggedy Ann doll into her lap and buried her face in it. Instead of sadness, Katherine felt a stab of anger. She was old enough to realize the way her mother felt about her, that it wasn't a passing phase and if it weren't for her father, there would be no love, there would be no vacations or happiness.

Bruce jogged back to the car, jangling the keys in his hand. "Right on the beach, my lovelies." He started the car and looked over at Ruth expectantly. Somehow, he never gave up on her. She may have been the wrong woman and he may have strayed, but it

A Woman's Ring

was never too late to start again, to make things right between them.

"How was your sleep, Ruth?" He asked the question carefully, knowing all too well that treading lightly was necessary if you didn't want to agitate her.

"As good as it can be in this old car." She huffed heavily and stared out the window. "Are we close Bruce, or are we going to spend the remainder of the week without food and water?"

The light in Bruce's eyes dimmed. He glanced back at Katherine, whose eyes held the same lack of light in them. "We won't let her spoil things for us, will we, Katie?"

Katherine gasped as did Ruth, who snapped her head back to Bruce.

"What did you just say?"

"I *said* that I won't let you ruin this for our little girl, Ruth. For either of us, actually. I've worked tirelessly to take this trip, and Katherine and I will not let you ruin this. It's about time you learned to let go of the fact that you –" he glanced back at Katherine, lowering his voice to a whisper – "that you couldn't have a baby of your own, and start loving the one we have now. Or so help me, you'll regret it for the rest of your life. Or rot for it."

Bruce slammed the car into reverse and peeled out of the office, driving intently. Katherine couldn't keep the smile from her lips, couldn't keep the pride from swelling in her chest for the way he'd stood up for her.

Ruth stared at him open-mouthed, too shocked to utter a word. After a minute of awkward silence, she began to speak. "How dare you chastise me when –"

"Keep it to yourself, Ruth." Bruce held up one hand and refused to look at her. "I didn't say I was perfect, and I know damned well I've made tons of mistakes, but they're not without reason. And *you* are the reason – you and I both know things could have been much different if you'd wanted them to be."

Ruth crossed her arms, muttering under her breath. Katherine sat silently, realizing that the only child in this car was her mother – but that she couldn't hurt them anymore. That they were going on vacation and there was nothing anyone could do about ruining it. They were here and she and her daddy were going to have the best time ever. And her mother could just sit in her room and sleep the days away. She was like the walking dead anyway. It would only be a matter of time before death truly came and took her from the world of the living.

A few minutes later, they pulled into the magical subdivision of houses, theirs a Disney World pink, bordered by others whose colors filled every spectrum of the rainbow. Big blue and green houses with fanned out balconies and intricate white roof trimming. Barbie's palace with a Ferrari in the driveway, big custom vans and floats strapped to roof racks.

Their rental house was two levels, bordered by small patches of grass and chipping paint, a testament to the many passing tropical storms. Bruce gave Katherine the key, and lugging her small suitcase and doll, she ran to the back door, fiddling with the lock before she finally wrenched it open and ran into the garage. The second door was positioned beside the washer and dryer. Katherine could still smell fabric softener and mildew from previous guests. She fumbled with the second lock, hearing her father outside unloading their bags, her mother no doubt still sitting in the car in a state of shock from the way he'd just talked to her.

Katherine finally got inside and was faced with a set of stairs that led to the main floor of the house. She ran up as quickly as she could, gasping when she met the landing. Wood floors spread in front of her, a large, open kitchen to the right, dining room table to the left, a living room with big, painted shells on the wallpaper and two dark blue couches that looked soiled from so many visitors. But the row of glass doors was what took her breath away. They led out onto the deck and a gray set of rickety stairs that descended down to the soft, white sand. She didn't care about the bedrooms or even the second story of the house. It was this – the pearl sand and gently rolling waves, the families that splashed in the water and sat under umbrellas, sipping cocktails. Katherine jumped up and down, waiting for her father to get upstairs so the two of them could venture onto the beach. The ocean. Her first time seeing the magnificence of it all.

A Woman's Ring

As if on cue, Bruce bounded up the stairs, struggling with two suitcases, a duffel bag, and a cooler. He whistled as he entered the house, dropping the suitcases and bags against the loveseat that sat against the center wall.

"Look at all this, Katie. Pretty nice, huh?"

Katherine grabbed his hand and pointed out the doors. "Daddy, I have to go out there! I've never seen anything so beautiful. Can we go now, please? It's still sunny! We could go for a swim!"

Bruce glanced over his shoulder, as if he expected Ruth to be stalking him. For once, he didn't care where she was. For once, he had said what he'd really wanted to without worrying about how she'd treat him for the next month as repercussion. He ignored the minute part of him that still wanted to take her in his arms, to guide her out onto the beach and sit until morning. But Ruth had chosen her battles, and he didn't seem to be a part of that fight anymore.

Bruce kneeled down in front of Katherine, placing a hand on either shoulder. "I'll count while you put your bathing suit on. We'll race. You ready?"

Katherine squealed in delight and ran to her suitcase, hunting around on the ground floor for a bathroom. She found one nestled off to the back corner of the house and changed quickly. Her father was already in his trunks, equipped with sunglasses and a hat when she emerged in her two-piece blue and pink polka-dotted bikini.

"Aww, you always beat me, Dad!" She stamped her foot and crossed her arms.

"Dad's always win, you know. But look at you, Ms. Katherine! All grown up!"

Katherine immediately dropped her arms, prancing around like a model. He laughed and reached his hand for hers.

"Let's get you to the ocean, Princess."

The two of them ventured outside, Katherine tipping her face up to the sun as it warmed her skin. There wasn't sun like this in Ohio. Too many trees, too many storms, too many clouds. This was her idea of heaven. Her first family vacation. She bounded down the steps, feeling the heated sand slip between her toes, gruff and perfect as it smoothed the bottoms of her feet. Her father watched her prance over the sand, feeling such love swell within him. He followed her out to the ocean's mouth, came up behind her as she let her feet sink in the wet sand.

"Daddy, this is the best day of my life. The best."

She spoke so seriously for such a little girl, looked so peaceful here staring out at the vastness of the ocean, the absolute magic of the sea. "Can we go in, Daddy?"

He answered her wordlessly by taking her hand and walking her into the ocean, the froth leaping at their ankles, their knees – Katherine's squeals of delight so pure, so free as the waves leapt at her. "It's so cold!"

He laughed and splashed at her, sinking deeper, but only as far as Katherine's belly button. He knew the strength of the waves, the way an undertow could whip a child in its grasp and keep her there.

From the porch, Ruth watched them, tears running off her cheeks as she looked at the simplicity of her family. Why did she not feel like they were *her* family? Why did she keep such a distance? She gathered her dress and sat gingerly on the edge of a white plastic chair. There was a bucket with water to wash off one's feet, a green hose attached to the house. Ruth looked around her, down at the hands that shook on her lap. Why had she come here?

She stood again, leaning against the worn wood of the deck as she watched Bruce. Once her love, just as quickly a man. A father. She watched the muscles in his back, the slight bulge at his middle from lost metabolism and age, and at their little girl bouncing in the ocean, giggling helplessly. Ruth had never seen Katherine so happy. Not playing in the tree house, not anywhere. As a little girl, the ocean had been a favorite place of Ruth's. Her parents had been kind and wonderful – listened intently. When had she turned so cold, so reluctant?

Ruth began to walk down the deck, toward the stairs that led to the beach. If she stepped onto that sand, perhaps she could join them – flock in the water and feel the weight of her little girl wrapped in her arms for the very first time. But if she turned she'd lead the same monotonous life, the same journey. Her feet

A Woman's Ring

hesitated on the deck's flooring. One step in the right direction and it could begin again. Her life could begin again.

She hesitated. Katherine screamed in the water. Bruce picked her up and set her on his shoulders. Together, the pair waded out a little further, the two of them happy and resilient. Ruth's momentary opportunity seized in her feet and then scuttled backwards. It was too late for her, for this family. She reentered the house and made her way upstairs. There, she locked herself in the master bedroom and sat on the bed, rocking back and forth as her husband and daughter played freely in the ocean.

Rea Frey

A Woman's Ring

Chapter Five

Katherine stumbled up the porch steps behind Brandon, whose feet shook in his socks from drink and too much jealousy. Beneath the grim moonlight, her hands moved in circles over the back of his limp t-shirt, bringing him to a gentle seat on the rear steps of his home.

"What are you *doing*, Katherine?" He slurred his words as Katherine watched him – remembering those elusive moments they'd spent each summer of their lives in this small, hindering town: moments when he'd fathered her the best way he'd known – seen her through sickness and heartache until she began to feel so deeply for him, groveling for his attention, wanting to occupy the dirt he walked on, to be good enough for all the soft, unseen parts of him; his heels, pink and tender, the white space of his knees, a rib, burrowed under tight, blonde skin, the rough patches of his elbow, the salty places behind his ears.

To Brandon, she was a neighbor, a best friend, someone to share dreams with. A girl he'd picked up and brushed off after tragedy, and cared for like a sibling. Where had the years gone? The innocent nights of playing flashlight tag and camping out in the backyard? He missed their former selves, when complications were whether to have a chocolate chip cookie or brownie for dessert and whether they would ace the weekly science quiz.

Now Brandon wished only for piloting, where he'd dress in a crisp, blue uniform, flying the world while carrying the lives of hundreds beneath his wings. It's what he talked of and studied for – that great day, where the city of Urbana would crumble below his long, slender feet so he could make it in New York or

Chicago or Dallas, in Europe, Africa or Hawaii – away from this place that kept you stuck in its web, that kept honest people lying, their wants and needs trampled upon, as the grit of small town life booted what could be to what couldn't.

Through all the moments they'd spent staring and wondering, holding each other back with their eyes, Brandon and Katherine had never entertained romance, though they'd felt that urgency deep within them; beyond the heart and blood, beyond the bones and intuition, so deep there was no name for that place – the place that love crept, swelling until it pressed against the skin, bulging, daring, neither of them releasing, always safely contained. He'd been there for her since her father's death, warming the frigid nature of her mother's whitewashed shadow.

Katherine had always felt that solitary pain of adopted children when even an adopted parent didn't want you; she knew the pain that death brought, she and her mother alone on their middle-class carpet, fidgeting and sighing like mothers and daughters will when no conversation is left between them.

As a teenager, Katherine was now parentless, depending only on Brandon, on his love for her that she knew he kept hidden somewhere deep within him. Now she kneeled before her friend, his clammy, white hands clutched warmly in her own, prepared to release the truth.

"Brandon, I'm just bringing you home because you're drunk and I need to tell you something."

He grunted, giggled, burped.

"I -- I realize this might not be the best time seeing as you're, um, drunk and won't remember this tomorrow, but here goes."

He looked at her beneath shocks of blonde hair that covered those stark, gray eyes, the most fascinating part of him. This was the only time he'd ever been drunk, had made himself as numb as Katherine felt when her world had crumbled, when her mother quit talking and she had no father to run to. Brandon released a strand of indecipherable words and placed his head in his hands, thinking of the cause of all this jealousy. The cause named Andrew. It seemed like only yesterday he'd rolled up in his red Cadillac, a toothpick balanced out his mouth, hollering at Katherine to be his girl.

A Woman's Ring

Katherine tried to ignore Brandon's mumbling and concentrate on what she had to say. This moment was hers - to tell him what she'd ached to tell him since she was eight years old – and if she didn't do it now, she might never tell him. She knew his anger stemmed from Andrew; the man who cruised the streets and called to her, begging for a date or a moment of her time. Brandon couldn't fathom the thought of any man having her, taking care of his best friend as he'd done for all those years, yet he would not reveal his own want of her; rather, it stayed bottled inside the thickest cavities, the deepest spaces. He would never tell her, only sigh and laugh and wrestle her in their soft, green backyards, Katherine so tired of waiting she knew it would have to be here, on this night, to change their relationship.

"Brandon..."

"What, Katie, *what*?" Brandon hinged over on the steps, a gurgle passing from his lips, a battle in his liver as the whiskey twisted and bit at it, destroying it cell by collective cell.

Katherine blew the hair from her eyes and leaned forward, the hard cement grinding her knee caps, yet she pushed anyway, pushed his head up to her level and leaned in for a kiss, forgetting the words, the sentiments, only the kiss, her lips connecting with something slimy and reeking of alcohol. This was not as she'd imagined it, her only love belching in her mouth, before pushing her backwards onto his lawn, saying, "get away," pushing her so hard there would be the phantom print of his hand for two days on the edge of her shoulder. Brandon pulled himself to standing, swaying and swearing beneath the moon. He looked at his shoes for a tottering moment, then up to the stars before retreating through his back door, slamming it against Katherine's shadowed profile. From the other side, his unsteady, drunken fingers lingered on the doorknob as if to say, "please don't go, Katherine, I need you."

The night closed around her as she struggled to sit up, tears of frustration pelting her chin and jeans, that moment gone, the moment she'd craved almost as much as boxing, where she'd fit gloves over her fingers, squeezing that leather with certainty, the punches she would one day throw clean, hard, and devastating; opponents stepping up, then smacking the canvas with a power wholly unknown to them, her rage imprinted against millions, jaws, eyes, and noses, the passion kept inside for so long erupting with those insistent throbs of her heart that would push with each punch thrown, that rhythm, ba-boom, singing every moment inside her -- *I am I am I am.*

Or the times when her father had been away on business, and her mother's laughter used to burn holes inside Katherine, teasing out emotions, only to be killed in the next second by some thought or somber moment, the whole house cracking a little from missing the vibrations of him. That laughter Katherine had often stayed up Saturdays for; sometimes crawling in on her hands and knees to the lip of the dining room, pressing her palms against the soft Berber carpet, trying not to burst into giggles as she slowly padded to make her way beneath the card table set up in the middle of things: away from the couch, the china cabinet, and the two overstuffed chairs. That long, shiny card table sat directly in the center, ladies around it, all that perfume and women's chatter in the air, the scent of Peach Schnapps evident in their pitcher of imposter iced tea. If Katherine ever found a way inside their secret space, it would mean minutes of admiring all the ladies' high-heeled shoes and stockings. They sat around it as guards, barely an inch between them: Mrs. McClintock, the piano teacher from down the block, Mrs. Crawley, a Sunday school teacher that worked with her mother at the local Church of Christ, and sweet Mrs. Baskin, Brandon's mom, who always knew she wanted under that table more than anything, who parted her knees to let her through, who often reached down and fed her ginger snaps between games.

There, in the heat of the pulled stockings and sweaty female feet, Katherine would sit wondrously, studying the shape of each woman's knee, the angles of their shin bones glistening beneath shiny hose, and wondering what it must feel like to wear such fancy skirts and proper shoes all day. There, in that quiet coven, she would wait for her mother's laughter, the rhythm shaking the entire table, their bellies, cards, and the pitcher of spiked iced tea. Under that sea of femininity, she would wait hesitantly until someone kicked out her foot but a mere two inches, and caught Katherine snooping on a night with friends.

A Woman's Ring

"You have no respect, young lady," her mother would snap, the lady who'd looked so beautiful from the knee down just moments ago, now pulling her daughter up sharply by the elbows, shoving her toward her room.

It was the room that sat close to her parents' at the back of their one lone hallway. From beneath her quilt, Katherine had often waited for sounds in the night, sounds of passion from a woman who knew not how to love and a man who had adored Ruth for an eternity, until his physical needs had seeped into other women in sloppy one night rendezvous. Tiptoeing outside their door, Katherine had listened for any life beyond what she knew of them – her mother, the Sunday school teacher, her father, the consultant. Before he died, she'd often imagined that those dreary facades would melt off them at night with their clothing – that they would nudge each others' soft skin, and that she might somehow listen hard enough to hear the awkward, urgent sounds of their lovemaking. Would he tear at her as he tore at legs of chicken, gnawing, spitting, and swallowing in one messy bite? Would she nibble at his neck and shoulders, sliding up against him with her tight, slim body, wrapping her knees against his hipbones, begging and laughing as Katherine had watched her laugh – that magic of her throat and eyes welling up, pressing down on him, her entire being overpowered in his arms, crushed into consummating what they'd created over twenty years ago?

It's what she imagined with Brandon, her legs wrapping around his body, squeezing her love into his ribs, showcasing that emotion that she reserved for him, for boxing, for the escape they'd make in due time. Only now, on the grass with the crickets and dirt, did she feel the beginnings of doubt inside her, doubt like she'd had her entire lifetime when remembering her orphanage, that place where unwanted children slept and cried for parenting.

"No one wants me," she'd often said, making an exception for the "orphan mother," a woman with curly red hair and big, soft hands who'd been her caretaker until the age of three. She'd taught Katherine to walk, her toddler's frame fastened between the bigger woman's thighs, holding onto the adult hands as she moved forward left foot, then right. There was the first time on the toilet, the orphan mother clapping eagerly as Katherine sprayed into a red, plastic training bowl; the beginnings of vocabulary lessons, her mouth learning to say such small words.

"That's my girl," she used to say before tucking Katherine into bed. "You're such a good girl." When she'd left that place with the bright rooms and hallways, she'd clung to the orphan mother, dropping tears and snot against her sweater, yanking at the woman's hair. For years, Katherine had expected to see that woman at her new home's window, saying, "Come here, my little angel. You're such a good girl." Katherine hunted for that phantom face as she would one day hunt for her birth mother. A small, tucked promise of some kind of rescue.

She'd thought of Brandon as her only real rescue since then, since her father's funeral, their bonds transcending the petty games and rules of teenage love. Yet he was playing them, throwing her away to Andrew, the man who perused the streets, searching for a girl with no hope, no love. Hadn't her father always said to follow her dreams? To make her way out of Ohio? Wouldn't Andrew be able to give her a way? A life outside mediocrity?

If Andrew were to drive past now, he would find her crying tears of a rejected girl – her hands fisted and punching the air with every burden, every pang, every missed opportunity of her youth. She wanted Brandon's love and not Andrew's, wanted that acceptance as deeply as she wanted to leave this town, as deeply as she wanted the dream of boxing, as deeply as she wanted the world.

A Woman's Ring

Chapter Six

The doctor regarded her head as he would a canvas – the blue hospital smock draped over her anesthetized frame. This was his art – carving the lives of patients into recovery. He stared down at the girl who boxed, who'd told him she'd be the best someday, recalling a little girl he'd just operated on two hours ago who had wanted to ride horses and marry a rich man. Now she was in Intensive Care, as Katherine would be.

"Boxing," he'd told Katherine in their pre-op meeting, "saved your life. If you hadn't developed headaches, if you hadn't come to me...it might have been fatal." What she didn't know was that this was, in fact, fatal. Going under the knife always meant a risk of not coming out again – his hands on her brain were the only chance to rid this thing from her life – but even then, it could reappear.

He began to cut in, slitting and stretching the scalp to saw through the skull cap, her head twitching as the skull greeted him under rivers of blood, his soothing voice calling, "sponge, sponge," to remove the fluid that shielded her cyst. There it sat, peeking up out of aggravated veins, a small iceberg whose depth went beyond the fillet into the coils of the brain, into the center of her life.

When he'd removed the damaged skull, he noticed its abnormal fragility. It was like an eggshell, probably worn down since birth. The intrusive vein wrapped itself around the mass, taunting his hands to do what they'd been trained to do, cut it loose from this net, as if that vein was the only thing standing in the way of her survival.

Dr. Hopkins cut slowly and deliberately around the vein, watching the monitors, moving with exacting precision. He waited, amazed at the swell of the vein that disguised the cyst, the vein which prevented his work from being done in a swift fashion. Finally, with excessive prodding and slicing, he removed the mass in four small clumps, some slimy, some smooth, some swollen, as the nurse caught them in a jar, the last bit hemorrhaging from all the prodding.

"Take the remains to the lab, Susan."

Katherine's eyes moved in her head. Dreamlike. The halo held her still, two drills lodged into her forehead, blood leaking down both sides of her head as if she'd been shot. Perhaps she could hear him speak. He always wondered if his patients could somehow sense him, could understand the mechanics of what it took to go in and not know your chances – people's lives in his hands.

As he was preparing the titanium to fit over the skull, he heard the head nurse, Gail, gasp and drop one of the IV bags to the floor. As one, the crew witnessed Katherine's body begin to tremble, the pulse plummeting on the monitor, her hands beginning to shake in small, anomalous fits.

"Christ." *He whispered, as he signaled the nurses for back-up.* "She's having a seizure."

A Woman's Ring

Chapter Seven

Why wasn't she under the bleachers with boys or getting big, blanched tattoos around her biceps and calves? Her father had died, her mother could care less if she jumped off the Brooklyn Bridge (though she'd have to get quite a bit of money if she ever expected to make it to New York alone), and yet here she was, behaving. Perhaps it was Betty and Brandon keeping her safely under control – always talking her away from the ledge, making sure she was well fed and comfortable. The closest she'd come to rebellion was when she and Brandon smoked cigarettes in their tree house and pretended to be stoned in school.

Katherine closed her eyes, thinking over the nine years it had been since her father passed away. She'd gone to school, attended church, cried in the night and wished a thousand dreams. She should have sneaked out more, run around with the wrong crowd, or had more experience.

She wanted more than a story to tell – she wanted a chance out of her own world before contaminating it by having some kind of bad record. Katherine took a long, shaky breath and thought of Andrew. All the girls in high school were dating regular boys – sometimes even in grades below theirs. If Martha or Christy knew she was dating someone twelve years older, what would they say? Would they be incredibly fascinated and finally ask her to hang out – or would they laugh and say what a freak she was because she couldn't date normal boys like them?

Katherine sat up in bed and stretched. It felt like she could never win. She didn't quite fit in, but no one exactly made fun of her either. She just blended, disappeared with the brick walls of school, the lackluster scenery of the town. She sighed, reaching to her night stand for an apple. She always stashed fruit, spare snacks and bottles of water in her room so she could stay out of the remainder of the house as much as possible. If only she had a bathroom, then she'd never have to see the creaking floorboards and grimy furniture that composed her home, or the woman that infested it.

She bit into the green flesh and pulled her comforter around her. Andrew. She closed her eyes and imagined his hands on her, what it would feel like to be fondled by the arms of experience. Could she let him seduce her?

As the hours bled into the early afternoon, Katherine got out of bed, stripped off her night clothes, and put a sundress on. She opened her door and peered into the murky darkness of the hallway – ghostlike. Walking into the living room, she found her mother wrapped in an afghan, watching muted television.

Startled to find her mother at home, Katherine awkwardly paused and mumbled hello.

Ruth's head turned slightly, her eyes still on the television. "Afternoon."

Katherine darted in front of her and exited the house, letting that shroud of stale life slip from her shoulders as the soft rays of Urbana sun, the aroma of freshly mowed grass and chirping birds encircled her. She made her way across the street to Brandon's house, knocking lightly on his window. Maybe they'd ride bikes today or drive across town. She looked behind her, at the house she longed to move from.

Or maybe, she thought, inching back from the window before Brandon could see her, she'd look for Andrew today –get to know the man who wanted her to be his girlfriend. He usually hung around Jilly's at this time on a Saturday. Katherine hopped on her bike, gathering her dress in a knot between her legs. She pedaled furiously down the street, avoiding the rare car that crept along the pavement.

What would she say when she saw him? As she pulled into the graveled drive of Jilly's, only a few cars graced the lot. Not Andrew's. Sighing, she made her way over to Thelma's, deciding to grab some coffee and head back to Brand's. They could study for midterms and play basketball. Pulling into the parking area,

A Woman's Ring

she skidded to a sudden halt, startled to see Andrew leaning against the trunk of his car, eating a muffin with one hand, scanning a newspaper with the other.

He looked up as she approached, tossing the paper behind him on the car. "Well, well, what a perfect midday surprise."

Despite herself, Katherine blushed, hopping off her bike and unknotting her dress – very deliberately and slowly. She saw his eyes travel to the softness of her inner thighs, the way she slowly brushed her fingers against herself in the process. He swallowed, willing his eyes back to her face.

"Um, so what's the pleasure of your visit?"

Katherine smiled, sauntering over to him. She opened her mouth and leaned in to take a bite of the muffin that Andrew extended in one hand.

"I'm hungry," she said, licking her lips while spraying crumbs into the cool spring air. He laughed and leaned in to remove a few flakes from her chin.

"Well, I can help you with that, you know."

She smiled, wondering why not, why shouldn't he be the one to experiment with, to fall into for a while.

Katherine swallowed and stood to her full height, which barely reached his expansive shoulders. "Help me, then," she whispered, moving a foot closer, so both their bodies were mere inches from one another. "Help me," she said, watching his full lips part into a smile – as he leaned down to her ear.

"I can help you do a lot of things, Katherine. Let's go for a ride and the lessons can begin."

Katherine felt her heart thrashing in her chest, felt a sickness settling in her gut. A million thoughts hammered through her head. What would happen once she was in his car? Would he throw himself atop her? Where would she leave her bike? She didn't have a lock – could she strap it to his car? Who would possibly have a rope nearby? Maybe she could fit it in the backseat -- was his car even big enough to fit a bike in? She backed up quickly, calling her own bluff. Why could she never just go with what she was feeling without some kind of rushed over analysis?

"Um, actually, maybe another time," she mumbled, hopping on her bike, the skirt of her dress billowing behind her. She raced toward home, feeling like an idiot, knowing he was sure to give up on her now.

She knew before her next breath that the real reason was Brandon. He was the one she wanted to kiss, to experience all those things with for the first time. Sighing, she entered the slope of her driveway and dismounted her bike by the garage. Once again, she walked over to Brandon's house, this time knocking twice on the front door.

He answered in jeans, a lime t-shirt and a smile, his hair rumpled from an obvious afternoon nap. "Hey, Katie." He opened the screen door and leaned against the frame.

"Want to play some ball?"

He smirked and nodded. "Always. Let me just get my shoes, okay?" He began walking down the hall then turned. "You playing in that dress?"

Katherine tipped her chin up defiantly. "Yes, and I'm going to beat you in this dress, too."

He laughed and continued on toward his room as Katherine retreated down the steps around to the small basketball court. This was better, she told herself as she picked up the ball and tossed it effortlessly through the net. Basketball was safer – for all she knew, she could be in Andrew's car right now, rounding third base. She shuddered, thinking of his hands all over her, though she had just entertained that scenario less than ten minutes ago.

As Brandon loped around to the backyard, she couldn't help but smile. He was what she wanted, she thought, as he boldly came up and staked a claim on his ball.

"To twenty-five by ones?"

Katherine nodded and opened her mouth to say something meaningful. To break the spell of their friendship into something more, as she'd tried to so many times. Instead she said "Sure" and checked the ball as their game began.

One day, she thought, *we will experience more.*

A Woman's Ring

Chapter Eight

Andrew was the kind of man who flicked gray ash onto the arms and wrists of passersby – a man who'd watch that flicker and sizzle from his own cigarette transfer to the flesh of arms or knees. Ash that melted the skin into craters the size of small, lucid diamonds.

Occasionally, he would turn to catch the expressions of small children and grown men who hunted the sky and small Urbana crowds to find the culprit of their pain. Andrew, with the cuffs of his shirtsleeves secured against his biceps, would flex and smile at the victims, an ominous reminder of the powers of men.

In that town, under that net of his father's company, where his only intention was to ebb the flow of his spending, to settle into a quiet spot, unnoticed, he'd found Katherine in her driveway, Katherine on the road, Katherine in front of her school, looking bored and angry as any teenage girl. He decided to pursue her – the girl who'd lope home after school with the gait of an insecure woman, who experienced moments of courage, then hopelessness, her looks a constant give-away. He knew those looks – his mother had worn them – the woman who'd walked the same dichotomous steps of Katherine, both their shoulders hunched, worry weighing down the bones, arms crossed then swinging, as if struggling to let on to that agony that memories could bring.

Andrew would have Katherine, even if she did not want him. He knew time could change the world, time could open that virginal slit of her emotions, that frigid mask where nothing moved unless prompted to. Time would erase that mask, would erase the walls she erected, those tall, lonesome buttresses.

For Katherine, this was the only time to entertain the what-ifs and conflicted emotions that young girls pondered. Inside her house with the loneliness of dusty furniture and tacky curtains, she'd consider her choices – the frightening prospect that she might not love Brandon enough for the both of them. That her heart could not speak for his – that in this small town, under that spell where college or moving was not an option without money, she had to find an escape, some way that would peel back the skin of Urbana into the tender state line, giving her room to explore. A purse of money, a reason. Andrew came as the only answer, that face that shone with lambent eyes and the beginnings of laugh lines. Lips that would trail over her hands at the ends of dates, where she'd waver between wiping away the wetness or kissing that same spot, still warm from his intentions.

"Andrew…what am I doing here?"

Andrew would often look at Katherine as she questioned her place in his life, most times from the driver's seat of his car, his hands moving centimeters across the red seats to tease at her skin.

"You're here because there's nowhere else to go." He almost meant those words, wanted to say, "Without me there isn't," wanted to love her as much as he could love a youth in all his thirty years. This girl that could seduce him with a curl of lip or wobbling of chin. This girl who he studied as his own father had studied wife number two, then three. The way he spoke of them, as objects, as ornaments, as legs that spread and popped out babies and were there for the sole purpose of pleasing a man.

"You find you one, Andrew. See how she fits before you decide to go on the prowl like I did."

Andrew was sick of the hunt, sick of the easy women who fondled his neck on business trips and pouted for the cash they knew he had in the pockets of every suit, jean, or satchel.

"It's just *money*, Andrew. You'll make more you know." They'd tease him like only women can, sucking on his stiffness, as if he dared say no. It was always the money, money like lightning that lit him up, money that ruined things, money that shook his hands in the night as if in need of pills or drink, that made him curl beneath a blanket wishing for someone who'd forget the cash, forget the freedoms and prisons it built.

A Woman's Ring

With Katherine, they were both part of a manipulation, in which neither knew the other's motives; while Andrew was part sincere in his search, Katherine was growing impatient to shed the anxiety of her life and begin anew. They were both on a mission to end the hunt, to build a life, Andrew wanting to try Katherine on, to burrow into those tight, covered places where no one else had been.

"Why am I *here*?" Katherine asked again, knocking her head gently against the passenger window, wanting to nail her fists through it, feeling the bleed, the sting, the relief from fused glass wrecked beneath her hands. Andrew inspected her thighs as she sat beside him, up to the birthing hips he wanted to grip, the small breasts beneath her T-shirt that might one day grow large. His, she would be his, he knew it as he stared at her from toe to head, from hip to breast, playing out the future in his mind.

"I'll take care of you, Katherine…God, I swear I will." He growled from that pit of truth swelling in the bowl of his stomach, a massive intrusion of honesty -- "if you let me," he promised, "if you let me." He would care for her the way his father cared for money and alcohol, the way Katherine cared for the meaning of a dream, the way Andrew suddenly cared to risk everything – opening that rusted place inside himself – for her.

A Woman's Ring

Chapter Nine

They'd been sixteen. It was an angry September, heavy with rain and burdened by storms. Despite the circumstances, Brandon and Katherine packed up a tent, a cooler of sandwiches and drinks, and the sleeping bag Katherine's father had given to her before he died. This was the first time in years she'd touched the purple fabric, stared at the Care Bears that dotted the front, the lavender zipper on the side. Together they ventured in Brandon's car, driving the couple hours to Laison Camp Grounds for a trip they'd been planning for weeks now.

Unsurprisingly, the site was bare, speckled with the few troopers who adored camping as much as they. Secretly, Katherine couldn't have cared less about the camping -- cared only for the possibility of romance. She'd even packed a sexy pair of underwear she'd bought at Dillard's, telling the clerk, Mrs. Shims, that they were going to be made into a headband.

"For design class," she'd murmured, before bolting out of the store.

Brandon pulled the car into a parking spot and killed the engine. The ground was moist from unending rain, but there was a pause in the weather, enough for them to set up camp and start a fire for roasted marshmallows.

They worked almost silently, with the rare joke or complaint about school, the recent happiness at both receiving their licenses.

All the while, there wasn't a shadow of closeness, not until the fire had died and they were snuggled within the triangular canvas of Brandon's tent, witnessing the night as it measured around them -- the cracking of lightning, urgency of thunder and raindrops that hit and dripped off that sclerous fabric like long, wet dreams. Both of them reveling in the freedom away from home, the closeness.

Brandon moved closer to cup Katherine's ear, whispering something under the thunder clap and heavy drizzle. His words, "make a wish," pushed her to the biggest aspiration of her teenage years. Wet panties and rubbed out thighs. Stiff parts and orgasms. Unadulterated, guiltless wanting.

"What do you wish for, Katie?"

"Lots of things. Escape, warmth, passion." Katherine spun off her answers, lingering a bit on the last word as if he could hear the pining in her voice.

Brandon clicked his small yellow flashlight on and off, pointing small breasts of light into the tent's pointed top, then off again, leaving only the faint illusion of a circle in its wake. "Escape." He sighed, rolling over to her again, gray eyes animate with the energy she loved him for. That independence he possessed, the capability to disconnect from the world, to differentiate longing from anger – the way he did that without effort or resentment – unlike her.

"Escape sounds nice, doesn't it? Kind of like what we're doing now?"

Katherine nodded in response, listening to the rain, remembering her father, her perfect vacation in Florida – how much love she'd felt. "Do you think I'll get out of Ohio, Brand?" Katherine stared down at her purple sleeping bag, suddenly feeling eight again. "I mean, do you think I can make something out of myself? Be a boxer? I know everyone else is going to college, getting an education, but I just can't fathom more school, more exams, more –"

"Katie, stop." He reached over and placed his hand in hers. "I promise you'll get out of here. We both will, remember?" He squeezed her hand, smiling in the darkness of moon slick perfection, Katherine letting the thunder and light seize her with its vigor, hoping to become as lively as the night above them. "Who knows? You might change your mind about school in a few years, find something you really want to do. Pursue both boxing and something else. You know, something to fall back on."

A Woman's Ring

"Hmm, maybe." A roar of thunder shook the ground then, rattled the tent, and Katherine found herself burrowing into Brandon's chest, still feeling vulnerable.

"Hey, it's okay, Katie. It's fine." He rubbed her back, fiddling with his other hand to find the flashlight, clicking it nervously. Here, he had a girl in his arms; they were alone and could do whatever they pleased. He wasn't blind. He knew the way Katie felt – saw it in her eyes, felt it in her every word, as if begging him to take her. Brandon cleared his throat, knowing he couldn't make a move on her. It was Katherine – his best friend, a sister almost. He shook his head as if affirming his decision, ignoring the weight of her head on his chest, the long hair spread like a fan between them, the sweet smell of her perfume. There was momentary silence in the campsite, as if the thunder had knocked out all life other than the two of them. "Know what?"

"What?" Katherine asked, ingesting the scent of his detergent and bit of marshmallow that had dripped onto his shirt by the fire.

"We're going to leave Urbana. I know we are. So let's just not worry about it now, okay? We've got plenty of time."

Katherine nodded against his chest and settled back to her own side, thinking back to what her father used to say about time. How you should seize it, because you never knew how much you had. But she had honestly believed his time would go on forever, that he would watch her graduate, walk her down the aisle, help her shop for her first home. Katherine buried the memories and felt around in her backpack for a candy bar.

"Caramello?" She asked, offering Brandon a warm piece of caramel. He took it, biting it straight off her fingers, his warm gums brushing her, the strings of beige candy slack and descending between them onto the tent's bottom. She felt her breath slip away, her finger warm and wet from his advances.

"Sticky," he mumbled with his mouth full, jumping as another bolt of thunder shook the tent, and sent them into nervous smiling.

"Most things are, Brand," she whispered, swallowing her bit, watching the rain outside, rolling away clear and tender.

Rea Frey

A Woman's Ring

Chapter Ten

She saw them after school.

Katherine had gone to Martha's Bakery for the chocolate chip scones Brandon loved. Sometimes, if the weather was right, they'd crawl up to the nook of their tree house, spread out a blanket, and gorge themselves on scones and hot hazelnut coffee, talking about anything.

Katherine balanced the coffees in one hand and the bag of freshly baked scones in the other as she walked up Mrs. Baskin's drive, waving as she came onto the side porch with a broom to sweep orange and yellow leaves into tiny, neat piles.

"Afternoon, Katie." Mrs. Baskin raised one fleshy arm and gestured at Katherine.

"Hey, Betty. Just bringing some nourishment after school." Katherine lifted the bag so Mrs. Baskin could see the treats from the bakery. Even though she only had two scones, she offered her one, not wanting to seem rude. "Care for a scone?"

"Oh no, Katie, that's the last thing I need." Betty pinched her upper arm and stretched it at least four inches. "You see this? That's from years of thinking I could eat everything and taking advantage of anything made with the key ingredients – butter, cream, and chocolate."

Katherine smiled and continued walking around the back of the house, not encouraging Betty to spill another one of her many "unfit" stories. Betty had never been fit. Even as a child, she'd been the one to eat donuts in the dark, slurp chocolate milk in the classroom, and hide candy bars in shoe boxes at the back of her closet.

Katherine rounded the back corner of the house, walked past the shed, hearing voices coming from their tree house. She stopped, immediately startled, but remembered Brandon was writing a short story for Mr. Larraby's class and perhaps he was just reading it aloud. Placing the scones in her backpack, Katherine climbed the ladder with one hand, balancing the coffees expertly in the other.

She pushed the top latch, felt its weight slip over her head as she set the coffees down and hoisted herself through. "Brand – look what I got!"

She climbed up to her waist before stopping, a witness to the scene before her. "What – what are *you* doing here?" Her eyes narrowed, fists tightening against the wood. "It's Stacy, isn't it?"

Stacy nodded, flipping her blonde hair over one shoulder. Katherine noticed how close she was sitting to Brandon, some sort of brochures spread just inches between them. They had two mugs of tea and the remains of cookie crumbs piled on a yellow plate at the rickety end table behind them. Katherine tried not to scream, to beat this girl in the face, to run back to Mrs. Baskin and ask why she didn't tell her that he had *company*.

Stacy. Brandon had met her at an Aviation class two months ago in Texas. He'd actually gathered enough money from summer jobs to make the weekend trip. She was older, they'd clicked immediately, and now she was here, though she didn't belong. Katherine couldn't help the jealousy that raged through her at the sight of this woman – she was breathtakingly beautiful in such a natural, simple way. Long hair, slim nose, full lips and a sultry attitude. She hated her.

"Hello, Katherine, how are you?" Stacy smoothed a hand over her hair and glanced at Brandon. "Um, I didn't know you were coming – Brandon and I were just looking at some possibilities for Aviation Academies and –"

"Oh, how special that you can share that with him." Katherine knew she was being petty, knew her jealousy shone in her eyes and spiked her every syllable. But she didn't care. This girl was after only one thing – her best friend and the boy she loved. "This happens to be *our* tree house, Stacy – no one else is invited in. Ever."

A Woman's Ring

"Katherine." Brandon said her name softly, looking first at her then down at the timbered floor. "Don't overreact. Stacy's just a...friend."

Katherine couldn't help hearing the inflection in his voice, the way his and her cheeks reddened on that special word *friend*.

"I didn't know you were coming, Katherine. Stacy and I would have met somewhere else..."

"But you know this is our spot, our place, *ours*." Katherine spat the words, felt the tears well as she picked up one of the coffees and chucked it right between them, the liquid bursting out of the flimsy lid as they both scrambled to escape the scald. Katherine scurried back down the ladder and began sprinting across the yard. She couldn't believe he was with Stacy. He barely knew her! Did Brandon want Katherine to know he was no longer interested in her? That it took blonde hair and tanned legs to attract his attention?

Katherine adjusted her backpack as she ran, not wanting to go home. She just wanted to be with Brandon. She always wanted to be with him. It was what they did – spend time together, laugh, eat, imagine. When had other women become a factor for them?

All through school, neither of them had ever been too interested in dating. Katherine had always been curious, but mostly for Brandon. And she assumed he'd given her the same courtesy. They'd made a *plan* -- one that couldn't be destroyed by some tall woman who shared the same passion as Brandon and encouraged him to move far away from Katherine.

Katherine felt the tears explode over her face as she ventured down the street. The cool air pelted her back, brought relief to the heat of her cheeks. She rounded the corners of the neighborhood, feeling the warmth of the scones in her backpack. The sobs caught in her throat at the thought of losing Brandon. What if he moved away without her? Was he sick of her moods, her own dreams, her obvious inadequacies? What would she do without her best friend?

As Katherine turned to come back home, a red Cadillac slowed in the opposite direction, the driver side window inching down.

Andrew.

Katherine wiped at her eyes and looked both ways before crossing the street. She walked up to his window, saw the glittering eyes and slick, black hair, the smile that probably brought women to their knees in any town.

She sniffed and he noticed that she'd been crying. "Want a ride, Katherine?"

Katherine glanced in the car, then looked down the street toward the short distance to her home. She thought of how she'd run away from Andrew just weeks ago – how she'd almost given up on the idea of him wanting her. Though it felt nice to have him constantly hounding her – to have him want her company every single evening (though she had accompanied him a few nights to the coffee shop) -- she figured his intentions were impure, that he would grow bored of her and move on to some other place. He had money. A life. Experience. But she did want a ride away from here – even if it was with a man she hardly knew.

"Katherine?"

She faked her best smile and leaned in close to Andrew, who stared at her tits with a devilish grin. He could practically touch them, they were so close, but somehow he restrained.

"So, how about it? Want a ride?"

"I'd love a ride, Andrew." She leaned in the car, and brushed her lips next to his ear. "As long as it's not home."

Chapter Eleven

It was too late for them. Brandon saw the way Andrew looked at Katherine, with such lying eyes. She'd already made up her mind to get him back for his time with Stacy, and as much as he resented it, he would have to let her purge her system.

He sighed. It was always like this with Katherine – one minute, you saw the whole world through her eyes and the next you were cowering from her evil glances, her sharp words. Brandon moved off his bed and picked up the brochure Stacy had given him – Westwood College in Chicago. She was going in two months – had a friend to stay with until she got a part-time job for rent. Though her parents offered her money, Stacy always thought it responsible to buy her own things, pave her own way.

"Come on, Brandon. We can learn together." Even as she'd said it, he'd seen the flirtation in her eyes, the way she held her hips in long, tapered fingers, her belly button barely peeking from the top of her low-waisted jeans. "You know you want to."

And God, did he want to.

Pack his things, board a plane and leave this town. It was what he and Katherine shared most intensely – their passion to pursue the world. But Stacy had never been a part of that dream until now – Stacy had never experienced the intense bond between lifelong friends.

Brandon raked a hand through his choppy hair and shoved the brochure back inside his top desk drawer. If there's one thing he was, it was honorable – his parents had taught him right from wrong, but most importantly, to keep promises. And he'd promised Katherine – promised they would venture together, that he would stick by her through other cities, through further years.

What had once been a sloppy pinky swear in their tree house was now a more achievable possibility. Money seemed the only issue, though they'd both been saving. And Katherine's father had set up a special savings account when she was just a baby, putting in money every week until he died.

Brandon picked up his keys from the desk and yelled to his mom that he was going for a drive. He had decisions to make, promises to keep, or break. Stacy or Katherine. Illinois or Ohio. There was only one way he'd leave without Katherine.

Brandon climbed into his car, clenching the steering wheel as he thought of Andrew and his quest for someone innocent. The man that reeked of ineptitude and sleazy intentions. He only hoped Katherine wasn't ignorant enough to fall for the appearance of wealth. And though he'd been startled with Andrew's attention for her, he hadn't expected her to actually go on a date with him. But he'd seen them at Thelma's, on the street, Katherine coming out of his car with her head down and a hint of a smile on her lips. Is that the kind of man she really wanted? The kind of future she'd have?

As Brandon turned onto Schute's Pike, he began to wonder. When Katherine got angry, she was likely to plunge into anything, and if that anything was Andrew, then he *would* go to Chicago – honorable or not, he would make his way – with or without her.

Chapter Twelve

Andrew watched the moon's rays reflect upon her face, as they lay on the hood of his car, barely touching – stars sentient above them. This was their sixth date and he was careful to move slowly, so as not to dissuade her from his true intentions: the wanting of thrusted fabric, the slide of his fingers beneath her bra, cupping what was soft and round, probing what was deep and wet, for superlative pleasure. He shifted his pants and sighed dramatically, knowing he would wait until he had her hand in marriage, because for Katherine that was the only way. He knew of her fixation with Brandon – but also knew that Brandon could not do for her what he could. This he attempted to explain with his subtle tactics, manipulating her thoughts – though when he talked, her eyes sometimes took on a steely glaze, as if she were impenetrable, his words worthless.

But still she remained. Perhaps she didn't have anywhere else to go, or perhaps she felt the heat of curiosity between her thighs, the enticement of vacations and travel – a way out of her hometown.

"What do you think, Katherine?" He fingered the strands of her hair, picking up the scent of florid shampoo. "What do you think…of us?"

Katherine released the breath she felt had been trapped in her for seventeen years. She knew she was softening. For once, she wanted to be cared for. And not like Brandon had cared for her all those years, because though he'd been there for every occasion, like a friend and father, she'd wanted so much more than comfort. It was as if Brandon had been and still was oblivious to the look in her eye – to the desperation set off in her every action and appearance. She wanted him. The way she dressed in slim lines and tight fits, intentionally brushing the hair from his eyes, her hands on his face, fingers on his forearms, laughing and hugging him – her whispers. His refusal as easy as anything.

She didn't want to crave anymore. With Andrew, the feeling was incomparable, because she was only curious. No maddening passion, no flutters – when he touched her, it was with the hands of a man, the hands that had turned down beds in hotels across the continent, had held different drinks and eaten the exotic foods of other cultures. This she sought – and with his promises to care for her, to show her, to love and give her the things she'd always dreamed of, how could she resist?

She had no one older or wiser to guide her. Though Mrs. Baskin had been a surrogate mother, she was as old-fashioned as they came. "A woman should be a wife and mother," she'd say. "Accept her place in this world. That's what women do, you know."

Andrew was a way to say goodbye to her own mother, a way to meet up with Brandon, when she and Andrew went their separate ways – when all had expired between them. It would take immediate travel to keep Katherine from becoming bitter, and for Andrew it would take settling down with prospects of marriage and family to keep his word.

A Woman's Ring

Chapter Thirteen

He loved her in the way older men loved younger women. The challenge of handling her, provoking a smile – taking preciously from that reserve of ambition she still held tight to: the disillusions of true happiness amidst certain despair. He wanted to rearrange her attitude, show her that she didn't have to run, though she'd most certainly fight him to. Katherine felt it was her right to explore as Andrew had, visiting posh shops and dining in fine restaurants, where she would order the most decadent item on the menu.

Some night, he would hold her close and relive his own travels – tell her of China, Quebec and Italy, New York, Boston and Denver. In those places, he'd squeezed cheap women against his chest, rolled over expensive bed linens while listening to their ramblings of big diamonds and summer vacations in Tahiti. He'd seen it all, felt the heat of women, the greed that often came when wealth was involved. He wanted to stop running as much as Katherine wanted to begin. Together, they searched the need in each others' eyes – the demand to be someone outside themselves – to slow down or speed up, where women didn't pine over the expense of Andrew's lifestyle, where wom*en* would fade simply to wom*an*, and where Katherine could step out of Urbana and on toward more thrilling prospects.

Urbana was the first town where Andrew had smelled the fresh, warm air and the blossoming flowers, where he had existed in the high rise of anonymity and the lack of attractive women. That's why Katherine had pulled him the way no woman quite had. Barely grown at eighteen, he could remember the sweet taste of youth and the way life seemed as though it would go on forever. He envied that. He needed that. She held such maturity in her bones and movements – the eyes that spoke of anguish that most women would not experience until much later in life. He learned quickly of her ambitions, yet somewhere deep inside him he figured that being a wife and mother would soothe her need – would squelch the fire for running because she would become content with the resolve. He wanted to make up for his father's mistakes – mold this young child into the kind of wife and mother his own had never quite been. Only then could he be romantic. Trust her enough to let her go on her own, to fulfill her fantasies when he was much too old and there were no more children to raise.

In Katherine, Andrew saw the possibility of a wife, of a respectful existence; yet he knew if he pushed her too quickly she would resent him. Andrew's selfishness prevented him from being truly sentimental, although he knew what it was to love. He knew the wounds it could inflict, how those words could lead to depression, cheating and nights spent alone – yes, he knew of love.

Katherine humored him on dates, accepting that he was a businessman first and boyfriend second. He couldn't comfort her in the way Brandon had so easily, with a draping of arm or small joke that could earn gigantic laughter. Around her shoulders, Andrew's arms were not welcome, although his words carried the weight of promises, of pursued passions. She seemed sedated by his promises, but reluctant to accept any physical ties. If it had been Brandon, she would have popped the buttons off her shirt, cupped her own breasts in warm palms, and spread her legs to demand he enter her with slow, even stroking. But with Andrew, she was uncertain in his advances – ashamed of her innocence and his experience.

He was a foolish man who understood basic needs but not a woman's will. He had only experienced his mother, who had crumpled beneath his father's hand and became one with her pills and powders while good old Dad seduced women when traveling. Who Katherine was could not be contained or placated by a marriage license or the patter of tiny feet on expensive tile. She needed the freedom her father had lost in his marriage, yet she wanted the security of finances, the warmth of a man, the

A Woman's Ring

closeness of a companion. She wanted what was deserved – everything.

On dates, she fooled herself into thinking he understood her. Perhaps deep down, he did – knew of her wishes and sorrows but was much too selfish to let her explore them. Though with Brandon she felt in one moment what she'd craved an entire lifetime from a man, she felt with Andrew the possibility – the catalyst to unfold her future. Didn't that take money and security?

Perhaps she was playing games. On those first dates, she'd wanted a gentleman. Andrew sensed it, and became one – reluctantly. He took her hand, popped champagne, and listened intently to her conversation, though his mind was on future endeavors. He knew he wanted her, and not for the purest of reasons. If he had been a good man, he would have let her go – knowing that she would never be satisfied with a man whose desires for himself were stronger than for her. He needed women. Without a slim body to shadow his, he could not concentrate, could not breathe. To Andrew, Katherine was a sign of new beginnings – and to Katherine, Andrew was a means of launching her journey, her kismet in a world whose faith had become unbraceable.

Rea Frey

A Woman's Ring

Chapter Fourteen

On her wedding night, Andrew pulled at the buttons of the dress Katherine had found in her mother's attic, the cream A-line tattered by moths. He slid the skirt to her hips, the white panties pulled over to one side. Katherine closed her eyes as Andrew pressed his thick, hairy hands between her legs, the tips of them wet for easy access.

"You're not as wet as I thought you'd be," he growled, running his whiskers across her neck, Katherine's skin rippling from the touch of this man, her *husband*. All the courting and promises and here they were, in a home just three miles from her mother's, where the furniture was exquisite but the fit of the town was the same – his excuses things like "It takes time to find homes in cities…just be patient." Katherine, wanting to leave but having nowhere to go, would stay until the opportunity materialized when she could abandon him, rekindle Brandon's affection and explore the life she should have led.

"You can trust me, you know," Andrew had said, flicking that oiled up hair off his forehead, running one finger along her jaw. "I'll take care of you, you know that, Katherine. You'll never have to worry about anything. You'll have more money than you know what to do with…you can go anywhere and do anything."

Those words had done it, had sealed her fate as she'd imagined another world with gloves and happiness; that Andrew was simply the source of her welfare and she could act on loving him, that it would never be real, though the splitting emotions of taking that bait or waiting for Brandon haunted her, even now. If she had waited, would Brandon have ever supported her as

Andrew could? Would they have stolen Andrew's cash and run away together, never to be seen again? Would he have forgotten Stacy? That's what she'd hoped and almost planned for, Andrew's money a scapegoat, Katherine leaving that squalid rich man on a sunny afternoon, no note or goodbye, just cash and bags, Brandon and planes, flying far from Ohio.

But there was only disgust as his hands mauled her. She couldn't deny that there had been an initial attraction – the teasing promises and unidentifiable charm of an older man – but he was not taking her slowly as she might have hoped for, all candles and romance and long, sumptuous stroking. He held with force, leaving her a heap of nerves on their bed. She couldn't help but wish for Brandon.

Her best friend's hatred for their marriage was evident, from the way he shot hoops in his backyard, slamming the basketball in the net until it bent from the weight of his hands on the rim, to the way he destroyed Katherine's name that was carved in their oak tree, chipping away the letters one flake at a time. She wanted nothing more than to run with him, to join his dreams of piloting and her dreams of boxing into one goal, moving away where the world would be their template for creating.

Yet she was in Andrew's arms, in their new home that was "only temporary," Andrew promised, Katherine's eyes tightly shut as he unzipped his black pants and shoved himself against her. Her first time. She braced herself for what was coming, fighting the urge to push him off her as victims will push off their molesters. He ground into her, cupping her bottom in his hands, pulling her into him, the sweat off his belly saturating her dress. She felt the burn of virginity part for his experience, and fought the urge not to bite down on the flesh of his neck, milling her pain into him. He poked his way inside her, slow then urgent, then like a teenager, a crooked smile on his lips as he moaned her name, "Katherine," spat it in her face, "Ohhhh, Katherine," that rip below her hips constant as a creamy river of cum threatened to vault inside her, Andrew not minding for the eighteen year old girl to become pregnant with his children.

She waited until it would be over and she could tear this dress from her head, bury it in the back of a closet to be forgotten forever. Until she could wipe away the blood she knew was spilling across her thighs and panties. As Katherine felt his legs tighten, he pushed her backwards on the bed, locking her wrists above her head, digging his fingers so deep into her, she'd carry the bruises for six days; first blue, then green, then brown, then pale. She struggled to move as he continued to explode inside her, banging her hips with his, the fabric of her coiled panties rubbing against his penis, making a rash of her, making a rash of this. He collapsed on top of her until she struggled for breath, all the while quiet, feeling the clumpy, white strings between her legs, counting the seconds until she could run to the bathroom and wipe this mistake from her.

"I'm hungry, Katherine," were his only words as he lay there, panting, his sweat a wet towel atop her, smothering, his limp penis still inside her body like a small, wet balloon.

"Andrew, let me up," she said, attempting to push him off her. He began to roll over, removing himself like a band-aid, quick and painful, the sweat and stink of him between her legs.

"I bet little B.B. is sorry he didn't get you now, huh?" he asked, as Katherine rolled her dress back over her knees and began to walk awkwardly toward the doorway.

She halted, digging her nails into the woodwork of the door. "What did you just say?"

"I said I bet your little Brandon Baskin wishes he had gotten you instead of me." Andrew leaned back on the bed as Katherine turned to look at him, propped up by his elbows, that flaccid penis hanging out of his zipper like a piece of excrement, a small, dark lump.

"Why would you *say* that, Andrew?" She asked, her green eyes filling with the mention of that boy's name; the name that she repeated each night, damning her mistakes, *their* mistakes.

"Please," he laughed, pulling a piece of hair from his eyes. "It's obvious the way you two were always all over each other. I'm just glad I got you before he did, because he will never have you, Katherine, or see you much for that matter." Andrew narrowed his eyes, pulling out a strand of his black hair, coiling it around his fingers before dropping it on the bed. "I just can't believe you actually married *me* – I thought you would have waited for him."

Katherine ran from the room toward the bathroom, slamming the door before peeling the wet, white dress from her body, balling it up as a tissue to soak up Andrew's semen and her blood. She looked in the mirror, at her naked body and red face bathed in his sweat, bathed in some kind of sin, asking "What did I do," to the face too young to understand the vows of marriage; a face desperate to leave her mother's home, so desperate she'd ruined her only hope of being with Brandon; asking, "What did I do," as that ignorance locked her to Andrew, locked her in ways that only resentment brings to young women who act before thinking, who think only of themselves.

A Woman's Ring

Chapter Fifteen

The night he proposed, they'd been in the gardens of Urbana, a small park with potted plants and a gazebo. They'd sipped champagne, each of them avoiding the other with perfect precision, as if some heavy secret lay between them, a bubble of mystery that no one wanted to walk through. Katherine closed her eyes, trying to let that cool glaze of the champagne coat her indecision as Andrew paced from garden to cement bench, lowering his hands, picking them up again, dipping one finger at a time into his champagne glass.

"I need to get home, Andrew." Katherine opened her eyes, looked at the sky and the stars she imagined couples had stared at for centuries – she was here, part of a couple, yet her mind was with her dead father, a man whose face she'd come close to forgetting, the scruffy jaw and bushy white temples, the man who'd had everything to do with Katherine, the man who'd made her cookies and told stories of childhood romance and lifelong aims.

Katherine had always heard the urgency in her father's voice to *do* something with her life, to move fast and work faster, until she was happy and attaining her ambitions. Was Andrew her ambition? Would he take her away from this place and let her explore every waking prospect?

"Marry me," Andrew had said, smiling that bright white smile that had women opening their legs for him, that had their faces sweaty and lined in makeup, their lips licked and moist, their clitorises big and throbbing, saying, "Take me, Andrew, take me."

Katherine sat with her legs firmly shut, swirling her champagne, devising, scheming. If she was to have money, to do with it as she may, to buy things and travel, then all she had to do was marry him – on her eighteenth birthday, just marry him – buy a house, live in it and do whatever she wanted to do with or without him.

There was no ring, just the offer – Andrew pacing now, Katherine downing the rest of her champagne, tapping her feet on the cement floor, a buzz in her head, those bubbles of bad decisions pushing her to answer him, and then Andrew, kneeling in front of the bench, his lips on her neck, his hands drawing ever so slowly her knees apart, saying, "Yes, Katherine, say yes. You know you want to. Marry me, marry me."

Katherine felt his hands, warm from the night, slip up her skirt, parting her legs, her mind reduced to fizz and a nagging suspicion that she was forgetting something. She wanted his hands off of her, that much she knew; they were creeping up as though her legs were a part of him, as though he would find something malleable in that space so he could yank it to hardness. But there was only dryness in Katherine, a dry, cold place that had never been touched by a man, and she did not want him to be the first – but that voice would not quit her, she'd had too many drinks, and his hands kept moving until she was forced to say yes, as he fingered beneath her panties, Katherine shutting her legs hard on his hand, moving backwards on the bench, saying "yes, I'll marry you, yes," him shoving his hands so deep she screamed and jumped up, running as fast as her feet would allow when slowed by alcohol, all the way to Mrs. Baskin's house where she collapsed behind the shed she and Brandon used to play in, collapsed and began to cry hard tears, a curl of excitement inside her as she willed Brandon to come outside and finish her off, make that dry place wet with passion, him stripping off her clothes as she'd often imagined, taking her in that drunken state while he was sober and aware, the two of them rolling in the dark green grass at midnight, her saying yes to him, yes that she would marry Brandon and only him, that she'd said yes to Andrew, but only for the money, only for *their* future, where she and Brandon would travel the world in the most

A Woman's Ring

expensive ways, kissing and cradling that precious thing called love.

"Katherine?"

Brandon stood outside the back door, illuminated by the porch light, a carton of ice cream in his hands. Katherine could tell he'd been bored or angry – he always ate ice cream like a woman: with emotion, not hunger.

"Are you okay?"

He came to her, kneeling by the shed, setting the carton beside them, brushing her hair off her pale face, those green eyes lusting so badly for him, her lips trembling as she whispered, "Make...make love to me, Brandon...please make love to me. I need you so much, Brandon. I need you."

She moved to him then, blaming the alcohol, blaming the one time she'd tried to kiss him and he'd pushed her away, claiming he was drunk; now she was the drunk one, but so caught up in her emotions, she knew she would die if he did not want her. Her birth parents had not wanted her, her adopted mother had not wanted her and could care less if she ran away. That left only Andrew; the man who was her only hope to get out of Ohio. Unless it could be Brandon, in this moment, on this night, two weeks before her birthday, two weeks before that makeshift wedding. If he could find it in him to do this one thing tonight, to prove that marrying Andrew was wrong, that she didn't need marriage for money, that Brandon could love her poor and messed up and lonely, then she would call it off and be happy with him, and only him, in Ohio, in any part of the world where he would have her, where they could roll in bed sheets and remember how things once were.

"Katherine...what did you say? Are you *drunk*?"

Brandon leaned down to smell her breath, his eyes knitted in that concerned way, and Katherine took the chance and wrapped her hands firmly around his lean back that was damp from the heat outside, Brandon gasping as she closed her mouth on the side of his neck, sliding her tongue up to his earlobe, sucking as if from a straw. He pushed her back, his hands hurting so bad on her shoulders, but there was no way she would let go, as this was her last chance to make him love her.

"Katherine, stop it! What are you doing?"

He pushed her back until she fell into a small trash can, crumpled and defeated, bawling into the palms of her hands. Those cries left her mouth unhinged as she looked up at him, screaming, "Why, why, why can't you just make love to me or kiss me, Brandon? Am I that disgusting, that *repulsive*? What? What is it that keeps you so close but so far away from me?"

Katherine stood unsteadily, brushing the hair from her eyes and dampened face. Brandon, stricken, stepped back into the shadows.

"I just can't Katherine...you know I care for you, but I can't."

"But *why* can't you?" Katherine bobbled forward, reaching out to him, opening and closing her fists, hoping to catch a cheek, a piece of his T-shirt, a whisper. "Is it because of *Stacy*?" she snorted, wiping her nose. "Why can't you just feel the same way I do?"

Brandon backed up another step, close to the door now. "Katherine, it's more complicated than that. I just..." He looked down at the dirt, kicking it gently into a soft brown cloud. "You're the only girl I know who I can tell things to and wrestle with and just...be myself with, Katherine. How am I supposed to change that? Everything would change – look at your mom...look at the world, Katherine. It's not some fairy tale that exists just because you love me and I love you. That isn't enough to make things wonderful. It doesn't just happen that way."

Katherine swayed back and forth, only hearing that last bit, the part of him loving her. "Did you just say you loved me?"

"Katherine." Brandon reached up to his blonde hair and gave it a hard yank, ran those long fingers over his face and chest and took one step closer to her. "You know I do." He only said it once, only whispered it loud enough that it could have been the wind shifting, or her own imagination.

"You do?" Katherine closed the remaining distance between them, and hooked her arms around his neck, felt the sweat in small streams down the back of it. She wanted to lick it up, to transfer her wetness to his body, scraping off the shirt, the pants, studying every part of him, because that's where all her passion lay – in his bones and feet and hands and teeth, in his blood and veins and tissues. "God, Brandon, you have no idea how long I've wanted to hear you say –"

"Katherine, wait." Brandon removed her hands from his neck and held them, gently. "I do love you – but as my best friend. I just want you to be happy…and we're both too young to even think about something so serious as what you're saying –"

Katherine jerked her hands from his, her head pounding with his rejection. "A friend? Too *young*?" she felt a searing resentment boil through her, her lips reacting before her heart could stop her, before she could hold back the words that came out in a death sentence, ruining any chance left between them. "Well, tell me Brandon, my dearest *friend*, am I too young to marry Andrew? Because he just proposed and I said yes, and I thought if you would only make love to me, then I wouldn't have to. But what else do I have, *friend*? You don't love me, so what does it matter anymore? I might as well marry him and get his money and go and be whoever I want to be!"

"Katherine." Brandon reached for her hands but she jerked them away, crying and shaking, her body a mass of nerves and alcohol.

"You can't marry that man, Katherine. He just wants you because you're young. We can still go away together." His voice shook in desperation. "You can box and I can fly like we always said we would, but you can't marry him, Katherine, you know that…"

"Then what *can* I do, Brandon, huh? Because if I can't be with you, what can I do? I will not end up like my mother, I can promise you that…alone and afraid and angry at the world. God, why can't you just *be* with me?"

Brandon stepped to her then, wrapping both arms around her as tightly as he could, hushing her sobs, his heart beating rapidly beneath his T-shirt. "Just calm down," he whispered, her hair blowing from his breath. "Just calm down, Katherine."

She rocked against him, her heart splitting as the truth of Brandon and her illusions began to break through the soft edges of champagne. "What a fool," she whispered, clinging to him. "What a fool to imagine love."

Rea Frey

A Woman's Ring

Chapter Sixteen

Seizures sometimes meant aneurysms – which meant going back in, locating the bleed and attempting to expel the problem. If someone was to come in now, to see their daughter or girlfriend lying on the table, scalp excoriated like the peeling of a tomato, all that meaty substance of brain gray as rock; if only they knew what he saw, what he dealt with. If she had an aneurysm, it could mean retardation, slowness, or permanent disuse of certain limbs. Since the location of the mass was positioned laterally from her motor strip, the strip that contained life within its nerves and functions, she could cease to be the same woman in a matter of seconds.

If Katherine were to wake, to touch her head – the fingers plunging into the slick, red and gray tissues, she'd know something was going wrong, that regardless, she was alone, that no family had come to comfort her in these times, no friends or companions.

The nurses continued to stabilize Katherine as the doctor watched, the tips of his surgical gloves stained from her insides. It had been six hours already. It should have taken three.

When she awoke, there would be pain – pain of the tube being ripped from her throat, from the surgery, from the drill wounds on her forehead, pain along her forearms from the numerous arterial lines, nauseous, fainting pain from the catheter that would burn and sting between her legs, and maybe even from her decision to go through with this – for the fear of waking damaged and aching, in a ward where ninety year old women and men waited to perish in hospital beds. Where the nurses were bored, where Katherine would be the twenty-something freak who needed those nurses more than anyone.

"Come on," he whispered, stepping back in as her pulse began to strengthen. Her parted scalp hung flaccidly off the left side of her head, hair dangling, oiled from Vaseline and excess blood, all this before him as he breathed, waiting for the signal to begin the surgery of implanting the metal plates against the skull cap – those plates that would remain with her to the grave.

A Woman's Ring

Chapter Seventeen

There had been one evening when she was six months along, when her belly swelled to impious levels and her feet and breasts ached beyond complaint. Andrew was at Jilly's, the bar her father used to go to before coming home to face Ruth – softening the edge that unhappy wives brought to their husbands. Is that why Andrew drank in the middle of the afternoon – to drown the uncomfortable moments they spent together? To melt the good times into his mainstay of emotion? It was as if he was waiting for a baby to change things. That with a child they would immediately become a family, whose happiness survived in the slight hands and wrinkled feet of their offspring.

Katherine had been feeling too vulnerable, too desperate, and decided to drive the short distance to her mother's house. Once there, she parked and knocked on the door, smoothing down the stretchy fabric of her black dress. It had been months since she'd visited, and Katherine knew her mother had heard the news of her pregnancy only by way of Mrs. Baskin. She'd been too nervous to tell her.

Katherine knocked again and saw the curtains flutter, saw an old, griseous face peek out from beneath the yellow fabric and press back again, a small whisper of movement against the dirt-stained window. Katherine waited, tapped her feet, jiggled the knob.

She walked around to the back door and saw the shades drawn, the lights dimmed. She glanced casually at the open back yard, the dilapidated tree house her father had built for her and Brandon when she was just seven years old. The boards now hung loose and mildewed, soggy from recent storms. She remembered how her mother used to garden in the summer afternoons, donning her shears and a cloth hat that flopped over her eyes. She would occasionally glance up at Katherine in her tree house, and Katherine would wave down, knowing if her mother would only wave back, that everything would be fine. She never would.

For the first time in years, Katherine felt tears welling not for her father but for her mother – for all the lost moments and missed opportunities. Running baths and listening to bedtime stories. Baking cookies and tossing batter into each other's hair. Shopping and talking about boys. Feeling the touch of a mother's cool hands on a fevered forehead. But their relationship had been dead long before her father passed away, for reasons Katherine never quite understood.

Katherine retreated slowly when her mother never answered, kicked a few spare rocks that littered the driveway, that familiar rejection pushing in. She looked over at Brandon's house, heard the dribble of a ball, the swoosh of net, and a rebound as he slammed it in again. Katherine brushed the hair from her eyes, felt the split ends dangling against her lower back that now ached from the bloat of her belly, the weight of a baby.

She hadn't seen Brandon since she'd gotten pregnant. Every time she came around, Betty said he was out with friends. Katherine would always linger on the porch, expecting his head to dart out from behind a vacant doorway or appear from behind a window shade, because she knew he didn't hang out with the Urbana crowd. She had to see him. Pregnant or not, she had to tell him the way she felt – let this passion escape, this commitment to him, her plan to have the child and then escape with him somewhere. She knew that Andrew would give her the money if she gave him her child – and at this moment, Katherine could do it, *would* do it, for another chance with her best friend.

At the edge of the barn, Katherine moved to the front left corner, peering around at Brandon in shorts and a tank top – surprised at the bronzed color of his skin, the weight he'd gained in his arms and shoulders. She felt her breath slacken, her fingers gripping tight to the wood. She realized how much she'd missed

A Woman's Ring

him, how incomplete her life had been without him – how much he'd meant to her and reinforced her purpose to dream.

"Hold tight to your dreams, Katherine." She could almost hear her father's voice, low and easy, making Katherine promise to never forget the dream. Brandon had kept up with that – pushing her onward in spite of everything. She glanced down at her stomach, imagining what was forming inside her – an actual human who would think and talk and cry constantly. Sighing, Katherine pulled herself back from view at the barn's side. What was she doing? Would he laugh at how fat she'd become? How had she gotten herself into this? She'd married for money and not one fraction for love. She'd devastated her best friend and was now carrying a child she wanted nothing to do with. Was that because her birth mother had not wanted her – had given her up to people who would? Given her to a couple where the wife was resentful and the father found the entire job left in his hands? What kind of parent would she be, if she'd never known what it was to mother or be mothered? And as much as she didn't want to admit it, she knew Andrew would be amazing. Saw it in the way he touched her stomach in the evenings, in the way he looked at her – with fond eyes that brought her to tears because try as she could, she could not love him. He had won her on a challenge of conquest, fooled into thinking he could fix her problems, and had simply fallen in love with the idea of marriage, with the possibility of a child. Marrying her had been the means to end an era – of chasing women and boozing with friends.

In her thoughts, she had somehow lost the rhythm of the basketball, Brandon's soft breathing and scuffling of his tennis shoes. She glanced back around the edge and saw him with the ball in his hand, staring up at the cloudless sky. At that moment, Katherine would have given anything to know what he was thinking – to gain back the privilege of talking to him at free will, picking his brain.

Katherine forced herself forward, tripping on a root in the ground. Brandon turned with quick speed, face bathed in sweat – a single drop rolling off his forehead.

"Brand?" Katherine inched forward, arms dropped awkwardly at her sides, knowing what a blimp she was, how her cheeks had grown fuller, her step slower, her hair long and limp, unwashed for days.

"Katherine." He said her name as if it aggrieved him deeply, as if that word was new and foreign but so familiar – like a lost childhood memory. "What – are you doing here?"

She continued to step forward, noticing as he quickly wiped his forehead with the back of one sweaty hand. "Where's *Andrew*?" He said the name with as much contempt as Katherine felt, and despite herself she smiled.

"Getting drunk, probably."

"Great husband you picked."

"Well, I got rejected by my first choice."

Katherine laughed and Brandon bit back an impulsive smile, jerking his hair out of his eyes. For a moment, Katherine had hope – hope that he could forgive her and help her figure a way outside this mess.

"Brand, I need to talk to you - I've got to tell you something and I really need you to listen."

Brandon paused, clenching the ball against his chest, his eyes traveling toward her stomach. They rested there, tortured, and she saw the tears well up in his eyes – such a heartbreaking reaction, such a horrific thing she'd done to both of them. Why couldn't she have waited? Pushed past his rejection and waited until he changed his mind – proving that he was worth the time, worth everything?

"Brandon, I'm so sorry." She hurried forward, wanting to throw her arms around him, drown herself in all their worry until they could both break free from it with absolute forgiveness.

Instead of stepping in to embrace her, he spun around and shot his last basket, both feet leaving the ground, hands arched, the ball clipping the edge of the rim and rolling in the grass behind the goal.

He ran to retrieve the ball, scooped it up and began the slow walk back toward his home. Katherine stood there, with her arms still open, begging for a chance to at least explain. "Brandon, please, I need to tell you so many – ."

A Woman's Ring

"Forget it, Katherine." He stopped three steps ahead of her, turned with his eyes cast softly at the ground. "You can't tell me things I don't already know – and I can't tell a man's *wife* all the things I used to wish for."

He said the words delicately, yet so heavy with emotion that Katherine collapsed right there in the grass, hiccupping on her sobs, burying her wan face in her hands. She heard the screen door bang shut and cried even louder at his refusal. In the back of her mind, she knew that if he just came out and sat beside her, made some kind of joke or nudged her with her elbow, that there could be a chance to start over. She waited until the sun went down, and the moon cast white radiance over the tips of things – until the lights went black inside her neighbor's home and she was left alone with her portly stomach and impermeable sorrow – waiting for a boy who'd never return.

A Woman's Ring

Chapter Eighteen

Frankie bobbled on unsteady feet, balanced near his mother and twin sister, Lily. His lips opened and closed, as if that cocked mouth could emit sounds other than cooing or spit-up or noise. He swayed close to Katherine, his toddler hands fully gripping her knees, Lily at her shins. She shook them off as women will shake off stray hairs or the feeling of a bug upon their skin, watching as they tottered on the kitchen floor, close to falling.

"What's the *matter* with you, Katherine?" Andrew stepped into the kitchen, rubbing his eyes still full of sleep from napping on the couch. "Can't you ever just let them touch you? Jesus, they're not *poison*." He bent down to whisper in each of his children's ears, as if they could understand his words, as if picking them up was the only form of protection that would keep them from her.

"I've told you to keep them out of the kitchen – there are sharp objects in here, in case you hadn't noticed!" Her voice shook as she turned back to the sink, feeling a sting rip through her womb, that sting that made her bawl in sleep, that made her hair grow thin, that made her eyes sag with grief; the grief of babies, the ache of mothers, the blood and stitches and twenty faint, white reminders on her stomach from their birth. The twins had altered her young body, her tight hips. The flesh had spread and accommodated for them – her babies now walking and falling, smiling and laughing, while Katherine moved loosely about, stuck in some irate confusion.

Andrew moved Frankie and Lily to the living room, their insignificant weight steady in his arms. She mumbled under her breath, the breath that shook as it often did, as she watched Andrew with them, rocking their soft bottoms before he came to Katherine, touching her while she slept, pulling her on top of him in the night, slipping inside her inactive body, with all that hair pulling and nasty talk, Andrew bursting in quick explosions before rolling over, naked and snoring beside her.

Scrubbing dishes, Katherine stared out the small window that sat above the sink, a witness to the diminutive snow flakes covering the garden she'd planted last spring. The very idea of what a marriage should be caught in her hands as she held a butcher knife, a fork, or spoon. She ached to cut herself from Andrew, to charge at him with these weapons, jabbing his stomach, his intestines, his loins. He had tricked her into becoming part of him – part of his children that had the same round faces and weak chins, the same green eyes as her, the same pale complexion, those births so intense her legs still trembled when remembering it. How she'd done all that pushing when she didn't want to, forcing out one then the other, crying as they were crying, a witness as the doctor caught the first one, but not the second, Lily coming so fast he'd nearly dropped her, only to be saved by the umbilical cord. She had slipped in his hands from all that afterbirth cream, and Katherine was now a mother, a tired, bleeding mother. The misery and fatigue seized her so fully she wished the doctor would drop them, would smash in their undeveloped heads, stamp their bodies in anticipation of their hearts and brains flying from those tiny orifices, ruined, until someone was kind enough to kick them into vacant waste bins. She did not want them. Simply. She did not want Frankie, her boy, Lily, her girl. She hated their looks, such a mixture of the man she loathed and the woman she was being forced to become at just twenty years old. The smell of their excrement, the spittle from their mouths, the way her bosoms swelled and leaked, one continuous drip, the pain in her vagina, the pain in her heart, all from birthing them, from saying "I do," almost two years ago.

If she'd known the consequences, these twins, these little people that would grow to hate her because she was incompetent,

A Woman's Ring

because their father smothered them with love and her with sex, because Andrew gave her money after those sessions, leaving it on the nightstand to make her feel like a prostitute, because she went to bed weeping, wanting only her time, her dreams, because she was, in effect, never alone yet always lonely, burdened, shaken, and completely afraid of never accomplishing anything, she would not have done the unthinkable and married this older man full of phony promises.

The moments after giving birth were the toughest. She'd stood over their cradles, forcing herself to touch them, to feed the mouths that opened and closed like puppets, but with too much sound. It was always one that started, then the other, as if their favorite hobby was to make Katherine weak in the knees, to make her fidget with the hands that wanted to roll them onto their bellies, hold pillows over their heads and watch that precious life leak from them, each breath dying beneath the pink and blue fabric; she was just a child rocking her children, those bars of their cradle the bars of her life – Katherine the prisoner without the crime, but always wanting to commit it, to hurt them for herself, if not to take out her hatred for Andrew.

The only words she ever thought as their small, insatiable fingers pulled at the hem of her dress or the soft middle of her back and elbows, the only words as they began to walk and speak and laugh her laugh she'd had as a child were "death, murder, Hell." She thought of the Bible, that book she'd forsaken upon marrying Andrew, the pages she used to rip from the big, black body as a child, crumpling up the passages she did not understand, but always remembering the words like bold tattoos inked inside her.

"You've got it all wrong," she wanted to tell it. "Hell isn't some sanguine place with a man in horns tormenting you for eternity. Hell is the feeling of your children's hands like leeches all over your body. Hell is going to bed alone every night, though you have a man sleeping right next to you. Hell is thinking of your life and having the gall to contemplate taking the razor under your sink and ending it all in a vat of warm water one Sunday afternoon. *I* am the embodiment of Hell."

Andrew never understood her anger, never blinked twice when she cried at night in their room, throwing tantrums, clawing at her throat and eyes until his arms would be around her, forcing her to the ground in her most frenetic moments, ripping off her clothes and fucking her, Katherine's tears mixing with his sweat, him licking at her nipples, biting them, she ripping through the soft flesh of his back, her nails then her teeth, pulling at his hair as he pulled hers, him choking her, the two rolling like the most violent couple, Katherine wanting that fight, those unseen gloves, that urge fueling the need for her escape into the world of boxing.

As much as she hated Andrew, she needed him that way; with all the force and maddening moments, the fingernails on her skin, and rough words they uttered that no child should ever hear. She glimpsed his love for the children and it took her to new dimensions in her own judgments, the dichotomy between hate and affection, the needy redemption they found at nights, when husband and wife raped each other with fractious words.

Andrew took what he wanted, worked when he chose, had the money to dictate what Katherine could and couldn't achieve. Those moments of rolling and thrashing were like challenges. He felt good inside her, yet she yearned to cut his pride off, to banish the extension, and replace it with Brandon's. "Why aren't you him, why aren't you him," she'd often moan while he sucked her neck and hips, scratching her pale skin with uncut fingernails. "Bastard, I loathe you, why aren't you *him*," and both so desperate, they plunged and plucked and thrust blindly as if the moment could alter them from what they were – desperate for contact – violent, impure contact, in which she'd give all she had to live a fantasy, yet the realistic touch of her husband, of Andrew, was the downfall, the face of hellfire, the psychosis that robbed any innocence.

Marriage, the bond that two people share, any two people, in love or out. Over time they will feel constricted, when looking at the other and wondering how they got there, how the mind played those tricks and made them say two words that would bind them forever, two words as simple as "thank you," or "I can," two words that muddled the rest of life and showed what young girls could become with older men if they let them. All of this and

A Woman's Ring

Katherine was a mother and a wife, her pregnancy a parasite, eating away at her youth, gnawing at the flesh of her swollen belly, Katherine still hoping for Brandon as she scrubbed those dishes, still hoping he'd be outside her door, coming to rescue her, those hands that had tackled her as a child and made tin airplanes, those hands that had pushed her roughly into his yard when she'd tried to kiss him, the hands that had held her not as a girlfriend but just a friend, when all she'd craved is *more*, those hands, more, coming to rip the foolish mistakes from sight and sound and memory.

But there was only resentment in Brandon, as that childhood friendship flattened with her ceremony, his face and laugh washed-up memories. If she ever took Frankie and Lily to see Mrs. Baskin, Brandon would not be there, always out, spinning his tires over some new road, trying to erase Katherine from memory. The days they'd shared, eating grapes under the big oak tree, riding bikes through Mrs. McClintock's backyard, smoking their first Virginia slim, making the Urbana cemetery their own, playing and acting along the tombstones, farting in church, talking about future ventures were now abolished, her choices ruined by another man's seed.

Brandon was her only grand passion – no moment, no dream or happiness could take her the way he could. She recalled picnics in that cemetery, moments as a teen when she'd closed her eyes and waited for an invitation to kiss him, to touch him and unleash the burden of hiding love inside her when all she'd ever wanted to do was share it with more ferocity and passion than even she understood. But he would simply eat quietly, staring at the random graves, tracing his long, attenuate fingers over the stone closest to them, telling stories, looking at her occasionally with such engaged eyes. That silence between them, needing to relieve the pressure that only words could, their love a release in which those words would be the turning – the beginning.

She needed to show him who she still was, the girl with the braids and strength, the girl who'd give anything for one more day spent beneath the sun. Marrying Andrew had been her biggest failure, a rushed oversight, and if Brandon didn't love her the way she loved him, she would wither into less than what she was, less than Katherine, less than hope, less than Andrew's wife or her mother's daughter; just an orphan girl who'd been dropped off with little hope, little love.

Only when she saw Brandon's car on a sunny winter's day, the back seat filled with gray luggage, parkas, and even his golf clubs, that car revving to pull out from Mrs. Baskin's driveway, did she chase after it, lunging at the exhaust pipe, tires, and rearview. He was leaving her. That betrayal bit at Katherine, eating her piece by piece, until she was lifeless as the rocks beneath his tires, spinning and crunching into the cement, bits of dust and grit and reminiscence.

"He's going to be a pilot, Katie – a real pilot, can you believe it?" Mrs. Baskin waved after him, Katherine standing next to her, hands in tight, shameful fists, her eyes and feet pulsing from too much blood in her veins.

"He didn't even tell me, Betty," she whispered, as his car sped down the street. "We were both supposed to go to Chicago…"

"He thought it would be better this way," she said gravely, placing a hand on Katherine's shoulder before turning slowly to go back inside with Katherine's children. Frankie and Lily were in Mrs. Baskin's home for the afternoon, Frankie and Lily, who to Katherine were not hers but additions of Andrew, additions of the man who raped her while she slept, who fed her so much money and misunderstood her grief, who fought her and adored the children she could not love.

Katherine remained in the driveway, halfway between her childhood home and Brandon's, exactly three miles from her own. She would never have one more chance to see Brandon's face as it walked from driveway to car, as it sat on Mrs. Baskin's couch, reading a comic book and slurping up milk from a cereal bowl; she would never again witness his mismatched socks, or the way his eyes crinkled when he squinted up into the sun; the lean arms that she used to make fun of for being thinner than hers, the pale skin, the knotty knees – all to Katherine worth it, worth running away from Andrew, worth forgetting her children, him like a drug she could not quit and never wanting to try, and

A Woman's Ring

yet he'd given up on her, on their great fantasy of pursuing their dreams together, Brandon making his way toward that grand city without her.

Katherine's breath slowed to the point of suffocation, her head pounding out her choices, voices of shock creeping in and out, the possibilities of some sought after freedom. Could she abandon this life of dinted choices? Could she walk out on her husband, her children, as easily as Brandon walked away from her?

On the way to Mrs. Baskin's door, she paused, hearing Frankie crying and Lily soon after, in the den of her neighbor's home, their little bodies waking from naptime. Katherine backed from the door, the driveway, feeling heat in her hands and stomach – her feet running before her mind made her legs move. The blunders swelled inside her, pushing her feet, her limbs – the body strong somewhere beneath the mistakes of childbirth. With each step, each mile, she began to think, to laugh at the sky that was aloof and hard. She would not stop running until the world changed, until somewhere untouched inside, she would be a girl finding bravery, in a place where men could not hurt, where babies could not find, where that sick melody of guilt would filter in and out of her ears that grew deaf from the journey.

Rea Frey

A Woman's Ring

Chapter Nineteen

She was an impersonator of the highest kind. It's what mothers were, at least all the ones she'd had the displeasure of knowing. She figured her own mother – the woman who'd given her life and then passed her on without so much as a name – had probably been young and irresponsible, pulled to follow the whims of childhood that slipped from your fingers if not careful. She'd probably developed a plan to make love with boys, to dance until dawn, to twirl magically along beaches and ride waves at dusk. But pregnancy wasn't part of that fun. Birthing a child would be a hindrance to her lifestyle, a burden in the face of freedom. The muscles, sinew, and impossibly tiny appendages that she could easily give away as the placenta oozed from her open legs.

She'd probably witnessed her pale belly, distended beneath baggy men's clothes, the swollen ankles and wrists – the longevity. Pushing the infant into the soft, warm air of a hospital room, she would be free – shaking and screaming, the walls of her genital flesh ripping from the pressure. There would have been only a glimpse of the child before she was carted off to the adoption agency, wrapped in a pink blanket, wanting the warmth of another human. Katherine's birth mother, watching, might have hoisted herself from the hospital bed that very afternoon, making her way to the local market for enough drinks to bury her decision.

Or perhaps, Katherine thought, perhaps her birth mother had gone on to marry and make darling babies, given birth to many,

many babies, still trying to bury what her first had become. That one glimpse of her newly born child, that one peek so many years ago as a foolish, selfish teen warping her memory, diluting her future children into replicas of the baby she should have saved.

Maybe the child had grown sick and passed away, her mother would suggest to her future husband or boyfriend. But a man would simply shrug his response and beg for sex, not understanding the enormity of a situation such as abandoning your child, simply giving it away as if it were an old, soiled shirt or sundress whose pattern had become too busy for the more modern world. It was a human being she'd discarded – a little girl who existed somewhere without her.

She would lay in baths worrying every possibility, plunging herself under the tepid water until her lungs filled with unsaid words, before breaking back to the surface, beet red and claustrophobic, thinking of other things besides her rejected child.

She would not trouble herself over such things, she'd say, she was still too young and marked for years of freedom. This was the person Katherine imagined her to be – regretful and capricious, full of stellar imperfections.

Her adopted mother, by contrast, was simply a crust of a woman, capable of crumbling when things got testy, persuasive when she wanted to be, or completely blank; she walked from living room to kitchen with the help of only bourbon or whiskey (the latter her choice after Bruce's death), sometimes a grimace on her lips and loss in her tawny eyes. She never wore beautiful clothing, sang songs, or laughed as she had with her few close friends. She simply drifted, sometimes frowning, sometimes moaning, but never showing more emotion than available to any one of her senses. She was cold and indifferent; a husk of a woman, a fragile, permeable casing.

And then there was Mrs. Baskin. A woman who played the perfect role of mother, but held such large needs behind her eyes. When she was knitting or scrubbing the pans, you could see the resentment build slowly, the battle as she tried to convince herself that yes, she needed to be a wife and mother to feel good about life, that yes, scrubbing pots and pans *was* important, and

A Woman's Ring

that living in a suburban town with no hobbies, an extra roll of lard around your middle, and a lack of talent *was* the ideal way to exist.

Yes, she insisted, *this* was life.

Katherine, however, was the largest impersonator of them all. Or perhaps she was just as needy and hungry and diluted as the rest of them. Scrub the dishes, sure; wash the clothes grudgingly while pulling for daydreams; feel her stomach grow to inhuman proportions, all the while failing to convince herself that there was something worthwhile blooming inside. Pregnancy had always seemed too alien, too surreal. Within her body was a baby, a person she would have to nurture for eighteen years when she hadn't the slightest clue as how to even care for herself. Not to mention the unspeakable pain she was supposed to endure during childbirth, the agony and depression all for the effect of adding one more human into an overpopulated world.

Katherine walked through the cemetery, bending low to scoop up handfuls of dandelions and weeds that to her, had always been prettier with their giant lollipop heads and disappearing consistency. Make a wish and blow. Watch that one breath scatter to a hundred seeds that would fly in many different directions. Feel the waxy petals of a dandelion, their wilt and green underbellies as they bake in the too hot sun. Watch them rise and wither as people do.

As mothers have.

There was too much Katherine didn't understand, not enough sense in the world. She walked from stone to stone, remembering her first kiss. It was in second grade with a boy named Jamison who'd been twelve at the time. They'd been in the woods behind school, and secretly, Katherine had liked it. Adored the sensation of lip on lip, tongue against tongue. She'd always looked at men with their gray mustaches and wrinkles walking their dogs, thinking – "What if I were to touch him? What would he do?" Often she wondered what sagged or lifted beneath the slacks and button-up shirts, the cotton boxers and cologne. It was very Nabokov, she learned in seventh grade after watching the movie *Lolita*, but with a small reversal in that she was the corruptor, the hunter, the impersonating child.

Katherine simply craved the attention of older men, craved what her father had taught little girls could achieve with their big, batting eyes and constant softness.

To others, Katherine always seemed the type to save her first kiss for marriage, or at least until the break after high school. Little did anyone know it had been on the playground, in a manmade ditch that held one scooter, a Frisbee, and a yo-yo when she was just seven.

Jamison had grabbed her hand, running along the freshly mowed grass, past the swings and monkey bars, past the chin-up bar and merry-go-round. He pushed her back into the ditch, his hands on her concave chest, shoving, her sneakers sinking deeply into the mud, a slimy chocolate river soaking her pink and blue socks. She gasped, exhilarated, stepping up to him as he leaned down to wrap his small paws around her bottom, giving it an ample squeeze (and imagining what would later fill the flat pockets in just a handful of years), and pulled her to him, crushing her insignificant weight with his more noticeable size, pulling his mouth down over hers, roughly massaging the corners of her mouth with his pointy, slick tongue. Katherine opened her lips in a loud, automatic wheeze, Jamison managing to slip his tongue inside that small, pink pocket, moaning and thrusting like she'd seen movie stars do.

Katherine kept her eyes firmly open, watched his brown eyelashes flutter, and a lone pimple glistening on the very center of his forehead, while containing her laugh as best she could. A bit of drool spilled onto her shirt, and dotted the fabric over the top button of her jeans. She stumbled and pushed him back, saw that look in his eye that she would later see in Andrew when he wanted sex and she was completely unwilling.

He looked over his shoulder, wiped the strings of spit off his lips and stepped further into the woods, casting them both in darkness.

"Take off your top." He said it almost nicely, as if he was asking her to move aside, or at what time lunch began. She stood there, hands fidgeting, saying the only thing that came to her mind.

"God wouldn't want me to."

A Woman's Ring

His eyebrows bunched together in confusion as he closed the gap of their bodies and unzipped her jeans instead, slid them down her invisible hips and pushed her panties aside.

"Fine then."

He slipped one finger against her and began flicking it in and out as if he had a caterpillar stuck to him and was desperately trying to fling it off. She let him do this peculiar thing, felt the sensations in her stomach, the slight pain between her legs. He finished and they both jumped when they heard the recess bell. Jamison sniffed his fingers before adjusting his shorts and running back toward school. Katherine remained, looking down at herself as if she'd suffered a fantastic miracle, as if her first period had arrived or she'd just given birth right there in the ditch and mud to a screaming, squiggling infant.

She didn't go back to school that day, stood there with her panties almost to her knees, looking at the area Jamison had brought to life with his awkward, inexperienced fingers.

That was the first time she became aware of the powers of a woman's body, of real sexual urges. That was the first time she skipped school, the first time she decided to do what *she* wanted to.

And now, with children, she could not make herself respond; could not find that simple pleasure her body had found all those years ago in the middle of recess. But she would find the strength to do what it was that women did, find the strength to mother and nurture, to give willingly.

Give until your bones were desiccated, brittled beyond repair; that exasperating pain of mothers which remained silent from morning to night, carried as a memory or lock of hair, straight to the arms of an open grave you go, utterly silent, utterly thankless.

Rea Frey

A Woman's Ring

Chapter Twenty

Lily would sometimes tear out the pages of fashion magazines – as if by ripping and stuffing the waxy sheets into her mouth she would somehow be noticed. Self-tanner, clump-free mascara, foot odor, tampons and body piercing ads – all split apart, the shreds floating up like confetti, coming down like rain. Katherine watched the infant play at her feet, a small rip gathering in her soft pink dress from throwing those arms up and down, flapping them as if to lift herself off the carpet, above the couch and chairs.

Katherine sat inches from Lily on the rocking chair, pushing her insipid feet back and forth along the rug. Her eyes she kept partly closed, as if to feign sleep, but she knew rest would not come. This had been the customary ritual of most afternoons -- where Frankie and Lily would nap or play staring games in the den. It was Frankie that usually napped, his whole fist in his mouth, drooling on the couch cushions, while Lily kept awake, as if she dared not miss one instance the world could give her, one second where she could flippantly play. It was a challenge almost, as if this solitary hour with her children could make Katherine want to stay – could erase the malevolence that secreted inside her, festering. She knew release would most likely come only with escape, with fighting, where she'd give boxing all she'd ever felt, in combinations like shoe shines.

Yet here, she struggled from the indecision of leaving, of proper morality, though she'd never been taught what ethics truly were, only force fed the Bible and the ever fading good faith her father had instilled. These times were the tests of an unfit mother, where no rules or booklets were given; only the sheer willingness to abhor or love. Circle A. Circle B. Either way, she'd have to leave something – the children or life.

Despite herself, Katherine laughed – a long, satisfying belly-chuckle where there were no sounds, only spasms of her diaphragm. It was a maddening cry, one of confusion and observance, a witness as Frankie ruined Andrew's expensive couch cushions with his slobber, her own life reduced to babysitting in the afternoons. Lily, sensing her mother's change in mood, turned back to look at Katherine, the pages of magazines still crunching and raining around her. Through the abyss, Lily leaned forward, identifying a chasm of opportunity, and as if to whisper a secret without teeth, she bent in to envelop Katherine's big toe, sucking hard over the nail. The greed of that child was shocking, as she wanted milk – the kind that didn't come from the bottle, the kind that Katherine let her bras and t-shirts steal, instead of the children. Lily brought both pudgy hands around the ball of her mother's foot, nursing the toe like a bottle, a bit of magazine stuck to her left cheek that was dampened from spit-up Katherine had not removed. For the second time, she smiled as the feeling of warmth worked its way through her body, Lily looking up at her as if a lover making sure that what she was doing felt good. And as if caught wrongly by tenderness, realizing her own surrender to this child, Katherine jerked her toe back, letting Lily's chin dive into the carpet, her hands still fisted around the imaginary arches of her mother's feet.

Katherine tucked herself tightly on the chair as her daughter began the slow act of crying – the mouth contorting, breaking apart, slipping out wails that soon woke Frankie. Katherine hushed her son without moving toward him, while Lily reached up to her mother, not yet able to stand, that sulking look only small infants can sustain – the bottom lip puckering, the tears crystallizing on the dough-like cheeks, the boxy hands and wrists stretching for its mother. Katherine squeezed herself tighter, as if to become invisible, letting Frankie settle back to sleeping, letting Lily cry herself to silence. Rocking herself on the chair, hearing the ticks of the clock behind her, Katherine felt her breasts begin to leak as if they knew her child was hungry. And with all the strength in Lily's tiny body, as if hearing that muted dinner bell, she tilted onto all fours, her chest still heaving, so determined to get to her mother that she pushed herself up – a tiny miracle – latching onto the chair's seat where Katherine's toes sat – Lily holding herself up by the dependability of wood.

Katherine was anchored to the moment, anchored to the ripped magazines and breast ache, almost willing Lily toward her, losing that fierceness if only for a moment, as she witnessed her daughter's hands releasing the seat to reach for Katherine. Lily cooed and glowered, afraid of falling, but Katherine, in a moment of powerlessness, worrying that her daughter's chin might strike harder surfaces, straddled the seat and pulled Lily into her lap, feeling her tiny body squiggle in triumph. Holding her daughter in one hand, Katherine lifted her shirt, her breast wet and warm. Lily lunged instinctively, her mouth fitting around and sucking the first juices of her mother; the eyelashes fluttering, the pink rash on her forehead covered by a soft, blonde curl. And with something like compassion, Katherine reached down to pet the fuzz of hair, to pluck the ripped page from her daughter's cheek, caught in a moment outside herself, where the only thing that mattered was that tug and gum on her flesh, the two of them linked by much more than blood, joined by the powers of deprivation.

A Woman's Ring

Chapter Twenty-one

He was simple with them. Walking the streets on weekends, the kids attached to him on either side – certain in their father's love, but occasionally glancing over their shoulders as if they'd lost something – a toy maybe? But it was their mother who wasn't there to latch onto the chain of hands – Lily's extended as if to clutch Katherine's shadow – as if her little feet and silken neck could brighten the condition of her mother's world.

Katherine imprisoned herself on Saturdays – waited until they were gone to run through the neighborhood or shadow-box in her living room. Reaching into old bins for the boxing tapes her father had owned, she'd watch the ones where rounds would sometimes climb from fifteen to thirty, the contenders and champions fighting until someone went or stayed down. In her living room, Katherine became the no names and World Heavyweight Champions – Meldrick Taylor, Riddick Bowe, Evander Holyfield, Lennox Lewis, Jack Johnson, Jim Jeffries, Pernell Sweet Pea Whitaker. Each round she'd be first one, then the other, examining the bouts of history, some black and white and gritty, others full of red and blue bright lights and millions, the ring girls in sequined tops and slutty heels with big white scorecards inside a Budweiser ring. She craved it. Compulsion pushed her farther and farther into that world where she'd be not white or black, but simply a fighter with the sheer ambition to win. What would that take, she wondered, as she slipped spirit punches and threw massive ones with improper form. What would it take to become what her father had always wanted – a moving target, a champion?

Amateur boxing seemed a world away from the professionals. The men half-naked with the intent to kill, making their way from unknown to Showtime, fighting for belts and titles. And the women, disrobing quietly in a holding room – where beneath their warm-up gear would be the modest trunks below the knees with a thick, fitted waist-band. T-shirt and sports bra, nothing flashy like the professional women sometimes wore – their camouflage or girly pink shorts that showed bare, toned thighs, tops that let people glimpse tan flesh and visible shoulder blades. How relieving as an amateur to be regarded for skill and not as an object – to expose the fears, tuck them in gloves and beat them out of your body. The special gift of a boxer. Could anyone truly relate to the stories told in that ring, where professionals had half an hour to tell their tales of sadness, of dedication and perseverance, while amateur women had six? Six minutes to illustrate the practice, the frustration, the ebb and flow of training.

The ring was stripped of time and place and consequence. There were only groups of punches, the stiff, controlled shots that would one day separate Katherine from the others, hoisting her up and over the trail of badly trained women, until she would be the best because she wanted it the most and had sacrificed too much not to be.

Only there could she own it all, her feelings, her place in the world – for no matter what happened, she could work through it in the ring but never outside of it. It took courage that no onlooker could ever interpret – courage her father had tried so desperately to identify with, sitting and watching with such fanaticism – if only he could feel what it truly took to be the prize they clapped or jeered for. She'd be a woman on her way, a single body providing points through punches, carrying violent, exquisite conversations with her fists as if she'd never again need a mouth.

It could not be learned, only bred inside her – and who could she share it with, who could relate? Katherine knew there was

A Woman's Ring

only one person – only one other man with that analogous fire in his eyes – Brandon – it was she and Brandon and no one else.

One day, she would train and share secrets through sparring, through fights and discipline, until soon she would be a woman without a past – on her way to that magic levitation where fighting earned not money or fame. This obsession was not monetary and never had been; it was a quest for esteem, power, and escape.

In those minutes where she shadowed the bouts on television, within those fantasies, there was so much more than Katherine – there was a prize pugilist capable of learning, trapped inside the jailed body of a lifelong dream.

Rea Frey

A Woman's Ring

Chapter Twenty-two

She was rabid with the world. In the dead of winter, she dressed Lily and Frankie, shoved them in the car and began to drive. Past the circular dead end where pairs of houses sat, up the small hill toward Lyndon Street, beyond the one lone grocery store with the sagging roof, past the Yearns' farmhouse, and straight out onto the highway. From the backseat, Frankie kicked his feet and began to sing a song Katherine had never heard. Lily sat composed next to her brother, staring at the back of Katherine's head, as though she understood her mother's quiet brooding.

Daddy never hurt her, but there was something inside her mother. Grandma had worn that expression many times, and Lily knew Katherine had to have some of Grandma inside her too. Just like Lily would have some of her Mommy's traits. Daddy called that genetics and often took her under the stars and promised the moon and heaven and explained that Katherine loved her as much as he did, but just had a harder time showing it.

Katherine drove madly, almost wishing to crash, to erase the small bodies that kept her so irrelevant to the world. She didn't know where she was driving – maybe to the next state, but she knew she wouldn't get far. That's why she brought them with her. If she had the children, then she wouldn't venture on toward other cities with real opportunity and life outside this imprisonment.

Only Andrew knew how to mother them – fix them up and give baths and read to them as her father had once read to her.

Watching him was torturous, because it made her realize that she was reenacting her mother's behavior – her reclusiveness. Hadn't Bruce taught her to follow her dreams? Maybe she should have gone on to college, moved away from this town, been strong enough to ignore Andrew. Yet she knew that even as her marriage continued in utter mockery, the children balanced him. Despite his womanizing, his consistent drinking, they gave him a purpose. So what was hers?

She made a loop back onto the highway toward home. Ignoring Frankie's persistent "Where we going, Mommy?" she fishtailed the car from lane to lane as the beginnings of sleet began to drift down on the streets and windshield. She made her way back through the familiar neighborhood, taunted by the possibilities of plane rides and car trips taken alone.

As she pulled into the drive, she saw Andrew getting out of his car. Hearing the kill of an engine, he turned and locked eyes with Katherine and she felt, for the first time in their marriage, remorse for all her deceit. Why could she not love him as he loved the children, as he might have loved her? Was she too bitter to carry any man's love?

She got out of the car and made her way toward the house. She left the children in their car seats, knowing Andrew would scoop them up and take them to a movie, or fix dinner and make dessert out of something left in the fridge. Katherine walked straight inside and locked herself in the bathroom.

This depression came with handcuffs and chains, came at unexpected moments that controlled her life and mood, ruined her. She shook her mind loose of her obligations. A small undertone passed through the anguish, straight to the expressions of distress tattooed along her lips and eyes – *follow your dreams* – it said. The words of her father, of Brandon. She would keep searching until she knew how – until nerve outweighed the obligations of being a miserable mother, a wife, and parentless child.

Chapter Twenty-three

Andrew stood behind her, digging his fingernails into the frame of the bed. He could sense the tenseness of her body, the jerky way she gathered her nightgown at her ankles and hoisted it into one hand. She began picking up stray socks and shirts, tossing them into the hamper as an attempt to ignore him.

"Katherine, look, we've got to start talking about this. You can't just keep running away every time something like this comes up. They're our children for God's sakes – not just mine!"

Katherine paced the room, holding her temper with every spare article of clothing she collected, with every breath she leveled, every step she took. "Andrew, I said I don't want to talk about this right now."

"Well, Katherine, sometimes you don't always get what you want." He closed the gap between them, grabbing her roughly by the arm. "Don't you get that? It's not always about you!"

Katherine jerked her arm free, her mouth falling open. "Don't you think I know that, Andrew? When has it *ever* been about me?" Katherine pitched a sock across the bed. "The only reason I married you was so I could get out of this hellhole town and make something of myself! I didn't want to marry you, and I sure as hell didn't want those children! I was a child for Christ's sakes – a child that you corrupted with your smooth talking and empty promises!" She balled up another sock and chucked it against the window. "Everything is always about you, not me! What *you* want and always manage to get – and I hate *all* of you for it!"

Andrew recoiled as if he'd been slapped. She knew she shouldn't have said those words – that no matter how poorly she felt, there was a couple out there worse off, that it wasn't the children's fault, regardless. She watched Andrew's eyes fill as they looked behind her.

In the doorway stood Lily and Frankie, two chocolate sundaes outstretched in their hands. Andrew's eyes stopped on Frankie's startled expression, his heart going out to his son. Andrew attempted to keep calm, to keep his face from contorting, to control the tears that threatened to spill over his sullen cheeks – tears for the pain his children were enduring, for all the things Katherine refused to provide. He covered his face with his hands, sinking onto the unmade bed. Katherine turned to look at her children who'd heard her inappropriate words, whose eyes welled with innumerable tears – Frankie throwing the ice cream against the carpet and pattering down the hall to slam the door to his room. Lily stood there, lips trembling, head held high as she walked forward and handed her ice cream to Katherine.

"Here, Mommy. Happy Birthday. I – I love you." Her voice broke on those last few syllables, her lips trembling as she went sniffling after her brother. Andrew was up and after them before Katherine could catch her breath. She stared down at the ice cream, the tiny candle, unlit, that was sliding into the melting vanilla. Her tears dotted the sundae, her cries breaking free as she slid to the carpet. Why did she insist on ruining these children? How could she continuously corrupt such chaste lives?

Down the hall, she could hear Andrew trying to talk them calm as he always did. He was the hero. But he wasn't always a good person, she wanted to tell them. He made little girls into liars and bitter before their time. Promised the world and provided mediocrity. And it was only when they'd been born, only then when he'd decided to grow up, to settle. Only then he'd resolved that being a good man meant ignoring his wife's pain and focusing solely on the children.

Katherine pulled herself off the floor, threw on a sweatshirt and grabbed the keys from the night stand.

She banged through the front door as Andrew called after her – all three of her family members silhouetted in the front door frame as she backed down the drive. Why could she never feel a part of them?

A Woman's Ring

Katherine drove for hours that night – missing her father, missing Brandon, but most of all, herself. The girl who used to ace her exams and put on plays in the schoolyard. The girl who survived the loss of a parent by a true best friend. The Katherine who had misplaced her laugh with marriage, buried her spirit with twins.

She wasn't like most women who could handle the challenge of motherhood – she'd never dreamed of it, never played house with her dolls. Hadn't her own mother given her away? And hadn't her adopted mother been unable to love her too?

Katherine had to admit that her birth mother's choice had been more tolerable. Because when a mother failed in front of you, choosing not to love but only to exist in her sorrow, it was an encumbrance – one that Katherine would most likely cling to for a lifetime -- one that her children would soon bear if she didn't change. She might never be fit for them. If she turned out like her father, staying in a situation he did not believe in because he'd been taught to suffer, she'd be resigned before her time. Katherine still wanted a chance, an opening.

As she pulled into the drive before sunrise, she let her thoughts sink in, let her ideas begin to form. She would do what felt right – for just a little while, she'd let the children and this life be the sole responsibility of her "perfect" husband.

Rea Frey

A Woman's Ring

Chapter Twenty-four

In Katherine's kitchen, Mrs. Baskin shifted in her chair, fanning her face with one fleshy hand. "I wish I could still exercise. I used to be so active but not since I had my hysterectomy…you wouldn't believe how that can mess a woman up, Katie."

Katherine let Mrs. Baskin carry on her familiar sob story, pulling down a mug for coffee. Mrs. Baskin droned on and on about her deteriorating health and Will, her husband, who was always away on business. All the while Katherine burned to ask questions about Brandon – why he left without her, if he was seeing anyone, if he would ever come back to take her with him.

"How's Brandon?" Katherine asked the question casually, pouring the carafe of water into the coffee pot, pulling the beans from the freezer to scoop three tablespoons into the filter.

"Oh, you know, living the big city life…whatever it is boys his age like to do. Working toward his dream, I suppose."

Katherine felt that familiar pang of jealousy upon hearing of Brandon's good fortune and the mere mention of dreams – dreams like water that everyone needed to survive, dreams like lovemaking, like those moments when she was alone and could only concentrate on her own breath, in and out, her own thoughts like vices squeezing.

"Yeah, Betty, he always got to do anything he pleased, didn't he?"

Mrs. Baskin smiled considerately as Katherine placed a hot mug of coffee, one cream and four sugars in front of her, sliding into a chair at her left side.

"I'm sorry Betty, I just get so fed up sometimes that I couldn't live like he did. I had so many dreams, you know, so many hopes and somehow it got so screwed up after my father died…I screwed it all up."

Mrs. Baskin reached one warm, wrinkled hand out to cover hers, tenderly patting the young knuckles. "Katie, honey, you'll get there. We all make mistakes, but you need to do what you have to, you hear me young lady? Do what *you* have to do."

Katherine stared into her wet, brown eyes, the eyes she had often looked to as a child, wanting her as a mother, wanting Brandon as much more than a friend. She cleared her throat, imagining acting upon what she wanted – it would involve so much, so little thinking of others. Yet deep down, that is what she needed, what she would do, as the oppression of her present existence kept trampling all over her; the children's demands, the husband's paws in places she ached to scrub free.

"I will, Betty. I know."

"Good. That's all I've ever wanted for you, you know. For you to stand up in this world, and put your little stamp on it like Brandon is doing in Chicago."

Chicago. It would take her a matter of hours to drive there.

Mrs. Baskin settled back in her chair with her coffee, voiceless. Katherine excused herself to check on the children, their diminutive bodies snuggled on the couch, reading a book given to them by Andrew.

"Hi, Momma," Frankie said when she entered, pulling his small hand up in a wave. "Lily's reading her third book this week, Momma! She's almost as smart as I am! Can you believe it? Her third book and they're *hard* books too!" That same child's smile would later be replaced with a frown only hours later, when Andrew was gone on business.

When Frankie had bragged of Lily's great accomplishment, she'd only passed them, not stooping to kiss their heads and whisper "I'm so proud of both of you," but moved away with her slow, tired gait toward her bedroom, in hopes of drowning out their chatter. Going to her closet, she pulled her suitcase down – a first step at saying goodbye. These were such loose plans for such a big move, where nothing would ever look or feel the same as it did to her. If she made it to Chicago, she would have to find an apartment, pack lightly, drain any money left in her accounts, and get her own insurance.

Katherine sighed, looking at the empty bag before rising again, knowing she couldn't leave Betty simply sitting in the kitchen. She walked down the hall corridor, Betty now on the couch with Lily and Frankie. They all looked up as Katherine entered the room, resting her head against the doorframe.

"Oh, hey, Katie. We thought you'd gone to take a nap."

Katherine smiled and took a seat on the rocking chair. She rocked wordlessly, Betty snuggled between her two children on the sofa. Mrs. Baskin always reveled in what was new with the children, what they were learning. It amazed Katherine that for all her social inadequacies, Lily and Frankie were nothing short of two geniuses. They worked at a tireless pace, playing, mastering puzzles, reading books that shouldn't have been read for a handful of years. Had she been that smart as a child? She couldn't even remember back that far.

For the next few hours, the children watched a movie as Betty kept up her string of conversation in the kitchen. Katherine attempted to feign interest, but found her stomach knotted and her mind elsewhere. She finally walked Betty out, promising to drop the kids off early the next morning so Katherine could catch up on the house work. She waved goodbye to Betty and sat out on the porch well after the sun went down, shivering from the brisk night air.

When she returned to the living room, Frankie was curled on the floor, his hands wrapped securely around the back of his neck while sobbing in the hot space of his knees. Lily was nowhere to be seen. Katherine looked up at the clock and saw it was way past his bedtime.

"Frankie, what's the matter?"

He moved, rhythmically, ignoring her question while silently wishing for his father – for arms that could pick him up from the carpet and comfort him in familiar elbows and forearms.

From the lip of the living room, Katherine watched him, stirred, but unable to step forward and retrieve him, afraid of the simple smell of a child's skin, afraid of its fragility and innocence and the ease in which it could be corrupted by a bad mother; as if it were already too late to do right by him.

Frankie continued sobbing on the carpet, a toy xylophone and a video tape beside him. Why he was crying, she could only estimate – for she too remembered the way it felt to be unloved by a mother, to be instead filled with hopes of the "orphan mother," and her unlikely rescue. Yet Frankie had only the video tape, the xylophone, the rare hope that his mother would erase his desperate need and drop down on him with encircling arms.

Instead, Katherine retreated, step by shameful step, feeling the violent palpitations of her heart, the knowledge that she was leaving tomorrow, and that in some way, he knew it too. He knew of her selfish dream, had seen her punching and studying past fights of boxing like her life depended upon it.

As she made her way to her own room, she passed Lily sleeping in her brother's bed, breath entering and exiting her lungs, that pillow of a body full of guiltless dreams. She stood and watched, feeling the pressure of tears as Lily's small pink lips pushed and pulled in air, questioning if her moving out of this place would ever make a difference, if she could leave them as easily as her own mother had left her.

"Goodnight, Lily."

Katherine made the rest of the way to her room and closed her own bedroom door, shutting off Frankie's cries that still sat in her like a dreadful weight, erupting with her every breath, blink, or sound.

"You have no grace, Katherine," she whispered as she slipped into the unmade bed, the stray chest hairs of Andrew dotting the covers beside her. She blew them aside, knocking his pillow to the floor with her hands, fingers shaking, wishing it was his face she was knocking into, that need spreading like disease in her blood.

As she clicked off the bedside lamp, she knew her son would be waiting at the door for her, pressing his expectant fingers

A Woman's Ring

around the knob, craving attention as she had in her life, where the love of a mother was inescapably unavailable.

Katherine pulled her own pillow over her head as she heard his small footsteps shuffle outside her door, his audible cries of "Momma, Momma *pleeease*," then the jiggle of the knob.

"You have no heart, no heart," she whispered beneath the cases, pulling them tightly to drown the voice of shame as Frankie's cries intensified. She pulled the pillows tighter, until her breath grew slight and her tears mixed with the cotton.

"Please go away," she whispered as Frankie's hands fiddled with the knob, his sobs causing him to hyperventilate, his words, "Mommaaaa, Mommaaaa," loud and desperate, that word, "please," inside of her, splitting her open, the pillows smothering – "please," her own voice begging to drown the wife, the mother; to be cut from the strings of confinement, to birth the sweet wings of faith and fly far from here.

Rea Frey

A Woman's Ring

Chapter Twenty-five

Midnight came with a thread of light. Andrew's absence made him all the more apparent – from the navy jogging pants crumpled by the chair to the scattered socks, mismatched and soiled, the hangers with half a suit draped scrappily over the wire and the long, silk ties that snaked along the dressers and bed posts. Unpaid credit card bills lay on the chest in crumpled envelopes. Files from work rested in old manila folders. Telephone numbers bulged from an oversized rolodex that balanced on top of their big-screen television.

She sat up, stretched, and dragged her feet, ghostlike, from the bed to the door, halfway expecting Frankie to still be crumpled in the hall when she opened it – hoarse from calling her name hours before.

She made her way to the children's room that had been Andrew's design, with twin basketball hoops and Barbie's palace, colorful drawings and baby pictures strung along the walls. Stars dotted the ceiling in chartreuse and navy – a telescope by the big bay window stepped out onto a screened in balcony. Frankie's eyes flitted open as she stood at the door, but he did not speak; only stared as if he had already made up his mind about her, as if that stare could knock her through the house and blow her away for ignoring him.

Katherine retreated, making her way from room to room. She studied things she'd never quite noticed before – the vase on the mantel that held the remains of Andrew's mother, the tile that was chipped at one corner of the kitchen, the brown stain by the couch's leg in the living room, a brand new wall clock that gleamed gold with inlaid diamonds on the second hand – the stainless steel fridge that had photo magnets in which the children and their father stood proudly, arms draped around each other – but none of Katherine. Where was she in this house? She looked from room to room, from ceiling to floor. Where was she hiding?

Katherine walked back to the mantel, removed the lid off the vase and stared at the bits of ash that fluttered as she inhaled and exhaled. Who had this woman been? How trapped had she felt? How had she died? Was it really suicide as Andrew had told her, or some sickness that ate her cell by cell? Katherine placed the top down carefully and tiptoed back to her bedroom, dressing for the day despite the moon still flirting through the blinds, the neighborhood still sleeping soundly in their bedrooms. She finished packing, hid her suitcases in the trunk of the car, and sat on the couch when the sun streaked over the horizon. She'd written farewell letters to all of them, explaining her needs, her wants and reasoning before ripping each word to nothingness, the pieces scattered along the trash bin's lining.

At 7:00a.m., she heard the pit-pat of Lily coming to rub sleep from her eyes, to watch a cartoon and ask for a bowl of cereal, please. Frankie would soon come behind her after brushing his teeth, asking for juice and then complaining about how terrible it tasted.

"Morning, Momma." Lily sidled up to Katherine, already forgiving her for the birthday ordeal, snuggling her face into her mother's shoulder, yawning dramatically. "Can I get you some breakfast today?"

Katherine dared not speak, knew if she did it would be all choked sobs and reactive words – that she might lose her nerve and fold into a life she so desperately needed to escape from. In moments like these, she thought she could do it – that mothering was simple as holding your daughter in the crook of your arm, watching a movie or making breakfast. That getting a divorce wasn't so bad if she could still pursue her passions.

"Mommy? Are you okay today? You seem weird."

A Woman's Ring

"I'm – fine, Lily. Why don't you go get your brother up and then make a bowl of cereal? Okay?"

Lily didn't argue, just disentangled herself from her mother and padded toward Frankie's bed.

Lily found herself oppressing giggles because she had different ways of getting him up. Today it would be a Nerf football in his face, tomorrow it might be a water gun. She picked up the ball from behind the door and lobbed it at his resting face, sprinting toward the kitchen before he could catch her.

"Lil-eeee!"

Katherine saw her daughter float past her into the kitchen, her eyes radiant, lips stretched back in a mischievous smile – and then Frankie's cranky voice upon waking. "Mommy, Lily hit me again!"

Two minutes later, he climbed up beside Katherine on the couch, complaining about Lily and how she was always bugging him. How it wasn't fair that a big boy like him had to share a room with his awful sister and shouldn't he get to sleep in his own bed without having toys chucked at his head?

Katherine wiped at her eyes, composing herself as her son fell silent, began fidgeting beside her, picking his toenails, scratching his hair and sighing like a grown-up.

"What? What *is* it Frankie?" she jumped up, hands in her hair. "Please, just stop fidgeting and go get ready to see Mrs. Baskin! We're in a hurry!"

Frankie looked at her the same way he had last night, the same glare as in his bed when she'd gone to check on them. He had to know, had to see that she was leaving him.

"Oh, Frankie, I'm sorry, just please get ready for Mommy okay?"

Katherine ran from cabinet to closet for baggies of snacks and toys for Mrs. Baskin's, wanting to hang herself for doing this, for acting this way when it had been done to her by a mother who chose to simply give up the job.

"What are you doing, Katherine?" she stared at herself in the bathroom mirror, noticing the small gray moons beneath her eyes – such disturbed eyes for such a young woman. A bottle of Andrew's cologne rested on the sink and it all came rushing back as to why. "Him," she whispered, dropping her head, smashing the bottle into the trash, dragging a hand over her face and exiting. No matter how hurtful this would be to the children, it would be more damaging for her to stay. Andrew would never give her a divorce, so she would be forced to live a lie, to be resentful. Perhaps part of her expected to run away only to come back again – to realize the rest of the world wasn't so great, that this was where she belonged.

She packed Lily and Frankie in the car, counting the slow, routine minutes of morning preparation. Her fingers trembled on the steering wheel. Lily watched from the front seat, staring at the startled pinkie, the vibrating thumb. Katherine looked over at her daughter with the rosy cheeks and sharp eyes that never missed anything.

"You cold, Momma?" Lily reached over from under her seat belt and placed her mittened hands on top of Katherine's, bringing her to immediate tears.

"Thank you, Lily, I'm fine." Katherine moved her hands out of touching range, and stared out the driver side window at a stop sign, wiping her eyes. She knew she would not kiss them goodbye. But their smell was on her already, in her hair, on her hands that she brought to her lips, the infectious scent of innocence. How had their quiet dispositions eaten through her bravery? That bravery that was actually weakness, that would plague her dreams and actions, that would test every cell and nerve, every decision. Wouldn't she miss them? Lily's laughter in the mornings, the way she sang in the bathtub. Frankie's constant art projects with crayons and markers. Their games of hide-n-seek in the back yard, the early attempts at riding bikes without training wheels, and Lily wanting to be a great ballerina by the age of nine.

As she pulled up the long drive to Mrs. Baskin's, she knew it was time to let go of the guilt, to seek her own destiny and slowly embrace change.

Part II

Rea Frey

A Woman's Ring

Chapter Twenty-six

The beat of Chicago was all-consuming, with its buildings that skimmed the bellies of airplanes, clouds that hovered near high rise windows, buses, cabs, and people making noise, the lake that moved wave after wave against the makeshift shoreline. Summer, where runners strapped on radios and treaded against the soft track bordering the lake, bikes and rollerblades guided by athletic legs. There were street signs and shops, more windows than Katherine had ever imagined. Trucks, ambulances, and construction workers hugged street corners, yet there was a calm about the city, a paradox of silence in chaos, peace in mayhem.

Boxing called – learning the sport which was one difficult dance, a rhythmic movement, an unending, scrupulous masterpiece. Ethan didn't train like the others, putting girls on the heavy bags or treadmills. He taught boxing with a subtle intensity – calmly explaining the components of the game, the importance of using your body and not your hands – whipping the arms at the end of punches, pivoting your heels, fighting Southpaw and left foot forward, honing the skills to be good enough to beat anybody, not just women.

On her first venture into a popular Chicago gym, Ethan sat nursing a cup of coffee, his gray eyes darting from the clock on the wall to the entranceway, and back to the clock again. Curls of steam rose around the bones of his face, his legs tightly crossed at the ankles, balanced precariously on the boxing ring's ledge. Katherine didn't know which she noticed first – this older man with the sloped shoulders and muscular arms, the small fists that held the cup as if he could crush it at any given moment – or the vibrant ring, its red ropes taut and shining, the ring floor dotted with stale drops of blood from countless sparring matches.

Ethan seemed like he was waiting for someone, his small lips twitching in and out, winding around his cup, opening, stretching into a frown, a grin, a grimace, movements that gave no indication of his thoughts or emotions. His patch of dark, silvering hair was cut short and receding above the forehead, an implication of his age, but the young, tight body led Katherine to believe otherwise. This man was a boxer, she knew, past or present, a man full of the knowledge she'd craved an entire lifetime; someone of stature who would teach her things.

"Will you train me to be a fighter?" was the first thing she asked him upon joining the gym. He looked at Katherine with those overcast eyes, like Brandon's eyes, not judging, not wanting, just seeing her desire for boxing. "Will you train me" turned into countless hours of talking, moving, listening, and learning. Ethan taught technique. How to lean out with your chest on a cross, how to slip punches, to angle and counter, to switch stances, to feint, to use your hips to execute a body shot or a hook to the head. Katherine was there with Maxx and Jake and Colin. In boxing class, they would work in pairs, quietly at first, Katherine only listening to their criticism, how to better her stance, her jab, her power. They took her in as the only girl serious enough about boxing, whispering behind her back, asking questions about the girl who never revealed a word about anything.

That initial moment on the heavy bags, hands ripping into the soft black leather, moving the brick weight with her fists, snapping her muscles with impact, picturing Andrew's face, then her mother's, and her own for wasting so much precious time – was sheer release. Hitting the mitts was the same, linking one punch to many, at first clumsily, later making noise off those mitts, her gloves smacking with accuracy, sweat racing between her breasts, fighting like a man, feeling like a woman, with the power to punch and move and dance and sweat, all a sweet rhythm of which she truly felt a part.

A Woman's Ring

After class, Katherine would watch the guys fitting on their headgear, gloves and mouthpieces, the intense looks in their eyes as they stepped in the ring to do what really mattered – spar. In their own private corners, they'd loiter, yelling out tips to each other, landing combinations, asking Ethan to show them ways to dominate round after round as real contact was made.

This was the corner entirely separate from the fancy cardio machines with the brand new computers attached to the front, so lawyers and traders could check their emails and stocks while burning calories. The weights sat in front of large mirrors, on racks that were a slick, waxy gold. Smooth black workout mats fanned out along hardwood floors, and on each wall were famous faces painted in vivid acrylics stuck in fancy frames.

Every day, Katherine would come into the club from her new apartment, after perusing the streets as though they were bookstores, partly afraid she'd see Andrew coming to take her back to Ohio, but mostly eager that maybe she'd see Brandon, alone and waiting for her.

Months perished, months in which she fought against thinking of her children, against seeking out someone she could trust enough to tell things to. Ethan was the only hope at first, his kind words and confidence in her apparent; after only two months, he wanted her to spar.

At first, it had been confusing, all that bouncing and feinting and moving like she'd never done before. She had trouble keeping up her defense, she wanted to hit hard and fast and not land accurate punches. The headgear would simply slide over her eyes, her mouthpiece a big, black chew toy that collected drool, those gloves the size of her head, blocking his shots. She wanted to keep throwing the same combinations, and then move away, too afraid of Ethan's power, obsessed with the quickness of her own retreat around the edges of the ring. Only his insistence to come forward and fight him worked, as she gingerly stepped in and learned what it took to spar. First it was Ethan then Maxx, then Jake she sparred with, each man a different entity, some tall, some slim, some fast on offense, some waiting for shots to counter. But each time brought new lessons.

"This is your sport, Katherine," Ethan would say, fitting on her gloves before tugging his own. "Just give it time."

Together, they would dance, his athleticism unlike any other man. If she closed her eyes and simply listened to the rhythm of his feet, it was balletic, them stretching, pointing, lifting lightly, his feet as quick as anyone's, his power of his punches devastating, his demeanor a cool, calm collection of experience.

Jake was the first sparring partner to give Katherine trouble, a gangly Latino with a small frame and a wild, unorthodox style. He never took a boxing stance, just kind of stumbled around the ring, left foot over right, right over left, landing big shots because he never quit throwing punches. Before the first round, Jake beat his gloves together, wiggling his eyebrows at her. Katherine bent to stretch her legs, as Maxx waited by the bell, flipping the switch to begin their round.

"You guys ready? Katherine? Jake?"

"You ready, killer?" Jake asked, slurring through his plastic mouth guard, which he pushed in and out of his lips with his tongue. "You ready for this?"

She snickered at his thin, tattooed frame, banging her fists together, looking momentarily at Ethan, who was slumped against one wall, talking to Colin. The distant hum of cardio machines was weak, barely audible. The gym seemed empty tonight, abandoned by the importance of business dinners and cocktails, nightclubs or movies and theater productions.

It was always the simple things. Hearing the ding of the bell, taking that one deep breath before meeting her match. The way she and Jake slapped gloves so calmly before trying to rip into each other's heads. The movement of her body as she faked a punch, then landed a beautiful clean left hand. The defensive moves. The connected punches. Slipping against the ropes, the other boxer floundering to find her head. The way it felt to get hit sometimes, that momentary fringe of blindness, like her brain erupted into countless stars, her vision black, eyesight torn. The recovery, deep breaths, retaliation, and then Ethan's pride revealed through a smile. Every sparring match was a competition, and though she had yet to compete, she was

A Woman's Ring

preparing, waiting for that day when she could fight another woman, a real boxer, like she assumed she was becoming.

But Katherine felt blind sometimes, dragging through the city alone, amidst high rises and law firms. During the day, she wandered the streets, thinking of the children and Mrs. Baskin, her mission of finding Brandon inactive until she'd made something of herself in and outside that ring.

Ethan seemed to be the only one to believe in her, always hugging or holding her, Katherine's mouth kept tightly closed as she listened for the next tip for boxing, then the next thing.

In the ring, she tried to forget the loneliness, tried to make her body do things they were just learning to do. She felt her mistakes sting her lips, eyes and jaw, tried to correct them by pinning Jake against the ropes, unleashing body shots to his ribs that would make him pee blood for days. She wasn't a killer, but she was searching for something. A love she only harbored for one man – an urgent, distant calling, a signal for him. If Brandon saw her doing the one thing she'd claimed she'd always do, if he saw her without the children or a husband, would he act differently? Would he take her in his arms and shower her with the words she'd always wanted, or would she find him engaged with another, off on a life of which she would never be a part? Either way, she was pulled to find him; pulled in the directions of her own longing, as she was here, in the ring, fighting her decisions as only a woman can.

A Woman's Ring

Chapter Twenty-seven

When Frankie and Lily still slept in their cradles, Katherine would often sneak into their rooms, toeing the soft carpet before dropping to her knees beside the wooden bars, clinging to them as if to plea, watching the air that she had granted them push in and out of delicate lungs. The twins slept together most nights, sometimes tangled like lovers, back to belly, other times foot to face, knee to shoulder blade. In the shadows, there was love, love she had never expressed when they were walking, waking replicas of her and Andrew. That disgust in knowing that these two people came partly from him kept her at a distance; that disgust for his body that grinded into hers with fierce, hot strokes night and day, him knowing her repugnance, but Katherine letting him do it anyway. There came a point when she could not fight the hands that left claw marks on her wrists and neck, a point when she guarded herself against his sperm, a point when she knew he was not faithful as she was not faithful; he in body, she in mind and spirit, and their nights soon became distant – no longer centimeters between their sleeping bodies, but entire rooms. When Andrew hogged the covers, snoring, or even when the occasional restless elbow slammed down on her head, she was better off with the children, their idyllic smells emanating through the bars of the cradles – only then would she become fascinated with their tiny hands and feet that twitched in dreaming, their small eyes and pairs of eyebrows like strips of white fuzz, pink pug noses and soft, budding heads. How had she birthed them? Pushed and screamed while her anatomy ripped open for the passage of their heads and shoulders? All those nights she'd sat in the bathroom with a warm washrag, rubbing her swollen stomach, saying, "Who would have imagined this, who would have imagined?"

But why did she stay? Why did she let them see her face and connect with it, let them pull on her and kiss her skin and sway her with their gentle nature?

With these questions, she'd fall asleep next to their cradle, curl on the carpet, one hand still clamped to the bars. When she awoke, Andrew was hours gone, the babies up and fed by Mrs. Baskin. On seeing those empty cradles, hearing dishes banging or Betty cooing at the kids, Katherine would fall into that foggy person she became during the day -- an irate, nasty mirror of the girl she once was.

Sometimes, she'd let Betty watch them for the afternoon so she could run down to the cemetery – a place she often went in times of solitude, a place she'd shared with Brandon as a child. There, Katherine would close her eyes as she lay on a soft patch of grass, the ground lumpy beneath her from scattered, unseen coffins.

Each day, Katherine would pick out a new person to lie over – Hannah Jenkins, 1925-2000. Peter Franks, 1895-1910. Celia Ward, 1934-1940. Cooper Neiland 1894-1952. Over their bodies she would rest, closing her eyes and feeling the sun beat over her body, feeling as dead as they were, seventy-two inches below the earth in big, rectangular boxes, reduced to bones and dust and memories.

A Woman's Ring

Chapter Twenty-eight

Boxing was a life inside itself. Standing in the ring learning, while the whole gym pedaled their machines and went through monotonous routines. How had she learned this so quickly? She thought it would be a giant climax, a bombardment of information. Yet she'd jumped in just as fanatically as she assumed her father would have, for who knew how much time was to be had? She fought through the motions, attempting to perfect every punch and move, never giving in to the frustrations.

She spoke little that first session, while Ethan took his time choosing gloves and mitts, wrapped her hands and told her what wrestling shoes to purchase. She stared self-consciously at the ground as he studied her from head to ankle – measuring her stature, her weight, and what would work best for her build. There was an art in deciphering – in teaching her to jab with her right hand, to bend at the waist, fake a low jab, back up, counter cross, change stances and fool whomever she was fighting in that fluid, awesome way – proving that her skills were indisputable.

"You never see boxers fighting well from both stances. That's why I want you to learn both ways. Even though you're a Southpaw, you'll be great from left foot forward. You'll beat anybody."

Katherine dared not ask when – when she'd know her hook from her overhand, how to relax and see what was coming, analyze her options and play with her opponent in the ring. When she'd feel the nip of a punch on her uncharted face, when she'd get her first bloody nose, when she'd be good enough to stand in the ring with a tight smile and confidence.

He talked like she was already a champion, letting her fists resonate against the mitts, throwing soft punches at her head, explaining the development of defending and the innumerable options she would possess in just a few months time.

"Options, it's all about options," he'd say.

Katherine nodded, attempting to retain all this new information. She'd been so secluded in Ohio, with her television and short runs and children's cries. This was her dream – in this expensive gym where no one knew her background.

"You ever do any dance or sports growing up?"

Katherine shook her head and brought her hands back in front of her face, the right dropped a little lower, so she could power jab. She already knew the names – jab, power jab, backfist jab, hook, cross, overhand, body shot, uppercut – these punches would be her new vocabulary – her knuckles inflamed in the evenings, shoulders iced, those first couple of weeks her hands shaking in the mornings, wrists sore, body unable to cooperate.

"You'll get used to it," he'd say, and for some reason Katherine always listened. Ethan didn't pry, just believed in her improvement – each day a demanding one – filled with setbacks like her lack of power in jabs, or right hooks. He learned to work with her body, make her hips and torso torque just enough to pull off each skill. Her stance was too wide, her moves choppy, but as if waving a magic wand over her head, she began to transform into something else – a smooth, confident fighter. The gym members would constantly watch her – nodding their approval and telling their friends about the quick girl in the ring.

Katherine lived and breathed boxing – thought about it in the mornings, afternoons, and evenings, drowning out the want for Brandon as she ran by the lake, burying the guilt of her distant children as she jumped rope before bed.

Would they ever understand the meaning of a dream – would Andrew explain that it took sacrifice to get there? Would he teach them what a bad person she was – and that she had never really cared about anything except boxing, except her father and

A Woman's Ring

Brandon? What would he teach them? How would he define love?

In her apartment, with the new furniture and sparse rooms, she began to worry about what she couldn't control – what she couldn't be present for. This had been her decision – leave one life behind and embrace another – because she knew she couldn't have it all – could not have dreams and a family – not without giving something up, twisting the paths of life and trying out the different roads, alone, hoping for the best, living for those revered moments of discovery.

Rea Frey

A Woman's Ring

Chapter Twenty-nine

Maxx and Katherine stood at the edge of the ring, watching Ethan and the new girl spar. Gretchen had waltzed in from the South side, packed with cash and an undeniable attitude. Two days and she was sparring, bullying the guys with her toughness, flexing her muscles in the locker room. Katherine kept her contempt bit back – kept the fake smile on her face in the audience as she watched Gretchen throw haymakers, grunting and stumbling foot over foot.

"What do you think?" Maxx nudged Katherine with his elbow, motioning toward the ring. "Pretty good, huh?"

Katherine shrugged, a frown pulling at her lips. "She's aggressive, but that's not always a good thing."

"Yeah, but she's got that fighter instinct – that killer attitude." He smiled, dropped his head, and shook it slowly. "You gotta have that to make it in this sport."

Katherine felt offended, as though he'd directed his comment right at her. Katherine knew her skills were paramount, had been crafted from a televised passion – and that should be enough to prove her dedication – her hours in this gym, beginning with private lessons and bag work, on to sparring and preparing for competition. But her instinct was far from threatening. Like Ethan, Katherine felt boxing wasn't about killing some opponent but making a story of the fight, beauty in each crafted moment, each round. The flight in the beginning, the restraint it took not to be wild with punching but patient with moving and watching – that elaborate art of observation. The bout in the ring's middle that suddenly formed when two people found themselves in an exchange, in clinches, on the ropes and off them. The ending, where the muscles fatigued, where breathing went unnoticed and the headgear, mouthpiece and gloves were now part of the fighter, of the round. Then the bell, when all was over and you didn't want it to be – when just ten more seconds were needed, ten more to knock them down, to land a shot, to dance brilliantly before you separated the ropes and left the shadow of a victor in the ring – a drop of blood, a roll of sweat, a recollection.

Why was it that people didn't take women's boxing seriously, that the crowd wasn't riled until the windmill punching unfurled? Did they want boxing or brawling? Would they boo her because she wasn't as wild and temperamental as this Gretchen girl seemed to be?

Listening to Maxx made her feel as though she'd never be aggressive or angry enough to survive professionally. "It can't be learned," he'd said.

"What are you thinking about, killer?"

"Hmm?" Katherine shook herself from her daze, smirking as Ethan landed a big looping overhand and pushed Gretchen against the ropes - teaching her the art of respecting him.

"Hey, easy in there, Coach!" Maxx laughed and turned his attention to Katherine, a genuine look in his eyes. "Seriously, why are you always so quiet? You never really talk much."

Katherine shrugged, suddenly feeling uncomfortable. "What do you want to know?"

"Um, I don't know – like where did you go to college?"

"I didn't. I couldn't afford it."

"Oh. Where are you from?"

The bell sounded and Ethan motioned for Maxx to jump in with Gretchen. He shrugged before suiting up, relieving Katherine of the pressure to lie about her past. What would these guys do if they knew what she'd done to get here? Was that enough anger for them to trust in her ability to achieve?

Ethan hopped out of the ring, removing his headgear and mouthpiece. "Hey, you sparring or what?"

Katherine shook her head and muttered something about not feeling well. There was something about Gretchen that threatened her, took this ring, this gym, this moment away from her on only her second day of sparring, belittling the sport somehow. It was supposed to take months of preparation, a certain level of respect, before you took on the challenge of sparring – yet here she was, with *Katherine's* men, battling it out in the gym.

Katherine gathered her things and left wordlessly, Ethan following her slumped shoulders with his eyes. Waving to the front desk workers, she let herself out the gym doors. Why did she suddenly feel out of place in her own surroundings? She'd worked to make this her home, despite everything. Despite her new apartment, this was where she could sleep and eat, where she could stretch and breathe and learn what it took to become someone. What happened if she did fail – if she wasn't as good as she thought she was? Katherine knew the alternative and couldn't fathom making the journey back from where she'd come.

"I can't go back," she whispered, walking the six short blocks to her building. "I can't go back." That night she sat on the couch, stiffly awake, as her mother had been after her father passed away. Something was beginning to annihilate her – perhaps fear, perhaps guilt.

A Woman's Ring

Chapter Thirty

The nurses strapped the soft booties around Katherine's ankles for increased circulation, moved the tubes in and out of her nose, stuck hands to her mouth to check for breathing – her body so motionless, her fingers swelled up red and goaded from the arterial lines in each wrist. Her head looked as though someone had struck it with a shovel, the imprint of a big globular body on her forehead, the side of it stapled and bloated, lime from bruising. The nurses could not imagine the pain she'd be in when she woke again in ICU, away from the other young patients with their televisions and cartoons, Katherine's healthy body almost a phenomenon below the damaged brain. The lack of hair made her face look strangely astute, a portrait of a child who'd lost its mother and knew of grief very intimately – those impressions in the contours and arcs of her face.

They'd woken her briefly at 4:00a.m. post-surgery to wheel her in for an MRI. This would be the vital answer to a very big question: had they gotten it all? And if not, then what?

Katherine was moved from her hospital bed to the cold, unforgiving bottom of the MRI, her head painfully thumping as it was situated and packed with Styrofoam blocks to keep still.

"Just hold on, Katherine. This won't take long."

During the impossible noise, she tried to remain calm, tried to breathe inside the packed tube, losing her composure, but regaining it before pushing the panic button in her tender hand. She was scared and groggy. The surgery had been the easy part. Take drugs, go to sleep and wake up less of a person. That's when the hard part began. Fighting the battle to regain control. The healing. The worry.

After what seemed like hours, the nurses pulled her out and hoisted her back onto the rolling hospital bed, cutting corners toward the elevators until she was hooked up to every available machine in ICU. Katherine could barely speak from the pain, and before she could ask what the results were, Nurse Jenkins came in and gave her a shot of morphine, the first of many. Katherine was drifting off as the doctor came in, his white lab coat wrinkled, his hair mussed. He placed a hand on her knee and squeezed it.

"How you doing, kiddo?"

Katherine smiled, her pain ebbing as the morphine kicked in. "Well, they just gave me morphine, so you tell me." He chuckled and looked at the results that lay in his hand.

"It looks pretty good, from what I can tell here. You may have some residual scar tissue, which will probably just dissolve with time. But we'll keep an eye on it. Monthly MRIs, that sort of thing. No exercise for a while after you're released, which you already know. Other than that, we just need to keep a strict watch on your progress because the first twenty-four hours are the most critical." He leaned in close, smiling. "You did real well, Katherine. You're going to be just fine."

She nodded off to sleep, worried that the cyst might not be gone, that she might have to go through this again, that it could grow back. But the doctor said she'd be okay, didn't he?

The nurses took turns watching over her – waiting for her next rise, as she'd first woken in recovery, all green vomit and yanking on her catheter tube, screaming and sobbing for her father – for someone named Brandon. Each nurse wondered why no one came, why there was an absence of flowers and calls. They huddled inside her door regularly, whispering about where she must come from, what she must do – where did she get the insurance money to pay for such an operation? Why was she alone? How had this happened to such a healthy girl? No one would have figured she had a family, a little girl who cried for her mother in her Ohio bed, a son who began to bear the resentment of unloved children – both listening to the new sounds

A Woman's Ring

of their father attempting to mask his sobs in handkerchiefs -- Frankie and Lily hoping for some grand entrance from a mother they were starting to forget.

On the third day, Katherine began to stir once again – her pulse dropped low, eyes trembling as she fought to open her weighty lids. She momentarily caught a glimpse of three nurses in her doorway, one holding a pink, plastic tray, the other two whispering excitedly. The taste of anesthesia burned her throat, and the foggy reminder of what had been done to her head.

She twitched awake, attempting to move the head that was cemented against her pillow, her mouth suddenly unable to form words – there were the choices of a mislaid girl blanching poisonous inside her, keeping her aware of the truth – of the sounds of sickness beckoning in her every breath and whisper.

Rea Frey

A Woman's Ring

Chapter Thirty-one

It was the type of thing she'd never do.

After sparring, Jake had approached Katherine, a smile slanted across his lips. For the past few weeks, they'd both engaged in mild flirtation, with every class ending with a new invitation. Yesterday, it was a movie, tomorrow it could be a club.

"Wanna get a drink or something? Maybe just hang out for a little while?"

Katherine hesitated as usual, thinking of what awaited her at home. A rented movie, a quick shower – a bed that would be filled with the shadow of only one body.

"I'd love to." She agreed, curious to discover the newness of this person, to forget Brandon and Andrew, if only for an evening. She felt Ethan's eyes on her as she left, the tight clinch of his hug lingering a second too long to be normal.

"Have a good night," he whispered, as both Jake and Katherine left together, scoring several looks from the gym members. Next to him she felt almost foolish – Jake with his tattooed arms and dark brown skin. To him she was just a stranger, a budding athlete.

The thought of doing something raw and unreasonable made her legs quiver. Andrew had been her first – awkward, forced, and completely destructive. Brandon was still a fantasy, undiscovered and untouched. Would it be so wrong to seduce her sparring partner, to see if she was capable of lust for a newfound friend?

They walked to the El, sitting side by side in their damp gym clothes, neither talking as the roar of the train guided them along the curves of Chicago. She closed her eyes, falling into a light sleep before jerking awake again. She turned to find Jake sketching in a notepad. His eyes were intent on hers – a deep, sad brown – and she blushed self-consciously.

"What are you doing?"

"A blind drawing!" He yelled as the train's whine intensified.

Katherine looked at his hands as they flirted skillfully over the page – but his eyes remained on her the entire time. She held back her laughter as he demanded she not move.

Jake glanced down when he was done, bursting into uncontrollable laughter that left his mouth unhinged, his hands clutching tightly to his abdomen.

Katherine snatched the drawing from his hands, but not before noticing the silver fillings dominating the lower half of his teeth, and the long cherry tongue that wiggled gleefully.

Katherine stared at the "blind" drawing.

"What is *this*?" She yelled, smacking him on the arm. "I have *three* chins? And I'm shaped like a *potato*?"

Jake could not stop laughing, even as the train slid to a stop, depositing them onto Diversey. They hit each other playfully, tossing insults all the way to his apartment – a small studio hidden amongst sparse trees in an ancient high rise. The framework was carefully decorated, the cast-iron doors etched in gold.

Jake high-fived the doorman as they entered, leaning down to whisper something into the man's ear, whose eyes traveled over Katherine's body indiscreetly. For the first time that night, Katherine bristled. Was this some kind of regular occurrence for him? Bringing women home, then casting them out again? And more importantly, if she did get naked, how would he react to her body? The stretch marks that were still visible, those small truths of a woman she had cast away. Maybe he didn't expect sex from her – just a relaxed evening of beers and conversation.

A Woman's Ring

Once inside his apartment, Katherine dropped her gym bag on the floor, surprised at the cheap worn out furniture and the closet posing as a bedroom.

Jake looked over his shoulder, sheepish. "Small, isn't it?"

Katherine smiled and shook her head. "No, it's...cozy, actually."

Jake moved to the kitchen, a small nook that was really just a stove and refrigerator separated by a slice of countertop. "I bet you live somewhere nice, huh?"

"I live downtown. Yeah, it's pretty nice, I guess."

Jake stuck his head around the corner, smirking. "And where does an amateur boxer get that kind of money, huh? Last I checked, living downtown was pretty expensive."

Katherine shifted from foot to foot uncomfortably. "Well, I had a lot of money saved up before I moved here – but I know I need to find a good job. I'm hoping I can make money boxing, though. I have enough until I can start boxing professionally."

Jake's head disappeared, and silence descended between them. Katherine's eyes danced over the Spanish rugs that were nailed to the walls, the cheap wooden crates that held books and sketch pads.

"Want a drink?"

Katherine jumped away from one of the crates, feeling as though she was snooping. She walked toward the kitchen, leaning against the doorframe. "I thought we were going out for a drink?"

"Why go out when the fun's right here?"

Jake moved from the kitchen, eyebrows raised, a bottle of cheap white wine in one hand.

"Wine okay?"

"Sure."

He moved closer and Katherine felt self-conscious. She needed a shower, she needed clean clothes, she needed to be drunk in order to do this with him.

"You're cute, Katherine, you know that?"

Katherine took a step back, looking at her shoes. Before she could look up again, Jake's mouth was on hers, his hands wrapped firmly around her waist.

Katherine received the kiss in surprise, unsure of what to do with her arms that were still crossed over her chest. She tried to relax into the kiss, moving her tongue with his, stunned at the softness of his mouth. Slowly, he pried her arms down to her sides so his hands could fondle her modest breasts.

The bottle of wine thudded to the floor as his head disappeared below her neck in one fluid motion. Before Katherine could utter a word, Jake had her shirt and sports bra yanked up and was encircling his mouth around her right breast.

She froze, realizing that a one night stand would do little for her level of experience. This was too uncomfortable, too impersonal. What would she feel like in the morning? What if he had some disease? From the look of his apartment, she couldn't be sure of his hygiene.

"Jake, Jake stop."

He was moaning so loudly she had to yank his head back up to her level. "Stop." She felt him press into her hips through his pants.

"What's wrong?"

"I – um – need to go actually. I've got to get up early."

Jake looked at her blankly, running a hand through his spiked hair.

"Why? What do you have to get up early for?"

"I just have to. I'll see you at the gym, okay?"

Katherine readjusted her shirt, gathering her bag and exiting without even a wave. Once the door was firmly shut behind her, she took off at a full sprint toward the elevators, feeling the spit from his mouth beneath her t-shirt. As she waited, she began to feel the slow mortification of what it would be like to see Jake again. What if he told Ethan?

The doors opened, carrying her down to the lobby. She breezed past the doorman and scrounged in her bag for some cab money. It was going fast. What she'd taken from Andrew, what she'd saved, and even the money from her savings account was nearly drained. She'd put an entire year's rent on her credit card, but the statements were beginning to pile neatly on her countertops. She needed a job – even if she did make it in boxing.

She needed Ethan.

A Woman's Ring

As she thought his name, an unexpected warmth spread through her body, stopping her on the sidewalk outside Jake's apartment. He was the man with the tough hands and smile of a child. Old enough to be her father, beautiful enough to be some sort of love. She closed her eyes and imagined his mouth over hers – moving slowly as Jake's had. Her knees nearly buckled. She opened her eyes, breathless. Shaking his name from her head, she hailed a cab, attempting to ignore the weakness of her body. She let the darkness envelop her on the way home, the soft seats of the cab, the lake that glittered off to her left, black, jeweled water under a lit night sky.

As the cab pulled up to her apartment, she stared at the cold rise of the structure, knowing that she would sleep alone tonight, that her bed would once again be stiff and uninviting. She thought of Brandon, of Ethan. Suddenly, her passion was not so easily defined.

Rea Frey

A Woman's Ring

Chapter Thirty-Two

Ethan invited Katherine over for one of his many weekend boxing parties. There, the guys from the gym would lounge on comfy couches and chairs, laden with beers, dipping into chips and salsa, conversations sinuous. A big fight was usually on, but sometimes Ethan would open his living room closet and let his guests pick from hundreds of video tapes of past fights that had marked themselves in history.

Katherine took the blue line to Austin, exiting up the long ramp at 8:00p.m. Oak Park quietly detached from the city with its quiet homes and questionable street corners. The occasional bum popped out at her from an alley, nursing a bottle of Jack Daniels while howling obscenities at the moon. Ethan had offered to pick her up, but she'd insisted she could get a ride. Even if that ride cost $1.50 and came with strange looks from men, she wouldn't make him come and get her. It was his party. He needed to prepare.

Katherine looked at the rows of brownstones rising identically along the block, while balancing a bag of cookies and a six pack of beer in her left hand. She smoothed down her jeans and slim red top, wishing she had time to check her hair and makeup before going inside. None of the guys had seen her dressed outside of gym clothes. It was always Katherine in a ponytail, Katherine in baggy pants and T-shirts, Katherine with a sweaty, red complexion. She buzzed Ethan's apartment and looked warily behind her, noticing a few guys on doorsteps catcalling and whistling at her. This was so different from Ohio, where you could walk down the street and no one would stare.

Katherine shook the thought from her mind and heard the relieving buzz of the intercom. She walked the four flights of stairs to his apartment, nervousness seizing her as she heard the loud thump of music and the raucous laughter of guys upstairs. She plastered a smile on her face and heard the bark of a dog as she rounded the last step, coming face to face with Ethan in a pair of jeans and white T-shirt. He looked comfortable in his skin, so strong and settled. The lines around his eyes crinkled as he broke into a smile and pulled her into a hug. She stumbled into the subtle hint of his cologne, the well-built arms.

"This is Daisy. Don't pet her or she'll pee."

Katherine nodded, looking down at a small brown mutt who wagged her tail ecstatically, shoving her nose in Katherine's crotch. Katherine forced a laugh and stepped into the apartment, immediately hit with scents of warm food and cinnamon candles. Maxx, Dave, and Jake stood upon her arrival, each coming in to give her a warm kiss on the cheek. Katherine's heart began to hammer in her chest as Jake bypassed the kiss and gave her a sharp slap on the shoulder. Ethan took the refreshments from her arms and disappeared into the kitchen as she stood awkwardly, staring at each guy who had left a warm sentiment on her face, the same guys who landed stiff jabs and took hers. The guys who yelled for her to get her ass in gear. One guy who'd had her breast in his mouth, who'd had his lips over her skin. The boxers.

"Make yourself at home, Katherine!" Ethan yelled from the kitchen, and Katherine nodded as if he could see her taking in the warm brown tones of the living room, the leather couches and gleaming hardwood floors. She wouldn't have expected Ethan to live somewhere this nice. It held such eclectic taste, such an African vibe. Maxx patted a seat beside him on one of the sofas and she nestled down into the plush leather, pulling a pillow closer to her arm. Daisy spun circles in front of her, begging to be rubbed.

"Will she still pee on me?"

Maxx laughed and leaned down to pet Daisy. "Nah, it's just the initial excitement I think. She should be fine."

A Woman's Ring

Katherine leaned in and gave Daisy a pat on the head, a scratch behind the ears. She'd always loved animals, but had never owned one. Brandon's two cats and golden retriever had always been like her own. She missed the simple, loving company of a furry friend.

"So, where do you live, Katherine?"

Jake sat across from her, a scarf tied around his head, baggy jeans on. He looked completely natural as he asked the question, but his eyes were cold and elusive. He obviously hadn't told anyone about their evening, or he wouldn't be asking her a question to which he already knew the answer. She looked uneasily around the room, glancing at Dave and Maxx. It was so weird seeing these guys in everyday clothes. Dave in a button up shirt and Birkenstock's. Maxx in a tight green T-shirt and loose, faded jeans. She realized shamefully that these people had other lives – that hers happened to be just boxing and nothing more – no real education, no job. Nothing but the ring.

"Um, right downtown. In a high rise. It's pretty nice."

Jake nodded and took a swig from his beer. Katherine looked self-consciously down at the pillow she was holding, noticing the stray dog hairs that were now attaching themselves to her shirt. She brushed them off and heard laughter from the kitchen, Ethan's laugh and a woman's. Katherine's ears perked up as she looked around at the guys.

"Ooh, does Ethan have a hot date we should know about?"

All three men lost their smiles and instead stared intently at the T.V. that held a fight of Ethan in his earlier days. Kickboxing. Maxx cleared his throat and leaned closer. "We thought you knew who would be here."

"What do you mean?"

Just as she said it, Ethan emerged from the kitchen, arms loaded with chips, salsa, hummus and a homemade cheese dip. Behind him came Gretchen – Gretchen for God's sake, in a midriff top and black pants. Her hair was down, and she was wearing lipstick. Lipstick on Gretchen. The tomboy.

Gretchen snickered as she locked eyes with Katherine's startled expression. Katherine attempted to recover by commenting on the spread of food. But when she spoke, her voice sounded high and uncomfortable.

"Ethan – this looks great. You didn't have to do all this."

"Well, it's for everybody, Katherine, not just you." He winked at her and went back into the kitchen. She could feel herself blushing. Gretchen plopped down beside Jake in the sofa opposite from her and Maxx, Dave sitting in a chair between the two couches as if preparing to mediate.

Why was Gretchen even here? She looked so comfortable, as if she'd known these guys for years. It had been less than a month and already she was chatting up Ethan in his kitchen? Dressing like a girl, when everybody knew she wore Nike pants and sweatshirts all hours of every day. Katherine felt her stomach tighten, saw Gretchen open her mouth to speak, but Katherine jumped up and walked quickly toward the kitchen. There Ethan stood, humming some blues tune as he stirred a big pot of soup, taking breaks to sip his beer. She was stunned to see how sexy he looked – such a man. The man she'd wished Andrew to be.

"Hey, killer, how's it going?"

Katherine leaned against a countertop and looked back over her shoulder, to make sure Gretchen wasn't behind her. "Um, it's good. I'm a little confused though. Why is she here?"

"She who?" Ethan sprinkled a couple spices into the soup, turned to look at the cookbook spread to page sixty as if he was forgetting a key ingredient. "Oh," he looked up, setting the bottle of spices back on the counter. "You mean your favorite new boxer. I had a feeling you felt uncomfortable around her. Why?"

Katherine snorted and tightened her jaw. "What do you mean, *why*?" Katherine lowered her voice and moved closer. "She waltzes in our gym as if she owns it, starts sparring after only two days and now she's everyone's best friend? I just think she's trying too hard, that's all."

"And does that make you jealous?"

She gave Ethan a lethal stare, noticing the twinkle in his eye.

"Come on, she's not that bad, Katie. What would you have to be jealous of, anyway? Her brutish good looks? Her charming, feminine attitude?"

A Woman's Ring

Katherine crossed her arms, knowing how childish she was being, but she also knew that she was, in fact, jealous. Jealous of another girl becoming Ethan's favorite. Taking this life away from her.

"Pumpkin." Ethan moved in to hug her, spoon in hand. Katherine's mouth fell open at the pet name, a name her father had called her so often. "You'll always be my star pupil. You and I both know that." He squeezed her tightly. "Don't worry about her. She'll be good sparring for you."

Katherine wanted to stomp her feet, shake her head, to scream no. Instead, she disentangled herself from Ethan and uttered, "You're right. I'm just being stupid. Um, where's your bathroom?"

Ethan pointed her in the right direction. Once in the bathroom, Katherine took deep breaths, composing herself. Ethan was right. Gretchen wasn't so bad. She didn't have to be best friends with the girl. Just civil. That she could do.

She flushed the toilet and exited, smiling at Ethan as she made her way back into the living room, plopping on the couch by Maxx. "So, who you guys rooting for tonight?"

Maxx and Jake jumped in with their thoughts on Mayweather and his boxing skills. Gretchen stared silently at Katherine, narrowing her eyes. Katherine pretended to ignore it, pretended to be interested in what Dave was now saying about Mayweather being talented but predictable.

"What do you do, Katherine?"

Everyone stopped talking as Gretchen asked the question, sitting up from her slouched position to stare intently at Katherine.

"What do you mean, what do I do? I box."

Gretchen laughed and looked down the mouth of her beer bottle. "No, I mean for a living. What do you *do*? You obviously don't make money boxing."

Katherine felt the heat on her cheeks, the panic at having to make up a lie so quickly. They would all laugh at her if she said nothing, if she said, "Well, I tried being a wife and mother for a few years, but that really didn't work out for me, so now I'm just looking to beat up women."

Katherine cleared her throat as the buzzer sounded and Ethan came running in to let the next guest up. He looked at Katherine, saw the uncomfortable way she was sitting, saw all eyes on her and the devilish grin on Gretchen's lips – something was going on.

"Katherine, could you help me in the kitchen for a sec?"

She let out a long sigh, her entire body relaxing as she escaped the interrogation.

"Figured I'd rescue you out there. I'm not sure what from, but you looked uncomfortable."

Katherine stepped forward and placed her lips on his cheek, felt the beginnings of stubble beneath her mouth, the hot skin of his face. "And you have no idea how grateful I am," she whispered in a husky voice, a voice she'd never heard rise from her own throat.

Ethan licked his lips, flicked his eyes over her face, an almost painful expression in them. He opened his mouth to say something, then cleared his throat and held out five bowls.

"Will you help me serve the chili?"

Katherine took the bowls and turned from him. "Of course I'll help – I'm glad to."

A Woman's Ring

Chapter Thirty-three

When Katherine first moved to Chicago, she'd surrendered to the urges of scouring every street, every corner and back alley in search of Brandon. Sometimes, she'd ride the trains to the airports, exploring unfamiliar faces, hunting for her lost neighbor. She'd walk those terminals, stare at the planes on take-off and landing, wondering if he felt that pride of pilots, of the big, silver planes scooping back air with their streamlined wings, the cerulean sky a fingertip away, the exhilaration of lift-off, the terror in turbulence, each landing smoother than the last. On those trips, she would get angry with herself for not holding back just a little longer, just a month more, until she was a champion in the ring, until he would truly want her. If he saw her now – without accomplishment – she would have everything to prove, little to say besides "I'm sorry – please love me," or "I've come here for you..." He would think of her as a pathetic, motherless child – an evil woman who'd abandoned her family in want of him. She would have to be strong and single, accomplished and ready in order for his acceptance.

This time she would not cry or tremble, she would not beg or stumble, she would simply stand next to him, looking so different, but still the same. She would take him before a moment's hesitation, and in that pressing of lips Katherine would filter in all of it: the months of training, the misery of her marriage, the pain of giving birth and the agonizing way her hands shook to hold her babies or crush them all in the same breath – but mostly that torture of watching him leave without her in a tightly packed car. Over time he would see his mistakes, how foolish he'd been to think it would never work between them, when really it was effortless and fated, that destiny a golden ring between them, a bond unbroken by the words of marriage and the passage of time.

Many nights, Katherine called Betty, only to hang up again, her neighbor returning those calls, tracking the number. She knew it would be easy to locate Brandon, dial him up, get his address – but if she was impatient, it would all be ruined and she would be stuck without him, achieving her dreams alone. It had to be on her own time and by her own measures; when that reunion would be stronger than anything, when she would finally feel him flesh to flesh, her bosom pressed against his chest, his stomach, his back, him turning her over and again over, taking her from the front, the back, the side; exploring and exhausting every inch of her. He would move against her like any young virgin who wanted so badly a release. She would be that for him, until death robbed them. She would be resurrected by his touch, resurrected by his vows to her, his love for her; that bond the bond of sex and friendship – the two of them a lifetime – but not until she'd done what she'd come to do – only then would it be time and never too late to take him, to present herself anew, to brush that hair off her face and say, "I'm here, Brandon, I'm here." And he would have to take her because it's what was meant to be – he would cleave onto Katherine, as she'd always wanted. The two of them would exist on so much passion, sucking and molding and making shapes of lust, of love.

A Woman's Ring

Chapter Thirty-four

Ethan and Katherine had dinner in a small Italian restaurant in Old Town. There, in the restaurant's glow that cast dim slashes across Ethan's face, making his soft crow's feet decrease then deepen, playing tricks with his age, they discussed the possibility of her first fight and how much improvement she'd shown in such a short time.

Yet Katherine knew that he somehow doubted her, could sense it by his eyes averting from hers, the way he watched her in the gym, with his breath held, like she almost had it but didn't quite yet, that while she was quick and accurate, she wasn't as hard and devastating as she could be – not as aggressive as Gretchen. She didn't have the warrior inside her to beat all these girls, and while she was a good sparring partner, he wouldn't brag to the other trainers of her skill.

"Just wait," he'd always tell her, critiquing and fixing her technique, Katherine hitting combinations and Ethan always correcting them, growling at her to do it right, to do it again and again until her only goal was not to become good, but to be the best, to compete in Golden Gloves and maybe the Olympics, to prove to him that she wasn't a lightweight, that she wasn't soft, that she was a woman who could bring rage to the ring, rage like fire that never stops burning, rage like love, too intense for words.

As she sat across from him, she fingered the soft hem of her dress, swallowing and listening closely, not daring to offer her own opinions. No, she wanted his words and only those; to listen to his stories of former competitions, where he had fallen before succeeding, coming now, at age forty-three, to be a better boxer, a better man than in previous years. They talked of his losses, his wins – how he almost drowned himself accidentally in a bathtub before a fight from sheer nerves. How he'd lain there as a younger man, breathing in the scents off candles, falling into deep nothingness in his relaxation, his shoulders slipping from that white lip of the tub, sliding under, his nose and chest forgetting momentarily how to breathe, until he was thrashing and waking – his ride for the fight outside his apartment, banging on the door to let him in.

He talked to Katherine about her improvement, saying, "You were so shy," while playing with the edge of his napkin. "You never talked, just wanted to train, train, train. It's only been what, a matter of months, and you've learned so much. You'll only get better, you know…a lot better." His voice dimmed with the lights, the truth of his feelings bursting forth. He thought her skilled but not enough to push forth as a champion. Was she too quiet, too angry, too white for success, for that call of athletic ability that people either had or didn't have? Did he doubt her dedication, the rage that she kept coiled in her belly, filled from end to end, ready to explode? If only he would give her a shot at a fight, where another woman would be Andrew, where she would tear at that image bit by bit, not backing off as her jabs set up crosses and overhands, body shots and uppercuts, the devastation that would tear the soft tissue of her opponent's face, through the headgear, through the mouthpiece, through it all, so that she could spit on the object at her feet, turn back to Ethan, and say softly, "I told you so," fly back to Ohio to tell Andrew, "I told you so," her mother, "I told you so," and then finally finding Brandon to make him understand why she'd done what she'd done, how it was a plan gone wrong, how everything could be fixed if he'd just take her on a plane to another country where they would settle; kissing, loving, and exploring like she'd always dreamed?

Katherine sat with these emotions, battling the breaths that rushed her, wanting to yell at Ethan that she was better than "okay," that she would be the best female boxer out there, with all her unknown secrets and unseen fury. Yet she only listened intently to his speech, knowing she would prove him wrong, and soon.

A Woman's Ring

"We'll get you a fight soon, Katherine, real soon," he said. "Just remember your record doesn't count -- remember that. First fights never really matter."

It was as if she had already lost the fight. His words made her mouth set at unnatural angles, into straight lines and frowns. She kept her opinions at the far corners of the restaurant, losing them in the lights, the plates of food and signs to the bathroom. Should she break and tell him all that she'd done to get here, that she'd committed the ultimate crime of abandoning her own children, the husband who treated her like a prostitute, who groped her in her sleep but actually loved her – taking her in that bed that she loathed, whose sheets were soft, petaled silk, in that house that was a painful reminder of the choices she'd made? Tell him all about Brandon, and how she was working *for* him to make something of herself in the ring? That boxing was all she had and *only* boxing and how dare he doubt her, when she gave it her all as she'd never done, this dream that she'd had since childhood, making it the long, tiresome years to this place, where her own trainer reminded her of losses to her record and how it didn't really matter, anyway. "Of course it matters," she wanted to shout, "it all matters, it's the only thing that matters, the only thing I have."

Instead she let the conversation turn toward relationships, toward Ethan's many sad tales of women, his tendency to fall and never be caught in the warmth that only a woman could provide.

"I'm a romantic, Katherine. What can I say?"

"I wouldn't really know about romance," she snapped, downing her glass of wine, wiping her mouth roughly with the back of her hand, her green eyes flashing at him, daring him to ask her why, to illicit one smidgen of curiosity so she could tell him where she came from, how she'd gotten there, and even the awful thoughts she used to have about the twins, how she used to want them dead, how she'd toyed with the notions of hurting them, because she was too afraid to love them. It's what she'd done wasn't it – hate what she'd created, what was close to her – hating the living, breathing replicas of herself?

"That's too bad," was all he said, paying the bill, both of them rising to shrug on their coats and walk back to his car.

As they stepped outside the restaurant, they found that a light sheet of snow had coated the streets and sidewalks, big, feathery flakes drifting down like shredded cotton.

"I love the snow," Katherine whispered, looking up and flicking her tongue out to catch a few flakes. "Back in Ohio, I never really played in it that much." Again, a hint of her past, but again he did not ask and she did not utter a word.

Katherine looked at Ethan, whose eyes held smiles in them; smiles of his own childhood with five sisters and two brothers and many snow fights in winter, smiles of sadness, of his mother, who'd passed away when he was just three, but mostly smiles from the hush that dropped through the footstep between them, a deep, meaningful lull. She stared up at him, defiant, lusting for a man, wanting him as a man and not a trainer, to take her in those boxer's hands and do with her what he may. The moment between them was thick with his grin and her silence, airborne with pure colossal wonder.

"Shall we?" He finally asked, offering his elbow for their walk to his car. She hooked her arm through his, and together they made their way over the slick roads and sidewalks. At a crosswalk, Katherine slid on a patch of ice, losing her footing, and in an instant Ethan righted her, holding her shoulders tightly in both his hands, the look of previous seconds intensified. His lips, stained purple from wine, parted into a smile.

"Gotcha."

"Thank you," she mumbled, looking down at her feet, then back to him. She let him hold her, those hands pulling her toward him, hands so unlike Brandon's or Andrew's, hands that had tapped her face with jabs and hooks and crosses, hands that had done all the screaming as they'd pointed at her to fix some poor technique, to pay attention, to do it better than the last time, a perfectionist's hands that she now succumbed to as they cradled her face, more softly than anyone ever had, softer and softer as he leaned in, both their eyes falling shut, Katherine letting her trainer's hard lips bear down against her wet ones. The mouth was stiff and urgent, not filled with grace or tenderness but with the simple impulses of a man. His hands tightened around her face, those fingers that had probably traveled over women of all

A Woman's Ring

ages, of all types, maybe even with boxers much better than her. She pressed harder into him, pulling him tight against her, wanting to bite his lips, to hurt him for doubting her, to devour him for allowing her to explore this talent, and then, just as urgently, infidelity swelled before her, pressed a shred of guilt upon her, as she'd now forsaken her vows. Not the vows between she and Andrew, not the vows they'd repeated as they'd clutched each others' clammy hands without affection, regurgitating words spewed from the Officiate.

No, in her mind, there was only Brandon – Katherine his betrayer and he the betrayed. He was her true husband, her beloved, whose trust she upheld – that invisible promise that existed between unknown lovers, between longtime friends. But she could not deny that Ethan's wanting, his pulling her closer than she was accustomed to was elegance in itself, uplifting the small girl who'd been petrified into the arms of the same man who'd helped her fulfill her dreams, who now challenged her with experiences yet to come, with doubts and wishes for her to be better than he'd ever been – a man who knew not of her excesses, only of her skills.

Katherine, in that moment, was too weak to stop him, too weak to let him know who she really was. To Ethan she was just an inscrutable woman, a boxer. Should she accept this affection – the man with the eyes of Brandon, with the talent of a boxer, a champion?

She let the kisses trail to her neck and collarbone, passersby watching them with sweet smiles before Katherine pulled back, the heat of his body still clinging to hers.

"Well," she said, dizzy from the moment, "Ethan."

He was breathing heavily, smiling like a boy in love and not her self-assured trainer. Appropriately, he offered her his elbow once more as they walked the rest of the way to his Jeep. She climbed in, shaking with feeling, the first in a long time with a man. On the way home, she couldn't help but run a finger over her lips, tasting the wine and garlic from their meal, the passionate surprise that had settled there.

"Here you are, my dear," Ethan said, pulling to the front of her building and killing the ignition. "I'll see you tomorrow?"

Katherine nodded, leaning in to hug him goodbye, amazed by how calm he was, how relaxed and easy and still drunk.

"You really are beautiful, Katherine," he whispered in her ear. He wanted to pull her closer, to make love to her, to pull her into his world and let her exist there, if just for a night, a day. But she drew away too quickly, her eyes full of guilt, her lips parting, pausing. "Ethan, I..." a loss of words Katherine had often had with Brandon – Brandon, her one true affection slamming back into her mind. *He* was her real husband, her dearest love, his familiar face a sudden portrait, the heat of him taking Ethan's place, reminding.

A Woman's Ring

Chapter Thirty-five

The fight doctor was old, maybe seventy, the skin dark and cracked around his eyes and ears. His lips sagged and pulled, contracting out of spasmodic habit. It was the liveliness of his mouth that drew her in – made her notice his soft brown eyes, watered by years of loss and disappointment, eyes she herself possessed.

Katherine observed him observing her, unaware for the briefest of moments the room in which she stood, the noise, men and testosterone, or her beastly opponent just now walking through the South side doors. The warm-up room was a long rectangle, flanked by pale white benches on all sides, a scale in the very back corner where boxers stood in their underwear waiting for weigh-in. Others were listening to music, hunched over on the benches, some pacing to the other end of the room where two tables were piled high with blue and red gloves. Old men with potbellies sat behind them, scribbling notes on clipboards.

Katherine concentrated on the cool metal of the stethoscope against the cotton of her T-shirt, the swelling of her heart beneath it, the bright pencil light shining down at her. She blinked, imagining an internal monologue of the doctor's thoughts – imagined him thinking what she was thinking, worrying like she was that she was the white minority, an amateur. Ethan's doubts of her ability pealed through every muscle of her being. Families of contenders milled around them, yet she could only look at the doctor, not the fighters with their mothers, their fathers, and their smooth, russet skin – it was only Katherine, with no one save Ethan and Maxx, who stood casually across the room. These were the only men she trusted enough to bring her here, to suit her up and throw her in the ring, stepping safely back into the shadows for the fight to unfold between two women.

"Take a deep breath, please."

The doctor's voice was slow, temperate, as were his hands, a clue that he had not been hardened by this game. She figured he had children, all grown now, but she could tell how those hands had once held their fragile heads and full bottoms with more love than she ever could; that he'd smoked fine cigars and held the stems of wine glasses, laughing with some extraordinary woman. Later, when his kids and wife were gone, those same fingers had probably dug into cold, tasteless dinners, chewing sorrowfully on microwaved food. There were help and loss in the fingers that domed around the stethoscope – help and loss in his eyes. They stared, lenient yet serious, across the panorama of her face, the pale white complexion, the nose pulling and pushing in air, her small mouth curling and tightening, as if free from bodily control. She was captivated by his careful interest, as if she was, at once, his long forgotten lover and not a patient. But mostly, she was captivated that by thinking of him, she could forget about herself.

"This your first fight?" He asked the question softly, but the words echoed loudly in her ears, prompting all those confessions to unfold – the truths, passions, and inexplicable fear. She wanted to win at something, to show the world how beautiful this sport was – that she was a communicator with fists and not words. Yet the truth of leaving bloody, broken, or with a loss to her name was haunting.

In a few moments, there would only be a footfall between she and her opponent, Katherine forced to protect the innocence of her first fight, manipulating it toward victory. Two women joined by the compliance of combat in a ring of wits, of wills.

Each woman had arrogantly stood in her gym only days before, shadow-boxing and battering bags they actually thought could resemble a thinking, moving target. Each woman a witness to the black or red leather giving from the force of their fists, both smirking and thinking, "I've got her so easily."

In the ring, foolish notions would give way to more realistic circumstances. In those trainings, they had not factored in the crowd, the smoke, the refs, the hard blue terrain of the navy-checked ring. The nerves that often made systems acidic, bathroom trips often, and that first sweet contact a battle of speed, not skill.

It was the rhythm that was a factor – like a glorified sparring session, where faster and harder meant survival for one of them. Katherine would not forget that moment as the bell confected her into one of them – the fighters she'd emulated back in Ohio, on a living room floor where the children were off on the hands of Andrew. Even then, she was learning the art of the sport – the pain and size and mastery it took to get here.

One punch that landed clean on Ethan could now miss her opponent completely – a hook aimed at the solar plexus might skim the soft padding of the woman's hip, safely guarded by the groin protector Ethan had insisted Katherine not wear.

"You won't get hit that low," he'd said, and Katherine, obsessed with his righteousness, would lie to the ref and knock on her high-waisted trunks, as if to say, "Yeah, it's here, it's here, I'm wearing it."

The actual fight would be far less intriguing than the build-up and aftermath that would erupt in a fistful of regret and adrenaline. As if caught on the inward ring of a tornado, there would be much motion but little memory. Katherine could have been an observer in the last row, the top bleachers, or the dirty stall in a bathroom. She would treat her opponent with such indifference, poking and gasping at her when she knew she could really tear her end from end. The ability to do the things you're taught was the mark of a true champion. She might fail her own ability, shaming the sport, lying to the world.

If she was to be called a boxer, to ever feel like a champion – then she could not lose to another woman. She could not let another mar what was supposed to be soft, symmetrical and feminine. She was not butch and tattooed, coming off the streets with something to prove; boxing was the dream she'd plucked from childhood – a witness to one fight on a street, and how two men had been lost in it, devoured by the power of themselves and another, the cold, hard punches branding and denting – the retaliation when all was weak within, the way they kept pushing for one more punch, and one more. The way her father had come alive while watching, as if boxing was the only way to live when all else wasn't an option.

As the doctor waited for an answer to his question, Katherine remained vaguely aware of the boxers around her; the small, dark bodies and the large, muscular ones; the Hispanics warming their limber arms, some dancing shirtless, some eating honey for quick, explosive energy, some praying, knelt down on dark, bony knees. In their carefully wrapped hands they fondled the crosses that hung around their necks, those smooth, innocent necks arched over in prayer.

But, there was the question: w*as this her first fight?* Competitors waited in line behind Katherine for the doctor, shifting their feet impatiently. She reheard the question, remembering the soft vocal cords that had produced it. Unable to look at him, she whispered the truth.

"Yes."

That word was a telltale sign of her tragic flaw; the first fight, the lack of her experience in this room full of hungry competitors. Katherine kept her gaze at her ankles that trembled and twisted with shame. She dared not look up, didn't turn to see Ethan or Maxx watching her, didn't hear the trash-talking of the other contenders, didn't see her own opponent sink into a chair against the wall, her heavy body solid and tired from travel. Suddenly, she was her mother's daughter again, being chastised for swiping cookies from the pantry, wanting to dance in the rain, or trying to sneak out her bedroom window. She was that little girl who'd lived for a mother's laugh, her father's presence, whispering "yes" now, utterly terrified.

She waited for some kind of response other than one of ridicule. She wanted that one beautiful word to illicit hope and wisdom – that somehow her truth might make up for her lack of experience, that the blaze within her might fuel the fight, the victory. She needed the wisdom and confidence she hadn't received from her parents or Andrew; a promise that this doctor would somehow – subconsciously or tangibly – be there, rooting for her.

"That's okay, girl. You just keep your hands up. Stick and move. You'll be just fine." The doctor reached out and lightly

A Woman's Ring

touched her shoulder, his hand a shadow falling upon her skin. The hand retracted quickly as Katherine jumped from the contact. He looked down at his own weathered palm, a sigh escaping his lips, staring so deeply at that hand, as though he'd been burned by her reaction.

"I'm sorry," she said, finally looking up at him. "You startled me."

The doctor nodded and moved his eyes from his hand to the patient behind her, as though she was no longer there, a specter remembrance. It wasn't until Katherine made her way back to Ethan, the doctor's slim eyes shifting to watch her leave, that she felt the knot stick at the back of her throat – that sudden ball of cowardice. Ethan placed one hand on her shoulder, the same shoulder the doctor had touched, his fingers a shade.

With that contact, Katherine saw her opponent, the only other woman in the room. There she stood, her skin rough and patchy, her hands older and more callused than Katherine's. She watched the girl shrug off the XXL sweatshirt that had *Ringside* printed on the front in red block letters. She seemed comfortable amongst all these fighters, as though inhaling the smells of competition, laden with sweat and smoke from downstairs, the sounds of smacked focus mitts, the wrapping of hands and the incessant chatter of excited children and family members were her everyday scene.

Katherine couldn't help but imagine the girl's gym, filled with several boxing rings compared to their one, rows of speed bags and dozens of intense, experienced competitors guiding her. That gym would be cramped and serious, the bags taped from overuse, the men unsmiling, never joking or taking it easy with this brutish girl as they did in Katherine's gym. Her opponent would stay all evening, shadowboxing, moving, intensely aware and passionate of what it took to make it in this game. Despite all of Katherine's hard work, the budding confidence it took to prove Ethan's doubt unnecessary, it wasn't until she was here, in this shocking reality of true amateur boxing, that she doubted her own ability.

Her opponent, Martha, pulled one thick leg behind her to stretch her quadriceps, rolling her neck around on masculine shoulders. She seemed too large for her bones, overflowing with flab and muscle. Their weight difference had to be at least thirty pounds, and all Katherine could think when she looked at her was "boxer." That word, so simple, kept pounding the shallow, flighty motion of her breath, the knotting of her hands, the relaxed laughs of Ethan and Maxx as they dipped into the bright red spit bucket to remove a pair of focus mitts and gloves for warm-up.

Katherine swallowed, having the distinct urge to run and lock herself in the bathroom, while surveying Martha's gnarled nose, her puffy black eyes, and ruddy skin that only seemed to light up under her stiff, brown mullet that balanced in a sloping helmet off her head.

From behind, Katherine felt Maxx's long fingers rubbing her shoulders in a signal to warm up.

"You ready to go, kid?" He asked, cocking his head at Ethan, who was waiting for her, hands hooked snugly across his hips, the leather focus mitts extensions of his arms, balancing there like flattened baseball gloves.

As though underwater, Katherine struggled to nod, everything a giant weight she did not have the strength to move through. She thought of the boxers she'd watched as a child – old fights of Whitaker, Dempsey, Marciano, Ali, Jackson, Robinson, Leonard, Jones, and Tyson in his early years. Had Ali or Whitaker ever felt this pragmatic fear seize their fists and feet? Had the look of an opponent roused them to win, or made them rethink their decision to step inside the boxing ring? What was she? A fighter or an imposter?

"What's wrong with you?" Ethan asked, gripping her shoulders with the focus mitts, shaking her. "You scared?"

"Have you *seen* her, Ethan?" She asked, pointing discreetly to the woman she had so cautiously surveyed. "You cannot stand here and tell me she's 125 pounds. Why hasn't she weighed in?"

Ethan looked behind him, finding Martha, who was already lacing up her gloves. He nodded before turning back to Katherine, shrugging his tight shoulders. "Well, that's Doug's girl, and he's heading up this fight, so maybe they're not going to weigh her in. I don't know, Katherine. Just trust me. You'll be fine."

A Woman's Ring

She stared at Ethan, incredulous. "What do you mean they're not going to weigh her? I worked to *drop* weight, Ethan! I'm not going to fight some girl who's had a million fights and wants to have fun with the new girl!" Katherine sucked the spit back into her mouth, covering her face with her hands, fisting them, composing herself.

Ethan stared at her with those level gray eyes, eyes that only weeks ago had looked at her as though she was the only thing that mattered. Maxx stood unresponsive beside him, as though his poker face could not break one second before Ethan replied.

"It doesn't matter how much some girl weighs," he said, looking straight at her for only a moment, as a man behind the glove table blew a whistle, silencing everyone.

"Fighters, the first bout's up in five. Second bout, get warmed up. You'll be heading down in ten."

Katherine looked back at Ethan, as Maxx shoved red gloves on her hands, and she shoved them off. "Wait! When am I going? I'm not ready yet!"

Ethan glanced around him again, as though embarrassed of her. "You're second, Katherine. You got your trunks on under those pants?"

"Ethan! Are you even listening to me?" Katherine waved one nylon wrapped hand in front of his face, blinking at him. "I said I am *not* prepared for this!" Though she was yelling, not many noticed, since the noise around them was heightened due to the announcement of the fights starting. An upsurge of voices occupied the heated room, baritones talking to their trainers, mouths spitting on the red carpet, limbs shadow-boxing, so much movement everywhere. Boxers shrugged their warm-up pants to the floor, revealing shiny gold, blue, and red knee-length trunks. She waited for Ethan's response, grudgingly shoving her own warm-up pants to the carpet. Katherine wore tailored black shorts, her muscular thighs pale beneath the fabric, hundreds of goose pimples raised from exposure to the cool room.

"I've told you a million times that you'll be fine! You spar guys all the time. There's no way this girl's going to hit that hard."

Katherine felt her chest tighten. She was suddenly shunned into the realization that she truly didn't know Ethan, though she wanted to believe him. She wanted to believe that he knew what she was getting into, that she could box, that she was capable. In just a few months, he had her boxing at this fancy club where men placed bets on fighters and the competition was twice her size. Was she justly skilled or did Ethan want Katherine to have some kind of experience, even if it was the wrong kind? She looked at those eyes full of intensity, the buzz cut, the tight body, the promises he'd made to never harm her in any way. She teetered between trusting and doubting him – bemused about what it was that she wanted in and outside the ring. The evening they had dinner together, she'd felt it in her veins that she was good enough, that she could do what other females couldn't do. But, inside herself she felt it – an instinctual feeling, a clue, that she would inevitably lose this fight.

"Ethan," she said, her voice low and more composed. As she spoke, she let Maxx slip on her gloves, left then right. He kneeled to tighten the laces of her boots, double knotting them, before standing again, holding out her new, smaller headgear.

"I really don't feel comfortable with this." Katherine said the words, never tearing her eyes away from Ethan's. She didn't even flinch as Maxx fit the headgear over her hair and face, pulling her ponytail through the top laces, tightening the back of it. "You've always assured me that I could do well, but I didn't think my first fight would be with someone so much *bigger* than me."

With each word that left her mouth, she felt her emotions building, the complete truth of her loneliness and inferiority spilling through every shaky syllable. Her opponent was bigger, this city was bigger, this life was beyond her handling. The noise around her continued to crescendo, but it seemed as though no one was uttering a word. The sounds emitted she could not decipher; she only felt an intense burning at the top of her head, from shame, nervousness, or the laces being pulled too tight – she didn't know. Katherine simply looked down at her shoes, as though it was a surprise to find them there; laced so tight the skin above her ankles began to swell. Her hands were gloved, her

A Woman's Ring

headgear on tighter than she'd ever had it, the cheek protectors removed for competition. Only a strap guarded her chin.

Ethan stood, focus mitts at his sides, Maxx beside him with the spit bucket, her mouth guard extended in his hand in a question of bravery. She heard a snicker from somewhere behind them and assumed it was Martha, watching Katherine's breakdown with a confident smile. That girl's swollen knuckles popping assuredly, her big, testy mouth snickering insults to her coach – telling him that Katherine was much too small for her and that this fight would be another victory to her record.

Katherine closed her eyes for a moment, ignoring that negative voice screaming inside her, remembering the reasons for being here – to seek the acceptance of this world – where no one could touch her except the opponent, where Katherine could slip and cover and step into a world where she was known as a boxer and nothing else.

Katherine opened her eyes and nodded at Maxx to go ahead. Their faces relaxed, Maxx jumping up and down, yelling "That's my girl! Yeahhhh!" Ethan slapping his focus mitts together, thinking of a combination for her to warm up with, and then Maxx again, leaning in to slip in her mouth guard.

His mouth steadied near Katherine's, one lone freckle dotting the right side of his upper lip. She smelled his breath, like peppermints and soda, and opened her lips to receive the piece with confidence. He smiled at her, revealing two rows of slightly crooked teeth, before sticking it in. Katherine bit down, accepting all of this before her – the sounds, the competition, and the doctor who was leaning against the wall, staring at her.

"Ready?" Maxx asked.

She nodded, smacking her gloves together. Ethan called out a combination, and Katherine danced toward him, her fists resonating expertly against the pads. Every single male in that room stopped to watch her, to notice the honed skills, the true technique, the torque of her body, of her hips and chest.

"I can do this," she murmured between every punch, every slip, every overhand. "I can."

In the ring, Katherine tried to block out the packed ballroom, the men that drifted like drunken penguins in and out of the aisles, their stubby cigars red-tipped and burning, voices screaming "Ooh, it's a girl fight! Girl fiiiiight!"

There were hundreds of blood stains on the canvas, a fresh one right in the middle from the bout before. She let the crowd's chants awaken her inner athlete as she climbed in, watched Martha's large frame hop into the ring at the opposite corner with her fists raised triumphantly. A reminder that it was only six minutes of her life. She could do six minutes of anything.

Round One.

The bell rang and Katherine touched gloves with Martha, tapping her blue ones to the red. She stared right into Martha's eyes, surprised at the warmth of them, open, brown. Perhaps there was a nurturer somewhere inside the athlete. Her opponent nodded as the round began, and Katherine, letting go, began to relax as a modest amount of weight slipped off her shoulders. She concentrated on all the things she and Ethan had worked on. All she had to do was remain patient, not attack into an attack, and land big, hard shots that would knock the mammoth down.

Katherine was alive then, so alive with the possibility of doing well that for a moment she forgot the taste of fear. Stepping forward, feeling her feet solid and steady, she met Martha in the middle. Who threw the first punch, she didn't know, but in that ring, on that night, she was not her body, her fists, or her legs. She was a heartbeat and strength, adrenaline and nerves. After one stinging punch landed near her eye, Katherine remembered she was here to box – to compete and not take her time like she did with the guys in sparring. She had to move, think, slip, and cover. Martha's intensity was shocking. She moved much faster than Katherine assumed she would, landing hard, crisp shots – but not harder than any of the guys.

They traded punches, Ethan's previous advice lost to her. Punches struck Katherine's jaw, then hers, shook Martha's temples, then hers, slammed her teeth into her mouthpiece – hers, then hers. She counted the seconds, trying not to back up but angle. Ten seconds left and Katherine landed one big overhand at the bell.

"Round!"

A Woman's Ring

The ref separated them and Katherine walked to her corner, gasping. Someone shouted for her, another for Martha. Ethan and Maxx brought in a stool and spit bucket, and she sat obligingly.

"Good job, babe. Don't just attack her when she's attacking you. Look at what she's throwing and then counter." Maxx rubbed her shoulders and gave her some water. She nodded, amazed at the fatigue of her body, the cotton dryness of her mouth. Ethan rinsed Katherine's mouthpiece calmly, patting it on her knee to shake the excess water off. "How you feel?"

"I'm just so tired. I don't feel like I can hit her hard. I don't have time to set anything up and she just keeps barreling forward." Katherine took another sip of water and shook her head. "She's moving a lot faster than I thought she would."

Ethan put her mouthpiece in and placed both hands on the side of her face. "Hey, look at me."

She struggled to look at him, feeling those hands on her headgear, the same hands that had held her tightly to him just weeks ago.

"You can do this. Just look at what she's doing. She knows she's bigger than you, so she keeps coming forward. All you need to do is fake, back up, *then* counter with a cross. Move around after you land a combination. Don't just stand there or let her back you into a corner. Double up on your hooks, wait for her and counter."

Katherine nodded, trying to calm herself as the ten-second bell sounded. She stood, her limbs heavy and depleted from the quick exit of adrenaline. She waited for the bell, wanting to scream and run and win and beat her senseless all at once. She blinked heavy eyelids, one sore, one watering. Her jaw was aching, a thin stream of blood running from her left nostril. Her mind was a broken record of advice: *win, Katherine, win.*

A Woman's Ring

Chapter Thirty-six

It rained outside, leaving slick scythes against the hospital windows. There was the lingering of medicine in her mouth, rubber between her legs, the yawning, assiduous breath of the machines. The room was bare and cold, save for the comma of moon outside her shaded windows. Katherine craned her neck to see its slight vanilla body, feeling a ringing in her ears, a hammering still present in her head.

She checked the clock by the table – 2:00a.m. She'd yet to have water, to taste the luxury of food. She looked down at her fingers that stung with medicine, that were swollen to the size of small red sausages. With her right hand, she called for the nurse, pressing the white button on her remote control.

What seemed like an hour later, one of them squeaked in, her hands folded primly in front of her white pants.

"Are you okay, Katherine?"

She nodded, swallowing down the bitter taste of bile that still clung to her throat. "Um, I'm not nauseated anymore, so could I get some juice or something?"

The nurse seemed to debate this for a few minutes by checking her stats, her temperature, tugging on the catheter that pinched between Katherine's legs, causing her to gasp in pain.

"Ooh, sorry, hon."

"Is everything okay?" As Katherine spoke, she heard the despondency in her voice, but fought to keep her tone even and steady. If she let on to how she felt, then it would all be over. The nurse would ask the questions she knew everyone already did: where was everybody? Didn't anyone love her? Why was she going through this alone?

As if sensing this, the nurse gave her a pat on the knee and left, only to come back with a tray full of crackers, a small bucket of ice and two cartons of orange juice. She left her with the overhead lights slightly dimmed and paused as if to say something before deciding against it and exiting. Katherine released a long sigh and felt her stomach grumble as she reached for her first package of crackers.

Hunger. It hit her viciously as she fumbled with the plastic, ripping it open and stuffing the pair of crackers in her mouth, choking on the enriched flour, the small grains of salt that rubbed against her tongue.

Thirst. She fidgeted with the first carton of juice, stabbing the foiled top with a straw, sucking the orange pulp with needy tongue and mouth, sitting back gingerly, ignoring the persistent thump behind her eyes. She fiddled with the remote control, flipping through the channels while ripping through another package of crackers. She wagged her feet and swallowed - feeling in that moment almost satisfied.

But when she stopped on a Spanish channel that broadcast a lightweight fight, two men raising their hands as if to signal victory between the rounds, her throat constricted, her eyes filled.

She would never be a name that passed through strangers' lips, a soft-spoken syllable, a respected athlete. A talent that could grace the paper's Sports section – a woman clad in boxing attire and a smile. Showtime. Coverage. Spotlight. For Katherine, boxing would always be an amateur affair, learned and then forgotten while the new wave of females attempted to become known and respected by the world.

Her skills would be the skills of slight remembrance – how the body of a gymnast could still perform a handstand or back handspring years past her prime, how the mouth of a musician could still blow the notes from his horn, still arrange his mouth and hands even in the face of arriving death – she would still be able to throw proper combinations due to the potent power of memory.

Katherine flipped off the television, feeling a wave of cold pass over her newly shorn head. She looked down at her hands that were unable to fist from all the I.V.s. Suddenly she felt sick. Those people on the screen she would never be, despite all her prayers that she would come out of this triumphant and strong.

A Woman's Ring

She began to cry, the tears spilling over her swollen face. She let her mouth fall open, her wails waking the elderly that were dying in rooms adjacent to hers. She'd tried living and failed. Marriage and failed. Mothering and failed. She had expected escape would bring the peace she had clamored for, that running away would soothe the pain. As a nurse hurried into Katherine's room, flipping the lights to bright, she sank deeper in her pillows, spilling juice and crumbs all over her blue hospital gown. The nurse clucked her tongue and came over. Katherine gazed up at her as if to ask why this life was so hard, why she kept trying and failing, why she kept failing without trying. The nurse's eyes held pity and nothing more as she cleaned up the mess of her patient.

Katherine knew she needed to finish what she'd started, with a husband who was married only to his children, living in a house in the smallest city of the world. She would train to "unlive" her life – to deal with every caustic outcome of life's decisions. For the first time, she would learn honor – and honor meant pursuing the choices her heart despised.

A Woman's Ring

Chapter Thirty-seven

They sparred only one time. It was two days after her first fight, her nose still tender but kept pale by makeup. The guys were busy running off to business dinners and cuddling their wives after boxing class. Ethan moved all the extra mitts and gloves back to their cages and came back with a sigh.

"You sparring tonight?"

Katherine motioned to the guys packing up their things, taking off their wraps and shoes. "Doesn't look like anybody's going tonight."

Gretchen jumped down from the ring, sneering. "I'll spar – unless you're still sore from your *fight* the other day."

Katherine felt her breath constrict from embarrassment, felt that uneasy defeat all over again as she looked down at her shoes. Slipping on the canvas. Nerves and failure. Uppercuts marking her chin. She steadied her breath and looked Gretchen directly in the eyes.

"Well, you know Gretchen – I may not have won, but at least I've actually *had* a fight instead of pretending" -- she slowly looked Gretchen up and down – "to be such hot shit when you've never even experienced what it's like to compete."

Gretchen clenched her jaw as Ethan stepped between them. "Hey now – easy, ladies." He pinched Katherine's shoulders, forcing a laugh. "If you two are nice to each other, you can go a few rounds. But remember, Katherine – she's gonna hit you as hard as you hit her, so keep it light."

Katherine nodded, stalking off to get her equipment. Why did Gretchen constantly try to prove she was so much better? She may have won the guys over with her tough attitude and aggressiveness, with her big muscles and giant, looping haymakers. But they all knew she was a better boxer than Gretchen – they had to.

Katherine took a deep breath and felt the tug of anger fade to nervousness as she prepared, the same unsteady emotion as on her first day of sparring, or her first night of competition. She ran through Gretchen's boxing style in her head – how she left her head open when she threw a hook or cross, the way she constantly came forward and only got caught off guard when her opponent went on offense.

Katherine shoved in her mouthpiece, secured her headgear, and was the first to jump in the ring. "Don't get hit and then hit," she whispered, loosening her shoulders. She would use this sparring session for doing all the things she hadn't done two nights ago – waiting for Gretchen to attack, so she could counter and then beat her smoothly.

"Take your time," Ethan mouthed. Katherine nodded, stretching her arms above her head.

Gretchen came back from the bathroom, gloved and masked, a concentrated scowl on her face. Katherine attempted to remain calm, to diffuse the anticipation she felt only with women and not men. With men, she felt their need to box, their encouragement and willingness to treat her fairly, to push her, to fight. But with women – and especially Gretchen – it seemed to be all about winning, showing off what little skills were possessed while appearing unbreakable.

"You two ready?" Ethan motioned toward the bell as Gretchen made her way to the other end of the ring, hopping on her toes.

"Yep, coach," Gretchen murmured, charging a need in Katherine. "He's not your coach," she wanted to scream – Ethan would never be her coach, because she couldn't appreciate the sport like the rest of them. Ethan had molded these guys and Katherine from regular people, had carved them into contenders. Katherine took a deep breath and nodded at Ethan, noticing a few of the guys loitering around the ring to watch the two girls spar.

"Brrring!"

Gretchen immediately lumbered forward, sitting back on her heels, hands tight to her head. Katherine smirked, awakened to the fact that Gretchen had obviously been watching her, too – knew to lean back and not in, that Katherine would take any

A Woman's Ring

available opportunity to rain down punches – the excitement causing her to pound and not always restrain.

Gretchen snapped out a jab and Katherine leaned out to her right, simultaneously throwing a giant left overhand. It connected with Gretchen's nose, hitting that breakable wall of flesh and bone, her eyes closing around the big red fist which made her knees buckle, the guys gasp. Ethan yelled "Easy!" while Katherine threw a body shot and another overhand, feeling fluid and powerful, closing the gap between them. She stepped back with her right foot and bounced in left foot forward, throwing fakes, moving back, coming in with two power jabs.

Katherine could visit the surprise in Gretchen's eyes, knew it was the hardest she'd ever been hit and that she would lighten her own punches if she didn't want to get hurt. Gretchen began to back up, flicking out jabs and crosses that barely skimmed Katherine's head, as she continued countering, covering, and moving laterally.

The ring belonged to just one of them.

Here, there wasn't a ref or men in suits making illegal bets and puffing on thick cigars. She wasn't sparring someone a foot taller, whom she could never knock down. This was her gym, on her own time, with her fists setting the pace. With one shot she'd earned Gretchen's respect, though Katherine knew she couldn't take it for granted. Gretchen had a right cross to be wary of – the shot Gretchen always figured would define her fame.

Katherine inched her opponent back to the ropes and unloaded six body shots, then an uppercut-cross-hook, and stepped in to pin with the opposite stance. Gretchen covered and pushed against Katherine, seeming to finally find her fists and unleash them on any available inch of Katherine.

She ducked, moved out, ducked in again. Avoided most of Gretchen's shots and landed her own with staccato accuracy. The praise from the guys fueled her cockiness, molded her suddenly into Ethan – relaxed and confident in his abilities. She was releasing her dream on this tough girl who was folding beneath the pressure.

The thirty-second bell rang and Katherine let Gretchen off the ropes. She came forward, launching a jab-cross combination which Katherine angled from, coming back with tight double hooks. Gretchen took them, losing her balance from the second blow.

This was her biggest accomplishment – beating the attitude out of this girl – humbling her as she wasn't able to humble her opponent in that ballroom – competing now in her comfort zone and landing with absolute precision.

Katherine felt her muscles fatigue but kept her concentration. She could gauge the frustration in Gretchen's eyes – was that a tear rolling off her cheek? – but she kept faking, letting Gretchen punch before coming in with her own hard, crisp shots that tested her stamina.

"Round!"

The bell sounded and Katherine held herself back from landing her last big overhand. The guys clapped and hollered as Gretchen slumped to the edge of the ring.

"What, no more?" Katherine asked, fists raised at her sides. "Only one round? Come on! I wasn't even hitting hard!"

Gretchen didn't say a word, just waved her away, stumbled from the ring and went straight to the bathroom. She stayed there until the guys had thinned out, each of them patting Katherine on the back, whispering their praises in her ear, Ethan the leader of those remarks.

"You're already better than you were in that first fight, Katherine. And you'll just continue to get better, stronger. Just gotta keep you in the ring."

Katherine nodded, drinking his words, memorizing his confidence.

As she unwrapped her hands and packed her bag, Katherine made her way over to the bathroom, waving at gym members who gave her the thumbs-up or ran over to comment on her boxing. She waved them off, insisting it was nothing, all the while glowing inside. Once at the bathroom door, Katherine hesitated before knocking lightly.

"Gretchen, you in there?"

"Go away!"

Katherine ran a hand over her eyes, sighing. "You know the gym will close, so you'll have to come out of there eventually."

A Woman's Ring

"Well, then I'll wait until they force me out, cause I'm sure as hell not going to talk to you."

Katherine leaned her head against the door, knocking softly. "Come on, Gretchen, it was one round. It couldn't have been that humiliating. You did some good things – and I just got beat the other night in front of a whole crowd of people who lost *money* because of me, so I don't know what you're so embarrassed about."

She heard Gretchen laugh bitterly, and then pause before speaking. "Katherine, that's exactly my point. You got beat and yet you still beat me in one round! What does that make me?"

"Gretchen, please. You'll get better – it was one stupid round! Everyone has their off nights – ."

"Look, I said I don't want to talk about it! Just go back to your rich little apartment and leave me alone!"

Katherine slapped the door one last time, feeling annoyed. "Fine, run away then, Gretchen! You know, I thought you were tougher than this – just admit that you lost and get over it! You're not always going to be great every time you're in the ring – it's just a simple fact. And if you can't accept it, then maybe you should find a different sport."

She turned and moved back toward the ring, not waiting for an answer. Ethan was still there, hitting the heavy bags. He stopped punching as she approached him.

"You want a ride home?"

Katherine nodded, throwing her bag over one shoulder.

"Gretchen's locked herself in the bathroom."

Ethan shrugged and kicked the bag with a roundhouse. "Well, what do you expect? She's never been humiliated before. Her ego's just been crushed and she's embarrassed. It happens."

They walked wordlessly out of the gym toward his car, soaking in the cool night breeze. Katherine kept her gaze forward, not daring to look over at Ethan, to feel the neediness creeping up inside her, that fear of going home alone. She wanted to ask him to come up, to fall into bed beside her, curling his body tightly to hers so she could sleep inside a man's strong arms.

On the ride home, she tried to form the words, tried to ask him to stay with her – if just for one evening. He pulled the car to the curb and looked over at her.

"Here we are."

"Yep." Katherine's fingers hesitated on the door handle and she turned to look at him. "Ethan – "

"You – "

They both began their sentences, but Katherine trailed off first, losing her nerve somewhere in the moment. "Go ahead. What were you going to say?"

Ethan smiled and dropped a hand on her knee. "I just wanted to say that you really did a great job tonight. You were thinking, focused. That's what we have to work to maintain." He squeezed her thigh and released his hand.

Katherine swallowed the large lump in her throat and gave him a quick kiss goodbye. "Thanks Ethan. I'll see you tomorrow."

As Ethan pulled away from the curb, Katherine stared at the sky, spotting only one star amidst all the city lights. She stood like that for a while, thinking and staring, thinking and staring. For the first time in the ring, she'd carried an attitude – she'd let all her insecurities fall to the ground and beaten Gretchen with glitter and skill. Though it felt good, she realized her insecurities brought an element not many boxers had – she respected the game and not the attitude – the journey and not the prize.

She knew what professionals could become – how money and fame could rob them of their sportsmanship. As Katherine turned to go inside, she swore she'd try to remain intact – not ruining the only good thing that had ever happened to her. There had to be a balance of self-confidence and humility, and she would work to find it, work to maintain that mindset.

Katherine took the elevator up to her apartment, the beginnings of a headache lodging behind her left eye. Every night after boxing, it was always the same: pounding in her head, a punch of pain that eased when sleep finally arrived.

After she got ready for bed, she stood out on the balcony, looking out over the city, realizing what a small part of it she composed. In Urbana, she'd been known and watched from every

A Woman's Ring

street corner, every store. Here, she seemed inconspicuous, guiltless, incredibly free. She gripped the railing of the balcony, staring down at the hard, unforgiving cement. What would come after boxing was done? How would she know when she was satisfied?

Katherine took a deep breath, her headache intensifying. She stepped back into her apartment and gazed at the furniture of this new life. It was almost as if Ohio had been a dream – there was no husband, no children. As she slid into bed, she felt the gaping emptiness beside her, the cold sheets and extra pillow that lay blatantly untouched. She traced the sheets, closed her eyes, and pictured Brandon snuggled up somewhere within the same big city. He used to be only one house away – where she could sneak out her window and crawl through his, where they would stay up talking the entire night. Katherine emptied her mind and fought off the seizing pain in her head, thinking of nothing but the day, the moment until the lull of sleep robbed her of further thinking.

Rea Frey

A Woman's Ring

Chapter Thirty-eight

She received the letter a week after her first loss. A week after she buckled beneath the pressure of competition, her nose and chin still bruised purple, her shoulders and forearms shot from punching and receiving, from her sparring session with Gretchen. Katherine flipped the letter over in her hands, searching for a return address, but there was only her name and address scratched cursively along the front. Once inside her apartment, she sliced it open, spreading the single page before her, a smile on her lips – she loved letters but never received them. She often hoped that Brandon, having found her address, might jot his sentiments onto paper, searching for her address and sending his emotions via mail. That was her hope as she held the letter against her face, lost in girlish fantasies.

Katherine,
I found your address, I hope you're not upset. There are things that only a mother can deal with and this is not one of them. Where do I begin? I thought you should know that Andrew is seeing some woman, that she is often in your house, with your children, and they do not seem to like her. They ask about you constantly, Katherine, and I must say they're not resentful, they just miss their mother. You and I both know those children love you, and I can't preach to you enough how this is not the right thing for you to do. Whenever I told you to do what you have to, I did not mean abandoning your children. It is wrong, Katherine, the worst possible thing a woman can do. And as much as I want to support you on this, I cannot. Brandon once told me of your dream to box, and I can only assume that's what you're doing in Chicago. If you know what's good, then you'll come home, but that's all I'll say about that. You know Andrew won't come hunt you down, but those children need you if

you're to be a good mother to them – better than this new woman.

Now, Katherine, I don't know how to tell you what I must tell you. I try not to think about it and I don't want to write it, but I know you have to hear what happened, though it pains me more than anything. I figure you haven't talked to Brandon since you've been up there, and I know how much you care for him, Katherine, and how much he's always cared for you. He simply couldn't understand why, if you loved him like you and I both know you did, why you would marry that man. He never forgave you for that, Katherine. It ate at him, especially when you had the children.

Brandon's dead. He died in a car crash on his way to the airport where he was training. Dead, Katherine. My boy is dead. He was driving on the highway and some sixteen-year old crossed a median and hit his car. Both cars exploded – I don't know how and he...he was identified by his teeth, nothing left of him but bones and teeth. Katherine, he's dead. My boy's dead. How can something like this have happened to my family? I know he was the only real family you ever had, so I don't know what else to say. The funeral was last week, and I thought it best if you not be here. I'm sorry if that was the wrong decision, but I just could not handle telling you, or making this into more of a reality than I had to. Oh, Katherine, I'm so sorry. Please come home soon.

Betty

The letter crumbled in Katherine's hands, like tissue easily shredded by her strong fingers. She couldn't read it again, couldn't read the sentences that would plague her for the rest of her life. She ripped the sentences, the periods, the words, needing to extinguish the evidence as it fractured every piece of her. Brandon's dead, Katherine.Brandon's dead, Katherine. Brandon's dead, Katherine. Those words pushed her to the loss of sanity, her body turning to a mass of pruned flesh in the hub of the shower as she ran there, the water heating her skin through

A Woman's Ring

her clothes, fingernails pulling at her face, her hair, those words from Mrs. Baskin: *Brandon's dead.*

If she'd learned one thing about death, she knew it was swift and ultimately cruel. She would never again see that precious face swathed in moonlight, him holding her like a best friend, pulling her tightly against him, his beating heart that had so much life inside, now spent, gone. Why him? Why now? How could something as simple as twisted steel take him from the world he'd cherished so completely? Destroy the pulp and tissues and structure of his face, the face that had been so beautiful, the spirit so genuine, her one friend, her one love, her one escape in this big city, now throttled. And what was she left to do? She should have searched harder, looked faster, made up with him the moment she'd left him on that night two weeks before she married Andrew. She should have stopped his car when he left Ohio, because it was truly her fault – she pushed him to Chicago earlier than he should have gone.

But he was burned too badly, identified by his teeth, his eyes gone, those perfect gray eyes, the color of thunder, gone now, from one car accident. Her entire life gone with him.

Katherine sat immobile, letting the steam beat her until new headaches pounded with every fist of water that turned her skin from pink to purple to ashen. She wondered if he'd ever gotten to fly a plane, if he'd felt that exhilaration, the power of the sky and stars and moon right next to him; if he'd felt the magic of love, the softness of skin, the lips and genital flesh of females; if he'd ever thought of her up in the air; if her face had flashed through his mind one last time as his life was being lifted from him; or if he had just as easily forgotten her.

The phone rang for days as Katherine sat curled up in a ball, her stomach weak from vomiting; Katherine's head a splitting blind spot, Mrs. Baskin her only murderess:

Brandon's dead, Katherine. Nothing left but bones and teeth, Katherine, he's dead, my boy's dead.

And she is with him, a fragment of a body, parted from the earth as bodies will, just bones and teeth, sight and sorrow – the ash of him, of her.

Rea Frey

A Woman's Ring

Chapter Thirty-nine

They finally removed the catheter. It's what she'd been hoping for as she wiggled in that bed like a victim, finding the resolve somewhere between waking and vomiting to want to fight harder than ever before, to rip the I.V.s from her sore and swollen wrists, to run around the hospital ward like a child on fire – to live.

Nurse Jenkins came in some time in the afternoon, checking her vitals, administering the frequent strength and mobility tests which Katherine passed with absolute ease. When they said kick, she kicked the nurses into a wall, watching their astonished but pleased faces. When they said squeeze, she nearly broke the long, skinny fingers of every nurse or doctor. When they said follow the light with your eyes, she watched like a hawk, daring them to give her bad news.

"This is like a fight," she'd think. "Never show them you're hurting."

Nurse Jenkins prepared Katherine for the catheter removal, told her to take a deep breath as she deflated the balloon, that chafing rubber, the constant tugging that made her feel like she always needed to urinate. The nurse deflated it in a single pump and Katherine squeezed her eyes shut as the giant bulb was yanked from her insides, leaving Katherine gasping for air and squeezing her thighs together in pain.

"You may feel some burning – that's normal. We just need to make sure you urinate consistently to prevent infection. Lots of water, okay?"

Katherine nodded, her mouth hinged open as the pain swept over her. It felt like someone had brutally fisted her with a knife and removed it in quick, jagged motions. She pressed the button on her bed to sit up and looked over at the small white toilet that sat adjacent to a counter, out in the middle of a room like a decoration. She licked her lips and motioned to Nurse Jenkins as she was leaving.

"Umm, can you help me to the toilet, please?"

Nurse Jenkins smiled and returned, letting down the bed rails on the left side, wheeling Katherine's I.V. machine around to accompany her. "Alright, swing your legs over."

Katherine did, feeling the complete lightheadedness as she sat fully erect. "Jesus."

"Head rush?" The nurse patted her shoulders and helped Katherine to the ground. The tile felt smooth and cool beneath her thin socks. She felt as awkward as a child taking its first majestic steps along a corridor. She felt her stiff knees, the exertion from walking five feet to a toilet that sat so openly in the room.

Katherine felt a small flush of embarrassment at having to urinate in front of the nurse. Of course she'd just pulled a catheter from her bladder, but still. This was different. Nurse Jenkins lifted the lid behind her and lined the seat with a paper guard.

"I'll be back in one minute," she said as she helped lower Katherine over the seat, placing her hands on the guard rail.

Katherine nodded in relief and sat there, too nervous to pee, overwhelmed by the sudden sense of loss she felt. She was peeing for the very first time since brain surgery – on her own – and not one person was there to hold her hand afterwards, or congratulate her for taking her first real steps toward recovery.

She would have done anything to have the sweet hands of her father cooling her forehead in the hospital bed, whispering that she was a fighter, that she was going to beat this thing.

Katherine managed to finish her business, wincing as the sting of liquid splashed into the bowl. She flushed and, too impatient to simply sit and wait, walked herself back to bed. Before climbing in, she did a few calf raises, rolled her shoulders around. She was fatigued and restless, her limbs so unused to constant sedation. Had it only been a few weeks ago that she had been training six days a week, for hours on end? It was as if her

A Woman's Ring

body had already forgotten its reason, had begun to defy all the intense training. She pulled herself heavily back into the bed that adjusted every fifteen minutes to prevent blood clots. The vibrations threatened to rock her to sleep as she waited for the nurse.

She felt an overwhelming urge to call someone. A friend, Mrs. Baskin, maybe even Andrew? Even though she'd gotten her own insurance after leaving, he was sure to find her. Would he come if he knew? Would he flatten his hand over hers and promise to be here every step of the way?

Katherine closed her eyes and sighed as the nurse came back, stunned to find her patient back in bed. "Well, you sure are a strong one, huh?"

Katherine waited for the next part, the hourly steroid and antibiotic treatment. It burned up her arms, the drugs coursing through her veins, acidic, warding off any and all infections. They offered her Vicodin, but she refused to take any extra medication. She already had enough foreign substances in her body to last for eternity.

"I'm fine," she'd say, struggling to see through headaches, to fight the nausea after even one piece of bread. She went over facts in her head, boxing, math, poetry from high school. She was testing what they'd done to her. Seeing if all was intact. Inside, her mind was a whirlwind of information. Memories, funerals, trips as a child. But to the public eye, she was only a shaved and swollen creature, fighting to recover from something that had taken her legs from beneath her, a piece of her mind – had confined her to sitting and brooding with no outlet, no way to expel the guilt and loss that were weighing heavily upon her.

It was time to move on.

Rea Frey

A Woman's Ring

Chapter Forty

After Brandon's death, she found herself in a world inhabited by memories. Not the memories of her wanting, always working so selfishly for his romance; she remembered only the best of him. The boy who played basketball and mowed the lawn, the one who was always there to listen when Katherine needed him.

Sitting on the balcony of her apartment in only a robe, she cast off paper airplanes into the warm, Chicago air, remembering the boy who grew up in Urbana, the boy who'd first showed her how to spit, how to smoke, how to smile in the face of death and form the miniature airplanes she was now chucking from the thirtieth floor. The swift white bodies lifted from the railing, rising and swirling in steady circles toward the tires of taxi cabs, pelting shoulders of pedestrians.

She was hit with cherished memories. Their fourth grade play in which he'd been dressed as a turkey and tripped while waddling toward the microphone, causing a domino effect for all the cast of the Bradbury Thanksgiving play. Sixth grade band and his awful talent for the trombone which made Mr. Smith say that he may want to take up sports instead. His mother had gotten so fed up with his refusal to give up (as he thought the trombone was a great instrument), and his constant late night practicing that she sold the instrument and brought home a Nintendo in its place.

"Play this instead," she'd said.

Katherine smiled, wiping a tear from her cheek. They'd met at age four, and she actually remembered the way he'd extended his hand, shook it firmly and said, "I'm Brandon Baskin, your neighbor. Do you want to come play trucks with me?" From that first moment, she'd felt a little of her fear slip away. Being a girl from an orphanage in a small town should have made her strange. Instead, Brandon made her well-loved and respected. They were always together, but never a couple. And, until her teenage years, she never wanted to be. Never noticed the way the girls in school giggled and whispered when he went by, pouting their lips and fluffing big bangs. The way he always hid notes in his back pocket – notes she realized now had been countless love letters that he'd never pursued or wanted to show her.

He was always mature for his age, so considerate. A boy with the eyes of a cloud and the heart of a saint. Even when playing games and climbing trees, he was often contemplating other worlds, bigger entities. As if he knew his time was limited – that his journey was heading only one way.

In school, the teachers doted on his dependability and the students flocked to his lack of cockiness, his honesty. He played baseball and soccer, but wanted more than those sports could offer him. He volunteered after school at the retirement home and worked on the weekends at the ice cream parlor. When he got promoted to manager, he knocked on Katherine's window late one night, long after the parlor had closed, and the two sneaked uptown, where he giddily produced a set of keys to get them in. They spent three hours sampling from tubs of ice cream, making sundaes, throwing sprinkles in each other's hair.

When he got three scholarships for college, he simply folded them up in his desk drawer and told Katherine he wouldn't go away until she would. He'd sacrificed his life for her.

Brandon Baskin. Her best friend.

His smile made old ladies soften, those lips that were full and pink and impossibly round – all the more precious now that they would simply be a shadow of memory, a photograph tucked away in an album somewhere. He would never be remembered by a child, never carry a little one on his shoulders and feel the pride of fatherhood, of hearing his baby say, "I love you, Daddy." Never entertain the love of a woman, although maybe he and Stacy had ripped the clothes from each other's bodies and reveled in the magic of love. Her hands on his shoulders, her eyes below his waist, watching his desire for her swell and strengthen, pointing right at her. Perhaps they'd tumbled in the grass, in his car, in Chicago. Beneath lit candles and the influence of wine. Naked limbs discovering for the first time what they were made to do.

A Woman's Ring

Never again would he wake with his arms wrapped firmly around Stacy, holding two soft bosoms, smelling her fragrant hair. She would not cook him breakfast and he would not come up behind her, circling his strong, tanned arms around her middle and say, "You mean the world to me, you know."

There would be no air trips to London, no ventures to Hawaii or L.A. All he'd wanted was to feel the complete control of a plane from his position in the cockpit. The machinery that could change a boy into an adult. The flying.

Katherine pulled her robe tighter against her body and for the first time in years missed her life as a child. Before her father died, before she'd fallen in love. When things had been so inconceivably simple. Sure, her mother didn't love her – but lots of children's mothers were gone or missing. Hers just happened to be visible but fading into the horizon one day at a time. Brandon had made it bearable, had filled her life with laughter and goofy trips, with presents and friendship.

She missed his calloused hands and conversation. The way he would salute her father, though Bruce had never been in the Army. He learned to cook at twelve and would always make loads of rich desserts, sharing them only with her, bringing them to school, driving to parks and cemeteries for picnics.

The two had been the best kind of friends – the ones where love was second to commitment, where anger would always dissipate no matter what the cause.

Katherine found herself sobbing as she realized Brandon would have eventually forgiven her for marrying Andrew. That he had just been frustrated with her constant pity party, her impatience for life.

If only he hadn't gotten in that car. If only she'd found him sooner. If only. He had put off college for her and she never returned the favor. She hadn't postponed her life – she'd created it, created two babies and a husband though she didn't appreciate them. What he'd known that she didn't was that while she thought she was gaining money for their future, she was actually tearing herself away from Brandon one poor decision at a time.

All he'd done was give to her from the moment her father died, from the moment she'd come to him with a purple face and a deadly moan, saying, "My daddy's dead, my daddy's dead."

Brandon Jay Baskin. 1979-2003. Would she one day lie over his grave, as she had all the others? Tracing his name under her nails, whispering down to him, letting him know once again how she felt and wished for what could have been?

If she did, she would carry a red rose and an apology. For stealing his life, for loving him so selfishly, for giving up on the dream of a life with him.

A Woman's Ring

Chapter Forty-one

She had her. Belly up, gloves and boots writhing on the canvas like an upturned centipede. Nose flat and peach as smashed clay, stars in those wondering eyes of hers. One short cross, and Rita slapped the canvas, wiggled upon it. In the middle of round three, she was down but not out, Katherine's blue, competent gloves cocked above her, the buzz of promoters and spectators among lovers and lights and blood. Drops of blood the size of pennies bubbling onto the ring's worn floor, blood from her nose, her lips, blood under the fold of her creased left eyelid.

"Three, four, five, six." The referee stood, fingers flexed above her, his bald head as shiny as the baby's in the front row, who sat on his father's knee. Rita splayed as if for crucifixion on the aging, yellowed canvas.

There she lie, fidgeting on tired elbows, rolling to her one good side. All that gold – gold shorts, gold top, dressed for victory, her cut arms and broad, handsome face that had mocked Katherine in the dressing room now squirming, lost inside the twisted headgear.

"You fighting?" she'd asked, popping her knuckles like four rough peanut shells, her dark eyes crossing slightly, the proof of her fighting marked along her tilted features.

"Yeah – I'm fifth."

"Well, well," Rita said, looking at her friend on the other side of the bench who was stuffing two ham hock thighs into a pair of purple trunks. "You're fighting me, then. 125, right?"

"Yeah," Katherine said, bringing one arm up to scratch her chest, flexing her bicep, so her opponent could see that she had just as much, if not more, muscle than she. Rita's top lip seemed to connect with the tip of her nose, an ugly, long nose that dipped where it once was smooth and feminine. They stared at each other, in that moment her reasons for being there much different than Katherine's.

"Well, good luck."

"Yeah," Rita said, grinning wider, "see ya out there, *amateur*."

Now she was bleeding from three places, the ref in her face, counting slowly. "Six, seven…look at me, can you go on?"

Rita nodded, stooped, then stood, bringing her fists to her temples. The ref moved closer, squinting under the bright lights to tip her chin upwards, those lights that split over their heads like God's great flashlight – so many beams and directions under one yawning, yellow tent.

If Katherine turned, she would see Ethan in her corner, spit bucket ready and clutched comfortably between his short fingers – a smile over his thin lips – a smile because Katherine was winning, angling, and thinking second by second as if this fight would determine the outcome of her entire career as a boxer.

The ref sent Rita over to the cut doctor at the edge of the ropes who prodded and jabbed latex fingers on her nose, beneath her eyes, against her chin, mopping away the blood, yelling, "She okay! She continue!"

The ref, rejoining them, separated their bodies with the width of just one hand.

"Fight!"

Rita lunged at her, throwing wild windmill crosses that she slipped, countered, and angled from.

"That's right, babe! Get her! Take her out!" Ethan encouraged from outside the ropes; it was only yesterday that he and Katherine had been sparring in their gym together, only last week that he'd taken her home. But rather than hug her goodbye, they'd kissed for the second time. A sloppy kiss, their mouths wet and wanting, their teeth clinking and grazing the soft flesh of gums. There, they'd sat in delicate leather seats, sweat escaping from beneath her arms, his nose pressed so tight against hers, his with all those dips and bumps from years of careless punches.

"Well," she said, lowering her arms. "Well, well."

Ethan had rubbed his thumb under one of Katherine's eyes, scooping a fallen eyelash on his fingerprint.

A Woman's Ring

"You have no idea how much I've wanted to kiss you again," he said.

In the ring, it was just she and Rita – not sparring, but fighting for victory – Ethan in her corner, screaming, "Come on, babe, come on!"

At the thirty-second bell, Rita kept punching, her knees permanently knocking, her head snapped back and turning, like a slowly spinning coin.

"Do it!" Ethan yelled as Katherine sat back and waited for Rita to jab. As she did, Katherine leaned out with a giant left overhand. There was heat before it landed, heat before the cracking of her jaw line, a splitting apple's crunch, the bulge of her eye filling like a heavy, wet balloon. Katherine felt her opponent's body rock and press against her chest, pulling her down, her blood on Katherine's neck, and her own panting, like making love, making it in the ring with hundreds of people pushing, wanting her outside of it. She watched Rita descend as she disentangled her own limbs, that repugnant face bouncing three times against the canvas, her jaw broken, shoved over at strange, indefinite angles, her headgear shifted and stained from her own blood.

"Stop! It's stopped!" The ref came between them, sealing Katherine's first victory. Rita remained on the canvas as Katherine backed toward her corner, hearing the crowd's roar echo above the rafters, Ethan's arms wrapping around her waist. She raised her fists above her head, feeling weightless, bringing them back down to beat her chest, making crazy clucking sounds; clucking because she wore two hard breast plates inside her sports bra, yet she continued knocking, rousing the crowd to its toes.

Moments later, she was waiting for it – the call of her name over the microphone, for those relentless hours of boxing, where the heavy bags were her daughter and son, her mother, her husband, all unshakeable, now shaken. She knew in a few moments there'd be promoters lining up in the wings pressuring her to become the next big professional, but all she could search for was that baby boy in the front row, on his father's shoulder, clapping for her. That small face like Frankie's had been, trusting his parent to never leave. But mostly, there was Brandon, a treasured memory, his love beating this woman to the ring floor, surpassing Ethan's doubt to actually fight, to take that rage, that fuel, and feed the metronome of boxing, that click her every punch, every moment a crescendo of action, every hook, jab and cross the tight pulses, the beats of her life, the reminders of what she had to do to keep living without Brandon.

As the announcer called the women to the center of the ring, Rita loped toward her, a blood-stained towel draped around her head like a hood. Katherine blinked as her face came into view, her jaw the size of a softball, her eyes swollen and disproportionate. She shook Katherine's hand, mumbled, "Nife ob," which she translated to mean, "Nice job," before retreating, humbled, across the ring. Those bright lights strung around them like pearls as Ethan's hands fit around Katherine's hips, lifting her.

"You did it, Katherine," he whispered, pulling her down against him, holding her. The crowd recognized her victory, men and women rushing over to toss their congratulations from the stands. She took their pens, their paper, their questions; knew in her heart that this could be her last fight as she stared down at the little boy that had kept her attention so closely throughout the rounds. She longed for her children, for the first time in her life, their spirit like two small ghosts trapped within her memory.

A Woman's Ring

Chapter Forty-two

The day she left them was cold and dim, the sky patched with clouds. Katherine had hurried their legs and arms into snow pants and jumpers, frantically moving them from the doorway to the car, pulling snacks off shelves, shoving spare socks and sweaters into a day bag. Yet her only business was the drop-off, the escape route from Urbana to Chicago. Andrew was to arrive back from New York at nine, but she would be gone by then, cruising down the highway with only one bag in the trunk and enough cash to begin again.

She put the children in the car, leaving their seatbelts unbuckled, driving the three minutes to Mrs. Baskin's house, parking, breathing, trying to wick the sweat off her forehead and neck. In their jackets, the twins looked like infant snowmen, white and plump with their heads both turned upwards, tongues out to see if snow was falling. Katherine pushed them forward, checking behind her for a sign, something to prohibit her journey, something to bind her to the chains she'd just begun to saw through.

At the door, Mrs. Baskin welcomed the children with a smile, her usual Monday morning ritual, the twins hugging their mother's legs, clinging to her as if to kill what was left of her bravery. Frankie's eyes were still swollen from crying last night, and he stared at her now, whispering, "I love you, Momma," quietly, before turning to run inside the house. Lily kissed her mother's thigh and rushed off, tackling her brother with a glorified cry.

"Be good for Mrs. Baskin..."

Katherine's last words came out in one long monotone. Mrs. Baskin looked at her strangely, asking if she was alright. Katherine nodded and suffered a smile as Betty shut the door, Katherine's whole life shutting with it, her breath gone in the cold squeak of the door that separated her from them, freeing her to everything. Her mother's house she left too, sitting at that crooked slant beside Mrs. Baskin's, separated only by a slender strip of driveway.

"What are you doing, Katherine," she whispered as she walked back toward the car, overcome with guilt for knowing that she would not be back for her children, knowing that she had let Frankie cry and scream all night for her, that Lily would become strong and silent, that Andrew would realize she was gone and never try to find her. She knew in her heart that this was not right, but right for her, slamming the car door and backing down Mrs. Baskin's drive, not sorry but grief-stricken, not indignant, not Andrew's wife or the twins' mother any longer – just an escapee on her way to independence.

A Woman's Ring

Chapter Forty-three

The mirror held a reflection of a beast; bulbous forehead with two bloodstained butterfly bandages over drill wounds, a single strip of gauze over the rows of slate gray staples, the prickly hair stained red from the incision. Katherine's arms, pierced in seven places for I.V.s and arterial lines, were now scarred and swollen from the removal. Nurse Jenkins had pulled four-inch plastic tubing from different areas of her arm, shocking Katherine from the size and blood that spurted onto the blue hospital blankets.

On the fifth day, when she was able to walk around the ward, catheter removed, I.V.s capped, she couldn't help but stare at the creature so unlike herself: the coquettish smile that revealed nothing save the reality of removing a cyst that had probably existed since birth. She'd been saved by boxing, the fateful headaches and occasional blows to the head a swelling device, until soon, she was having her first MRI, then her second, her third, her body stagnant in that hospital casket, inducing a feeling of claustrophobia, and then that harrowing decision to remove it, to stop boxing, some small part of her hoping that she'd pass away in surgery, that she could be with Brandon wherever he went, still beautiful, still smiling, sharing all the parts of themselves never revealed.

The steps Katherine took were those of a tired woman: each door around the wing a depiction of what she could become.. Elders hooked to life support, hacking up breakfast, breathing through machines. Her footsteps now marked the same paths of their sicknesses, every step laden with fire in her skull, a pit of blackness stapled to her very core - the cadence of grief.

As she rounded the last corner, Katherine felt the thickness of her feet against the carpet; her insides emaciated from helpings of I.V.s and small scoops of mashed potatoes the nurses fed her twice daily. Katherine was to live with this pain as she would live with the metal plates, the scar, wound with guilt and the hurt of a lost love – this new life of a diminishing athlete.

Ethan stopped by on the fifth evening, bursting with shame for not being there sooner, rubbing Katherine's knees, saying, "It's all spilled milk, kid. You'll be right back out there." She listened to him speak, felt the weight of a present press into her lap, a new pair of gloves with her name embroidered in gold along the wrists. The tears came, making trails over Katherine's unwashed skin, patches of dried blood made slick from tears.

"Thank you, Ethan."

It had seemed as though she'd come to Chicago only yesterday, ready to learn the sport of boxing. There were such foolish moments in the beginning, Katherine shadowed in a corner, taken by the way the men hit the mitts with such ferocity.

With Ethan by her bedside, she dared not ask him the real question she wanted to ask: how was Gretchen doing with boxing? It had been months now, both women preparing for Golden Gloves while sneakily sizing up their other competitors all over town. And now only Gretchen had the chance to become a true contender.

The two had become even more competitive after their battle in the ring. Somehow, Katherine had lost a little of her fire after they sparred, as Gretchen always demanded a rematch, constantly working one more combination after Katherine finished, smacking the mitts just a bit harder on her cross or overhand, wanting it, she thought, more than Katherine did.

Katherine soon grew numb to her; the power of Gretchen's movements, her straightforward boxing style, the challenges, the fact that Katherine could beat her with ease. Yet she shrank from the pressure, letting Gretchen spar and hold tight to her opinions while Katherine quickly untied her shoes after class, still burning with the jealousy of Ethan cheering on the new girl as she landed a solid body shot, defended against the ropes, or changed stances like he taught her.

After Brandon died, Katherine had hidden in the locker room, masking her jealousy through mourning, recognizing that as much as she wanted to abandon it all and fight her way to a

A Woman's Ring

new existence, it would be of no use. No amount of fighting could bring him back again.

Nothing harbored the pain in one firm spot; not winning her second fight, missing her children, or ignoring Gretchen during boxing class. She wanted to pummel her in that ring as she once had, demonstrating her learned experience, show that she could now be calm and rational, that she loved this game more than Gretchen could ever love it – that it was Katherine's gym, Katherine's guys. Ethan held the faith of the greatest gift in her, because he'd created her from a mother, a daughter, a kind of widow. He'd opened up the black holes and poured in the great sport of boxing – plugged her wounds with hours of his companionship, of pinning, movement, countering, and relaxing in the ring. Only when she felt true victory did she understand the power, only when she saw Gretchen enter on that same canvas that Katherine had slaved on, looking unkind and muscular, coming day after day, bonding with the same males that she'd worked a year to bond with – only then did she feel that white hot rage well to the tip of her skin, blooming to tears and perspiration, for the need was in her as it had always been. She could not erase it or dim those lights; even in the hospital, held tight by confusion and pain, she would not dare let Gretchen beat her.

In Golden Gloves, Gretchen would be the one to compete, but with Katherine's heart and soul: Ethan would stand in her corner, pushing her, but it would be Katherine in her trunks, her hands in those gloves; if Gretchen won, that victory would carry only Katherine to Nationals, and there she would make her name. Yet here Ethan stood, presenting her with tokens of personal affection, and Katherine, vulnerable and needy, asked him about Gretchen, the roll of her name a memory she longed to purge.

"She's doing well," he said, looking at his shoes. "Going to the Gloves in a month...you know, training hard."

"That's good." Katherine looked at her new gloves, scratched her shaved head, the tears falling out her eyes and onto the light blue hospital blanket. She finally felt the shock of Ethan's reaction about her hair loss, the bloody and swollen forehead, but only when she started to cry did she let him *acknowledge it; did she let him look her full in the eyes and come to the bed, holding her lightly so as not to hurt her, kissing her bald, gory head, the head that had seen doctor's hands and been knocked by his. He soothed her with his words, his promises, sprinkling kisses here, then there, and Katherine, caught in a moment of weakness, spilled forth the entirety of her distress, let him hear it from end to end, from her father's love to Brandon's death, to the awful way Andrew had felt while on top of her, the weight of two babies in her womb, the tug of the gloves on her wrists and the look in a competitor's eyes when she stepped to them. The tale was hers and she uncoiled the long, repressive ropes, letting him see who his student truly was and asking that tormented question she had never before asked: "Ethan, what do I do?"*

He moved back, wiping his hands along his jaw, eyes at the floor, the window, the gloves, and back to her head again.

"Katherine...this is a lot to absorb."

He kneeled at her bedside, a stance for him she never imagined, a romantic gesture from an older man that she cared for as a mentor, boxing coach and friend. His eyes, Brandon's eyes, stared back at her, thunderous, and she knew that whatever suggestions he gave, she would run with them. She would.

"Katherine, you will always have boxing." He swallowed and swept his eyes across her face. "I know you're going to be the best out there in time. You're so young and you'll only get better." He picked at her sheets, plucking the soft fabric before continuing. "I can't completely understand all this, but you have to get your children -- as far as Andrew, I would say get a divorce, but you have plenty of time to do that, too. Just go get them, Katherine, if that's what you want – if you want them, if you want to be a mother to them. Bring them here if it's easier, or move home, but don't run from it. You'll never make it that way."

Katherine processed his words as she clung to the covers. Her head was a ticking bomb of suggestion, of answers, and when she shut her eyes to think them through, Ethan's hands closed around her fingers, squeezing them.

A Woman's Ring

"You'll never make it if you run," he said again, whispering it, trancelike, a reticent reminder of what her responsibility was as a mother, a boxer – as a woman.

"You'll never make it if you run." Once more, a lullaby into sleeping, where the only dream was the gulf of silence that met her, one gravitous pull toward home.

A Woman's Ring

Chapter Forty-four

They'd made their way to Jerry's Gym, the place where most boxers trained in preparation for Golden Gloves. It was a place where railroad tracks and run down cars littered the sides of parking lots, where patches of grass and flat land grew brown and withered, stray tires and homes that looked like pieces of junkyards with drug dealers shaking their shoulders, heads dropped low on their front porches, getting high or just coming down, drinking 40's clutched in dark brown paper bags – secrets inside their mouths.

"You ready?" Gretchen asked, sauntering into the gym as if she owned it, the same way she had sauntered into Katherine's: possessive. Straight ahead were three boxing rings, one blue, one red, one white, set up like the points of a triangle. Boxers loitered in packs, some moving like factory workers in and out of the aisleways of the gym.

Gretchen ignored the lady slumped against the check-in counter, who was scribbling something on her clipboard, her eyes moving from each ring to the girls, then back to her notations. Together, Katherine and Gretchen walked through the wide gym wings, speed bags strung up like rows of ripe, dark grapes hanging off vines. Blue mats were doctored with duct tape, spare jump ropes strewn about the hard cement floor that was stained with sweat and dirty towels. The members were in the grit of it all, doing sit-ups with wrapped hands and medicine balls. A litter of promoters hung to their left, slapping each others' chests and shuffling tennis shoes. A few female boxers were fitting on gloves at the tip of the triangle, where the red boxing ring sat. The whips from the jump ropes resonated with the steady da-dum, da-dum, da-dum of the speed bags, making a music Katherine had come to know and love. As the two made their way to the back, the lady with the clipboard caught up to them, breathless, tapping Katherine on the shoulder. As if tapped herself, Gretchen turned instinctively.

"You got a problem?" she asked the lady, pulling Katherine forward.

The lady widened her eyes, fastening two pudgy hands against her waistline. "Excuse me?"

"We're boxers," Katherine interjected, as if those words would explain Gretchen's outburst, the look of them in a place where they were not welcome.

The woman, obviously annoyed, shoved a pen behind her ear and retreated quickly, screaming the name "Jack," again and again.

"Jack – I *need* you!" She barked, breaking up the pack of old men with bubble noses and crooked jaws.

"Jesus," Gretchen whispered, unzipping her windbreaker. "If we're gonna see Nora spar, we better do it fast, before we get our asses kicked out of here."

On their way toward the back, they dodged several muscled boxers, some of whom lowered their eyebrows and bit full, split lips, swatting and whispering to their friends about the new girls. At the red boxing ring, both girls slumped against a wall, inconspicuous, flicking their fingernails. Subtly, Katherine looked for her girl, Nora. Her next big opponent for the title at Golden Gloves. Her challenge, her glory, her day. Beside Katherine, Gretchen fingered a sparring-induced knot on her nose.

"You sore?" She asked Gretchen, watching Nora with hawk eyes. Nora's rigid body mimicked most of the girls in the gym, the muscles compact but defined, her dark hair pulled back under a red checked scarf. The others around her drank water and stretched out their limbs by the ring. The white ring sat emptily, the blue one holding two heavyweights that threw slow, detrimental jabs.

"What do you think?" Gretchen asked, rubbing the knot gingerly. "How come you never got any bruises? The guys take it easy on you cause you're *fragile* or something?"

A Woman's Ring

"Right," Katherine said, folding her arms across her chest, feeling that familiar annoyance, that competitive nature that prohibited any kind of friendship between them. "The point is *not* to get hit, Gretchen. Or don't you know that yet, since you're still learning?"

Katherine ignored her reaction, instead taken by Nora, who was warming up at the heavy bags, rolling the shoulders and neck Katherine had long since memorized. This girl had been boxing for seven years, had seventeen fights, of which only two were losses. She'd been the Golden Gloves champ three years in a row, that proud title more evident with every article written about her, every interview.

Katherine stood in her territory, unwrapping Nora like some great gift, anticipating Golden Gloves, just four months away.

"Hey." Gretchen slapped Katherine's arm with one hand, the blow stinging her shoulder.

"What?" Katherine turned, following the maze of boxers toward the front of the gym and the steady thump of the speed bags to find the clipboard lady on the telephone, gesturing at them frantically.

"If Nora's sparring, she better go before we have to. 'Cause it looks like there's gonna be a problem real soon."

Two girls climbed into the red ring, warming up with soft stretches before the sound of the bell. Katherine looked around for Nora's coach, but all the men were up front; a pack that moved like machine operators, hitting bags, checking equipment, filtering in and out the lanes of the gym.

Nodding at Gretchen, she made her way toward the heavy bags. There, Nora worked, smacking the bags without gloves, her arms ripped from years of practice. The lip of her shirt shifted with each movement, revealing hints of a dark angel tattoo on her tailbone. Coyly, Katherine moved behind Nora.

"You sparring?" She asked, keeping her voice soft and steady. Nora kept hitting the bag, her knuckles making clean dents in the leather.

"You sparring?" Katherine asked again, glancing back at Gretchen.

Nora turned after a moment, grabbing her towel off a bench. Her eyes were ice, ice blue, her hands carrying little bumps along the knuckles, old scars, maybe. As she patted her neck, Katherine noticed what a weak, feminine chin she had, so unlike a boxer's.

"Who are you?" She asked, studying Katherine before looking through the mill of boxers, all the way to the front of the gym where her coach stood, leaning against a wall. There, he smacked another guy on the arm, laughing, and the factory continued. Swinging bags and bloody noses, the pack of girls who started to notice Katherine and Gretchen in a place they didn't belong.

"Just a fan," Katherine said, smiling. "My friend and I came down here to watch you spar. Would you mind going a couple of rounds with someone so we can watch?"

Nora draped the white towel around her neck, patting her face with the edge. "Yeah, I can do that," she said, extending her hand. "What's your name?"

"Katherine," she said, placing her palm firmly in Nora's.

"Nice to meet you." She squeezed Katherine's hand tightly, and cleared her throat. "Uh, I just have to get my gear, and then I'll be ready."

"Thank you so much," Katherine said, turning to head back toward Gretchen.

At the wall, Gretchen was casually chewing her fingernails.

"So?"

"Nora went to get her stuff to spar."

"Hmm."

"What's wrong?"

Gretchen jerked her head at the stocky woman who now stood right beside them, breathing heavily.

"Who *are* you girls?" The woman bellowed. "Somebody send you here?"

Gretchen smirked, spitting a piece of fingernail at the woman's shoes. "No, but you want me to send you *there*?" She pointed at the boxing ring. "Cause that's where I come from, and if you got a problem then that's where we're gonna have words."

Katherine quickly interjected, sliding a hand in front of Gretchen's chest to separate the two women. "What my friend

A Woman's Ring

means is that she's just accompanying me here, cause I'm a friend of Nora's and she asked me to come watch her spar today. I'm learning to box and I hoped to get some tips from her." Katherine leaned in closer to the woman, as if sharing a secret. "I didn't feel very safe coming alone, so my friend here," she looked back at Gretchen, mouthing, "*please* shut up," and turned back to smile sweetly at the lady, "so, my friend here decided to accompany me. Isn't that nice of her?"

The lady's face relaxed momentarily, but she scribbled something on her clipboard and returned glaring at them.

"Well, you're gonna have to sign in, cause we can't just have *anybody* walking in here. This is a business," she huffed, flicking back her bangs with small, chubby hands. "And I'll get my ass in trouble if I don't follow the rules."

"Right," Katherine nodded, seeing Nora at the edge of the ring, suiting up. Expertly, she stepped into a groin protector, shoving in her black mouthpiece, laughing with the group of girls migrating toward the heavy bags. Inside the ring, the two girls continued to spar lightly, throwing only jabs and crosses round after round.

"You think we could sign in on the way out?" Katherine asked lightly. "She's gonna spar any second now."

The woman turned to Nora, who was slipping on her headgear. "Hey, Nora, this a friend of yours?"

Three other girls turned to look at the women standing by the wall. Nora shoved her headgear back up to her forehead, removing her mouth guard. "What?"

"Tell the woman she's here to watch you *spar*!" Gretchen yelled, shaking her head in frustration.

"Stop it," Katherine muttered under her breath, smiling at the woman. She looked at Nora expectantly, and Gretchen grunted, crossing her arms over her solid chest.

"Oh, yeah," Nora nodded, slipping her headgear back on. "They're fine."

When Nora sparred, the ring came alive. Accurate punches and real technique; slipping and angling, and an occasional all out brawl. She was aggressive but relaxed, poised yet confident. Katherine fished her small note pad out of her jacket pocket and scribbled notes on the way she sparred, writing and watching until the entire gym disappeared. She burned holes in the back of her headgear, memorizing when to throw her own left hand, when Nora left herself open, what her tendencies were.

"She's not bad," Gretchen whispered, cracking her knuckles against the wall. "I wonder who's gonna get her at Golden Gloves this year?"

"I am," Katherine whispered, moving her head to the rhythm of the round. Her jabs, her movements, her combinations were the only focus; Katherine's body in her opponent's body, working.

"You girls boxers?"

Gretchen turned to the sound of a young Mexican girl, a lightweight with a faint bruise along her chin. A taller, wider boxer stood behind her, a lazy, unimpressive smile pulling her rough face upward.

"So what if we are?" Gretchen asked, standing up to her full height, which was far from threatening. The way her broad shoulders held fabric taut was enough; that and the way she fought, talked, and took punishment like a man.

"Why you here, then?" the Mexican asked, moving her head back and forth, sassing her.

"We're just watching Nora," Katherine said, uninterested in the montage of boxers that kept closing in. From up front, Nora's trainers were migrating toward the ring as they saw her in the middle of sparring. Many men were already linking their arms around the ropes of the ring, coaching the two.

"Slip, Connie! Don't let her head hunt!"

"Stick and move, Nora, stick and move!"

Nora and Connie pumped their fists aggressively, but backed off with respect when either of them slowed to adjust her headgear or clinched from fatigue.

"You wanna fight her or something?" The Mexican asked Katherine in a reprimanding tone, the taller girl swaying silently in the background. "Cause if you do, we got some gear, and you can go through all of us. Otherwise, this ain't your place to be. Comprende, chica?"

A Woman's Ring

"What the *fuck's* your problem?" Gretchen asked, shoving the small girl's shoulder. Inside the ring, the two boxers were drinking from red water bottles, resting between rounds.

"Hey!" Nora called to Gretchen, as she turned to look at her girls, at Katherine. "*Hey!*"

The small Mexican fell back into the larger one, and then a fight unleashed in perfect slow motion, fists into female faces, necks and chests. As the small girl threw a quick punch, Gretchen ducked and came back with a nasty right hand. Katherine stepped back as Gretchen's fist landed right on the edge of the big girl's jaw line, shifting it, her teeth crashing together, before her pair of solid knees literally crumpled under her shorts, a giant mass of weight spinning before smacking the cement.

"Hey! Stop!" Two men ran toward Gretchen, as both Gretchen and Katherine sprinted toward the front door, dodging jump ropes and sweaty bodies, men lined up like cellmates waiting to make bail, grabbing for them and catching air.

"Stop them!" Someone yelled, but their legs took them far past the screams, past the clipboard lady who lunged for them on the way out, past the double doors and dry fields, shack houses and trick turners yelling, "Hey, you sexy mutha, let's play, babeee!" until the train station greeted their feet, slowing them, their breath coming out in long, difficult wheezes.

There was a tingling in Katherine's belly; a taste like fire spreading inside her mouth, fire for competition, for having just one more fight before she faced her children, one more fight before she went back to Ohio, reclaiming that girl she'd left rocking on her mother's floor, pages of the Bible spread around her, tear-stained. On the train, Katherine closed her eyes to the curves and the rhythm of the ride, hearing Gretchen moan about her hand in the next seat over, her only thoughts of Nora, her only taste of fire, fire, all the way home.

Rea Frey

A Woman's Ring

Chapter Forty-five

The doors loomed ahead of her, blurred white from her still unstable vision. She felt like a visitor in her own body – didn't seem to have the proper motor skills, sight, or simple logic to make sense of things. What was a word? A movement? Feeling?

Chicago blasted her with its stale heat and visible road chatter; taxis, cars, buses and pedestrians, all on a mission, laden with briefcases and purses, shopping bags and cell phones. Katherine clutched her head, felt the waspy hair beneath her fingers, the staples glittering beneath a blood-soaked bandage. She felt like a drifter in her own world – a prisoner seeing light for the first time in years. She stepped from the hospital's doors, alone, clutching her small bag in one hand, her keys in the other. It was only seven blocks to her apartment – perhaps ten minutes of walking at an even pace, fighting through the crowds of people who regarded her as some poor, homeless girl. Some people clutched their purses, indecisive as whether to toss her a five. Some bowed their heads in shameful unease; little girls tried not to stare, but tugged on their mother's sleeves and whispered, "What happened to *her*?" Men who would have once lowered their glasses or made some offhand comment about the sexy walk of a woman now widened their eyes in surprise and fell startlingly silent as she passed them. Katherine fought the panic rising in her chest, the horrendous throb of her injury, thinking, "It's too soon to be leaving the hospital. I'm not ready yet."

She made her way to her building, gasping for air from a walk that would have once left her antsy to run, to go to the gym, to sidle down by the lake and move her limbs, witnessing the muscles pounding over hard, even surfaces. Now she was inhabited by pain and weak from minimal exertion.

Upon seeing her, the doorman asked if she was a visitor or perhaps lost, all the time avoiding contact with the wounded head. With downcast eyes, Katherine told him her name and apartment number, and that she'd had an *operation*. He opened his mouth, muttered, "Ohhh, hello Katherine" in slow recognition and then pressed the button to release the big, wooden door. She held her breath all the way up the elevator, let herself into her stifling apartment that greeted her with stray dust particles. She thought about what Ethan had said about going home, about not making it if she ran. Was this home? This apartment? This city? Or was it Ohio, with a home of lost souls she'd purposefully abandoned?

As she collapsed in her still made bed, she cradled her head softly on the pillow. She felt fragile for the first time in her life. She had always been messed up and misunderstood, but never fragile. Now she was unaided, denied the looks of a normal girl and wrapped in weariness. Thoughts of the children slammed into her mind – if they had known of her operation, would they have come? Would Andrew have brought them – brought loads of white orchids and hugs?

Perhaps she should have told them, should have begged for forgiveness and ventured into another life, invited them into this city that changed people in a matter of days. They would have taken one look at what she'd endured, kissed her needled hands and said they understood, that she had just been confused. That she hadn't really left them, just gone on a vacation of sorts. Maybe she could even learn to be with Andrew now that Brandon was gone. Open that vapid hole where her heart used to be and fill it with possibility.

As she fell into a bothered sleep, Katherine contemplated her choices. Ethan or Andrew. Chicago or Ohio. The names scattering and colliding in her shattered mind one after the other. This or that. Here or there. She would have to choose.

A Woman's Ring

Chapter Forty-six

Mrs. Baskin answered the door in a flower print dress, creases of fabric bunched and hanging on her thinning frame. The lines of her face had deepened, the lost weight causing new skin to appear as no fat was left to plump it – the skin of her neck and upper arms dangling. Betty's eyes first registered shock, then mild recognition as Katherine reached up to adjust her scarf self-consciously, firmly securing it over her buzzed head.

This was not the same girl Mrs. Baskin had watched play in the backyard with her deceased son, but a woman far removed – for in those moments, the living, breathing child she'd been was without true baggage. This woman was older, more serious. From her position on the doorstep, Katherine dared not look past the trees and sidewalk behind her, to the green shutters she'd often looked out and in from, wondering what lay beyond the confines of her old home. Now she knew: loss and victory, lust and commitment, suffering and stagnation – that long, perilous path toward recovery.

"Betty."

Mrs. Baskin's arms were around Katherine in an instant, her sagging, smaller body so foreign as Katherine's own muscular arms wrapped around the woman completely. They stood in the familiarity of her doorway, Betty with the same clothes and excess skin, and Katherine with scars and a bald head, a body produced from hard, enjoyable work and sacrifice. They shook and cried as women will, pulling back to make sure the other was real, saying all those previously unsaid words, shaming and exhausting them, mourning their grievances through inches of tears and apologies, steeping in their losses, Katherine pulling off her scarf to show her old neighbor the stubble that was now growing in, the rough, jagged scar that was just now healing, the dented marks on her forehead, the story and agony.

"Oh…Katherine, come in dear."

She walked into the aromatic kitchen, filled with the scents of real cooking, the sound of a T.V. in the den and Will, her husband, talking to someone in small, careful words.

"Will home?"

"Yeah, he's been home ever since…well, since Brandon went." Mrs. Baskin, who was wiping the counter with a yellow dishrag, collapsed forward onto her elbows, sobbing without sound. Coming behind her, Katherine rested her head on Betty's back, whispering the words she herself found hard to swallow.

"It's okay, Betty…it's okay."

"Katherine." Mrs. Baskin stayed bent over, slowing her breathing, her tears. "Katherine…the children are here."

As if hit by that same bolt of truth as when she'd heard about Brandon, when she'd heard of the cyst, Katherine locked up, unconsciously digging her nails into Mrs. Baskin's dress.

"What – my children?" She stood, retying her scarf, clutching her chest, her hips, her head, both feet retreating slowly. "Betty, *my* children?"

Mrs. Baskin nodded, motioning toward the den where Will must have been with them, reading or teaching them all the things Katherine had never bothered to. Hurriedly, she stepped back into the shadows of the pantry, sinking to the floor with her head in her hands. Mrs. Baskin moved to shut and lock the door that separated them from the hallway and den, the sounds of Will now blocked from the kitchen. Katherine needed to hear just one sound of Frankie or Lily, who would just be turning six, one sound of their speech, that memory so far from her realm of thought, but brought back now as if resurrected. Mrs. Baskin pulled up a chair in front of Katherine, sitting withered and beaten. Leaning forward with her hands clasped between her legs, Betty waited until Katherine spoke.

"And Andrew?"

A Woman's Ring

Betty shook her head, sighing heavily. "Katie, honey, he's seeing some woman who runs a new beauty salon. I keep the kids during the day and the two of them pick them up at night. That woman smokes all the time. I think she even smokes right in front of them, blowing it in their little faces, forgetting to feed them sometimes. She's made Andrew lazy, if you ask me."

Katherine listened, lost in shallow breathing, shocked to hear that Andrew was with another woman, wondering if she'd even see him again – if there would be a struggle between them as she'd once imagined, often picturing his chin on others.

Then her children, ramming back into memory, those sweet, precious souls she'd neglected and despised. Perhaps they hated her or wouldn't remember her. But she knew of their intelligence, their memory, that her neglect would not be forgotten, just as her adopted mother's disregard was not forgotten and never would be.

"Betty...there's so much to say, I don't know where to begin." Katherine reached up to squeeze Betty's hand. "I'm so scared they'll hate me, Betty. What if they –"

"Nonsense." Mrs. Baskin patted her hand, pulling her lips into a smile. "I tell them where you've been and why, Katie, even if I didn't approve of it. Trust in me, they love you and have been waiting patiently for you. I've never seen two children who just want to love their mother...no child since *you*, I believe."

Those words brought back that familiar yearning in which Katherine was a child running, always chasing to capture a woman's affection, a woman who probably hated her life more than she hated her adopted child. And then Katherine running from her children, at first uncertain in loving them and now loathing herself for all her selfish choices.

Will began to knock at the kitchen door, and Betty, silencing Katherine with one hand, cleared her throat. "I'll be out in a second! Just hold the fort down in there! I've got a surprise for everyone!"

She waited until his footsteps were in full retreat before she pulled Katherine to her feet, studying her.

"You look so different, Katherine, so much removed from this world." She turned to unlock the kitchen door and Katherine caught her wrist, seizing an opportunity for the one thing she needed besides her children, an answer to a lifetime wonder.

"Betty, I know this probably isn't the right time, but do you know anything about my adoption?" Katherine stammered over the words that had ached to burst free from her lips to her own mother, her own father, begging them to tell her. "It's the only piece of my life that I still –"

Mrs. Baskin wiped her hands across the front of her dress and walked slowly out of the kitchen, and back toward the basement. She was gone for several minutes and Katherine found herself looking around at all the cupboards and even the tile that was cracked by so many years of use. How many times had she played in this kitchen with Brandon, making snacks or coloring at the table?

Another minute passed and then Betty re-emerged with a set of legal papers, a contract with the court of Katherine's adoption. Her adopted parents' names, along with her birth certificate with the blanks on it where they had later filled in Katherine Ann Sinclair. Enclosed in a small envelope behind the other documents was a letter addressed to her adopted mother, and before opening the soiled flap, Katherine knew what it would hold – a letter from her birth mother saying she knew not what, but her writing would be there, cursive or printed, the i's dotted in strange slashes or bubbles, all of it there, concealed for over two decades, away from Katherine's curious hands.

"Betty?"

"It's a letter from your real mother." She nodded as if to confirm Katherine's knowing, nodded as if to encourage her opening it, unfolding the back flap, bringing that paper to her nose, inhaling the traces of her as she'd inhaled the traces of Brandon's death letter, her elation deflating at the thought of those words, the cold way Betty had written them, the tragedy of ending all romance in a young girl's life.

"How do you have these?"

Mrs. Baskin looked at the floor, pausing, before looking back up to Katherine, small tears dotting her eyelashes. "Your mother was always afraid you'd find these, Katherine. I'm not sure Bruce even knew about the letters. And after he died, she

A Woman's Ring

gave me things – your birth certificate for one. It's like she wanted to erase all evidence of...well, anyway, I know she burned the other letters, burned any evidence of your adoption, besides your certificate, but she gave this letter to me a while ago, told me to hide it from you and to never let you see. This was the last letter I believe, and maybe there was some small hope in her that you *would* find it, that I would give it to you and that you could ease a little of that pain in not knowing by at least knowing who your real mother was in a way." Mrs. Baskin took a long breath, wiping her tears away. "God, Katherine, if I cry anymore about anything, I'm going to have to be locked up, I swear it. Let's get this over with before I kill myself in the process."

"Wait –" Katherine placed a hand on Betty's arm. "Why did my real mother write to my adopted parents?" Katherine turned the letter over in her hands, not wanting to open it quite yet.

Betty sighed heavily, dropping her hands at her sides. "Her name was Gail Peterson. Your parents had an agreement with her when you were first adopted – it was an open adoption, and they met with her in this very town, and agreed to stay in touch for the first five years to see how you were progressing."

"You mean they actually *spoke* with her?"

"Yes." Mrs. Baskin turned away from Katherine, placing her hands on the counter. "Though I'm not sure your father ever got a chance to. Your mother seemed to control that whole situation." She stood again, rubbing the small of her back. "When Gail gave birth, she was young, sixteen maybe, and she thought your parents could take much better care of you. The father wasn't around, I don't think, and she just wanted you to be happy."

"Yeah, well I don't think that worked out too well, huh?"

Mrs. Baskin lowered her head, shaking it slowly. "Well, regardless, they stopped communicating, even when Gail still tried to. They said that you were just fine and that she should get on with her life. I never met her, don't know where she went or lived. But that letter's hers, Katherine. That's all your mother gave me of her."

Katherine tucked the letter into her pocket without reading it, waiting for a perfect moment she'd have alone, to indulge in the words, memorizing each token of information revealed.

"This is all so much to think about, Betty."

"I know, Katie, I know."

Mrs. Baskin moved toward the locked door, her hands hesitating, waiting for Katherine to push her on toward the children.

"Go ahead."

Betty slowly twisted the lock, pulling the door back on its hinges, walking ahead into the den, making that long journey down the hallway toward them. Once there, she clicked off the T.V. and stood with her arms crossed over her sagging bosom. Katherine followed slowly behind, knowing she could not be seen if she stuck to the left side of the hallway, attempting not to look at Brandon's pictures that still hung on the walls in their cheap, gold frames. Shots of him in grade school, on the soccer team, in the science fair. In his cap and gown at graduation, a big smile on his face, but anyone could see the pained eyes staring back at the lens – from Katherine's recent decision to marry Andrew. All that misery she'd caused.

In the shadows, Katherine could make out the tops of the twins' heads, Frankie's blonde hair in a bowl cut, Lily's curls bouncing at her shoulders, that small, feminine voice begging Mrs. Baskin to show her the surprise. Will sat in the chair across from the children, a look of utter shock on his face as Katherine stepped from the shadows, her hands clasped into fists at her sides, taking centimeter steps toward the back of the couch, where she stopped, her breath catching sharply as Frankie turned first, that face with so little of Andrew in it, his eyes so like her own, fastening with hers, at once familiar and strange, his small voice uttering that soft, foreign word, "Momma," like the most perfect of names.

For that was what she was, Momma, a mother, a lost parent. Lily turned, both children squealing and crying, leaping over the couch's back to rush her as she fell to her knees, feeling the skin she had never appreciated rub against hers, their soapy smells, their fingers now encouraging, as they twisted at her face and

A Woman's Ring

chest, questioning, "What happened to your hair, Momma? Your long hair?"

And Katherine, laughing, drank them in, murmuring, "Oh God, oh God," while Mrs. Baskin and Will huddled together over them, all of them a mass of salty tears, the reunion of Katherine's blood beside her, them crying, "Momma," her name, "Momma," their love a life unlived.

A Woman's Ring

Chapter Forty-seven

They lay atop her like heavy blankets, pressing their skin into her armpits and fingers. In Mrs. Baskin's guest room, they snuggled in the same bed, Betty having told Andrew the kids wanted to stay over. Katherine did not see him, though she wanted to, wanted to walk right up to him, run her fingers through that oiled up black hair, pulling it taut, bringing his head down to meet hers, biting his tongue, his cheeks, spitting on him, cursing, reminding him of all those years when there was never a whisper of love, never a sweet, stolen look over coffee, or prospects of romantic interludes between them; the husband, inarticulate and distant, the wife, a replica of stone.

Andrew was her biggest purging – that face she would never forget, that weak jaw she'd wanted to tap so many moments until it bled from the same places she bled, until he could see what he was and what he'd made out of her, until he was beneath her even, beneath hatred.

Frankie and Lily's little feet dug into her hips and kneecaps, one on either side of her, snoring softly. Katherine's scar burned in the darkness, the jagged soft tissue along her close-cropped head. On the top of the dresser sat the letter she had hoped for almost as much as her mother's laugh, or Brandon's hands – there it sat, read over fifteen times already, as she'd sneaked peeks through talking to the children, reading "Dear Mrs. Sinclair" while making them dinner, "I just wanted to know" while getting them ready for bed, "how she is," all the while excusing herself again and again to reread a part she may have skipped over, closing her eyes in an eager attempt to reinvent her mother; for in Katherine's mind, she liked Gail best, unknown, young, and beautiful. So many times, she'd created a life for that woman, almost living through her imagined freedom. That was the way she kept Brandon; not dead, but simply in another world, still blonde, still shooting hoops in his backyard, still wrestling in the hypnotic summer sun.

Perhaps Gail would be the same; a gift she would keep in times of sadness, that letter a keepsake for contemplation – that search for her because she needed it and not to fill her loneliness. Katherine would wait until she felt that impulse inside her to find the woman who'd given her away.

Frankie's legs began to twitch, then Lily's, as if they were two minds sharing the same dream. Katherine wondered how close they were now, how close they'd had to become for all the anguish she had caused them. How could she have been so utterly selfish? Leaving Andrew, with his steady job and hectic schedule, to help these children with their homework, make nutritious meals, and tuck them in.

Their minds must have developed at such rapid paces, their first pre-school days burdened by taunting children and the rumors around town. Katherine would forever be the cause, the mother who'd run away and given up on them.

Maybe she would take them to Chicago – to share with them what had molded her into the person she had become, the person she had always been but never in Urbana. Perhaps they'd meet Ethan or Maxx and live in her high rise apartment, gawking at the tall buildings and trapped noise that existed on every street, take them to the toy stores and down to the lake to play on the beach as she once had.

The weight of their bodies was now crushing, gone from heavy blanket to concrete, as Katherine once again felt the panic of having to be so much for them. To always worry where they were or what would become of them – when really, she could only worry about herself, her own path that had been so full of self-destruction and loss; she didn't know how to receive them.

Mrs. Baskin's eyes, when the children had reunited with Katherine, had been filled with anguish; anguish like losing

A Woman's Ring

Brandon, like losing hope; anguish that only mothers may bear. She wanted these children in a way Katherine never had, fully and without conditions. That was her calling; her mind mad with a mother's passion and Katherine's with regret and unmet responsibility.

Moving from under their heavy limbs, Katherine slid the letter off the dresser and stepped into the kitchen for a glass of water. Her head beat, as it always did when she got up – still tender, her walk still dreamlike and unbalanced.

In the kitchen, she began to cry – feeling like she would never slip on another red glove, or hear the mitts sound from hard punches, throwing and reacting to shots of beauty, shots deflected and reciprocated. Would she ever be that lively girl again? In the ring, Katherine felt an utter sense of control, but outside it was sheer torment.

She placed her empty glass down on the kitchen table, feeling its smooth top, tracing her name in the shade of light dust, fingers pushing against wood. Unfolding her mother's letter, she read it once more, wiping her tears far from the paper so as not to blur the ink.

Dear Mrs. Sinclair,

It has been a while since I've heard from you and I must ask if Katherine is okay. I know I made the decision to give her up because I am young and wouldn't know the first thing about raising a child, but I can't help but tell you that after having carried that baby for nine long months, I feel I am attached to her in a way that you never can be.

Please don't misunderstand me, as I'm not trying to be rude...I just miss her. I realize she spent the first three years in an orphanage, and I could have just as well taken her back, but I did not and when I met you, I couldn't help but think she would be better off with a good, Christian family. I'm sorry this is full of sentiments and so unlike my other letters. I'm just confused, I guess. Please let me know how she is, and if there's anything I can do for her, though I suspect everything is okay with her and that's why I haven't heard from you.

Is it wrong to still want to be in her life, Mrs. Sinclair? To want the best for the child I carried? Maybe we could meet for lunch and discuss how she is in person, or maybe I could see her? She's four years old now, does she know about me?

Again, I apologize for all the questions. I hope to hear from you soon, Mrs. Sinclair. Please send the best to your husband.

Sincerely,
Gail Peterson

Her every word Katherine could relate to – that fiery resistance to give up something that was hers, but struggling with the massive responsibility at such a young age. She knew that if they ever met, Katherine would not face her with resentment, but rather with empathy, as though she was the mother and Gail the child, wrapping her in arms similar to her own, Gail's heavy with age spots, Katherine's still firm from the ring.

Strange, how she felt an urge to locate her number and beg for guidance on this decision – should she leave Frankie and Lily once again, if just for a little while, so that she might figure out what kind of person she would be with or without them? If she had just a little while longer, she could do it. Could be the mother they deserved.

That night, Katherine slept on the sofa, checking on Frankie and Lily every hour or so, their bodies still tangled as they'd been in the cradle as loving infants.

"My babies…" she whispered, dragging her feet back into the living room, plopping down on the ragged sofa, shaken from the choices before her; faced once again with leaving and returning to Chicago, where she might heal and collect herself; or staying in Ohio, starting again, raising her children while learning the art of love.

A Woman's Ring

Chapter Forty-eight

She dreamed on Betty's couch, of rising and walking into Brandon's room, where she fished through his sock drawer and found mounds of her panties, bundled up, with red marker on each of them that said, "I've always loved you, Katherine, I've always loved you." In the next drawer, she saw a boxing ring and the first day she'd been in it. Ethan holding up the mitts and Katherine standing there with her hands on her hips, embarrassed to be exposed when she didn't know what to do, but honored, too, as people stopped to stare at the tall, pale girl who seemed so serious. There was that first jab, her first cross, Ethan adjusting her legs and hips and hands, the hook that became her punch, the power of it coiled in her shoulders, whipping her arm like stirring a big pot of soup, resonating off that leather pad, bam, "again," bam, "again," bam-bam, the onlookers impressed, much as she was. It was a kind of sex in that ring, a climax when she got something right, when Ethan would rub her shoulders or smile a thousand smiles until she finally felt as though she belonged.

In the next drawer was a funeral – the funeral of her father and Brandon, two men sharing the same face, half of it weathered and lined, the other half smooth and innocent, dotted with stale drops of blood. Brandon was half her father, half himself. His face was still intact, peaceful, as Katherine would always remember it, and leaning ever so slightly toward it, she kissed the cold flesh that evaporated beneath her tongue, the skin like cotton candy, dissolved by the warmth of young blood.

In the last drawer were Lily and Frankie at birth, Katherine looking down on herself in the hospital bed, Andrew squeezing her hand that she kept wrenching free, her tortured screams clipping a vein in her head; then tears as out came one, then the other, followed by the long, hard depression she fell into after.

When she'd first discovered her pregnancy, she thought there was no stair high enough, no drug potent enough, no drink strong enough to erase it – her luck would be to break an ankle and not the babies, to destroy their minds and still have to raise them as slow, damaged children. She sulked and waited – nine long months of weight gain and fatigue, her husband often coming home smelling of panty hose and cheap perfume. She knew where he'd been and didn't much care; she was more upset that her magical plan had backfired, that money had prevailed over love, that Brandon's rejection had pushed her into marriage, into babies, who cooed and cried and messed their clothes and she hated that clean-up, hated that rocking, hated that washing and drying and fawning all over them; always knowing that in the end, Andrew would take better care of them than anyone, that she'd been wrong to think she could outsmart him, that he had probably pressed his dick into any open crevice in town and outside it, that his business trips were full of cocktails and breasts while her life had been void of love until she'd moved away, searching for another's face, thinking that maybe Brandon would change his mind for her. That boxing would fill her lonesomeness.

As she drifted from dream to dream, she saw Frankie ten years from now, he and Lily blowing cigarette smoke at the ground, their eyes rimmed black, their hair a deep, dirty brown. They were sickly thin, and as she looked at them, moved to them, she saw Andrew's face replace each of their faces, him smiling, saying, "Funny how I tricked you, Katherine. It just goes to show how impatient young girls can be." Over and over until she was shot from waking, until the smell of breakfast filled her senses, until her eyes opened and Frankie and Lily stood in front of her, both carrying the same plate of pancakes with syrup running off

A Woman's Ring

the sides and dripping onto Mrs. Baskin's carpet. Their eyes were so bright, their faces so eager, saying, "Here Momma, we made you breakfast," Katherine's own eyes wet as she took the plate, each kid an extension beside her, their giggles, their laughter, those familiar hands pulling at her skin, wanting to feel the newly shorn hair, wanting so much to be part of her.

She chewed quietly, feeling the syrup drip to her bare thighs and slip off to the couch cushions. She ate as they chattered – wondering if this was what it would be like if she stayed here – them serving her breakfast and her listening to their conversation; a mother with no home who knew so little of the craft of raising them; making so many mistakes and errors that she didn't know if it would be better to run away again or endure their lifelong resentment. She knew what that felt like; resenting a mother, wishing what could never be undone, and with Katherine's absence, at least, they might never know how bad she would have been. It was as her birth mother had done – run away from the child.

"Thank you for breakfast," Katherine said, as they quickly removed her plate, laughing heartily as their little feet pattered against the carpet back into the kitchen with Mrs. Baskin.

She looked at the drops of syrup on her legs, reminded of the drops of blood she'd seen in her dream on Brandon. A choice was now presenting itself once more. In a world where her dreams had become everything, where getting brain surgery was the sole purpose in having a slim chance to box again, could she carry on as a young mother, carry on as if none of this had happened?

She reached up and gently touched her scar, feeling the bumpy incision still inflamed and scabby. Katherine shuddered from the intensity of the pain, ignoring the dreamlike state she was still in, as if her limbs couldn't quite move, as if her brain was lost in a deeply disturbed fog. She slowly made her way to what used to be Brandon's bathroom. She stared outside the small square window, looking out over the backyard where she'd played so many times. Stifling a cry, Katherine dressed quickly and slipped out the back door to take a walk through the neighborhood. And there it was – the same streets, the same tired stores and backyard sales – the stifling town of Urbana at her every stride, stalking.

A Woman's Ring

Chapter Forty-nine

She'd made a plan. Once back in Ohio, she would confront Andrew. Apologize, and then place blame while explaining why she'd left them. Their marriage had been a farce and everyone knew it. It had been a means – and only that – to fill each other's selfish needs. But as selfish as Katherine was, she couldn't have terminated the pregnancy. It had been the thirteenth week before she even truly figured it out, as her periods had often been irregular, as well as her weight. She figured once they were born, it wouldn't be so bad, that she could be a mother and a boxer and a wife who traveled the world.

Once back, she'd told herself, she'd let Andrew know just what he'd done to her, how she'd felt when away pursuing her dreams, what a mistake it had been to marry him. But as she made her way to their old house, she faltered. Her hand hesitated before pressing the doorbell, knowing he'd be in there on a Saturday afternoon, taking a nap or doing some extra work while the children were off at Betty's.

She waited, twisting her hands into two rags, staring at the peep hole. When he opened the door, she saw the same man she'd married, except for the eyes that had softened, the spark that had gone. His hair was now past his ears, his skin a grayish pale. She swallowed as his face registered first complete shock, then submission, each of them staring with little traces of compassion. What had once been fire in Katherine's eyes was now contempt, and in Andrew's she glimpsed only anger for what she'd done to their family.

He took in her altered appearance, the sickly thin body with the exception of her newly massive shoulders that could only be attributed to countless hours of punching. The stubbled head was a shock, appalling, really, with the braised pink scar running from ear to hairline.

"What – what happened to you?" His voice was surprisingly warm. If he closed his eyes and pictured a cooler, softer Katherine, he could pull her into his arms and kiss her sweet scars to welcome her home.

But this had never been her home and he knew it. He'd always felt it, and blamed it on her desire to travel. He never wanted to believe she didn't love him, but any fool would have seen the way she looked at him, with adamantly resigned expressions.

He asked the question, eyeing her closely as she opened her mouth – the mouth he'd first kissed in the passenger seat of his car, the same mouth that could spit such harsh words and screams – now faltering for something to say to her husband.

She closed her lips and looked past him into the front hall, far, far removed from who she once claimed to be.

"I – had an operation, but that's not why I'm here. Actually, I don't know why I'm back, but I do know I want a divorce. As if that even needs to be discussed, but – "

She hesitated, losing the nerve she'd worked over a year to obtain. Guts and anger. Revenge. But as she looked at him, all she felt was a dull ache from the mistakes she'd made.

Andrew shifted his hand from the doorknob to his hip, a small smile curving his lips. "You really think I'll give you a divorce? After you just up and leave, deciding you want nothing more to do with *our* family, and now you're back so you can destroy it even further? You think I'll simply give you what you want because you've had some sort of *operation* and you look like hell? What about what *we've* been through, Katherine! Do you have any clue as to what I've had to tell the children!" His hands shook, his face engorged with blood and unkempt emotion.

A Woman's Ring

In an instant, Katherine remembered why she'd left. Why she hated him so much and herself even more for not being the kind of person her children deserved, and for tying herself to this man. She looked down at her shoes, then up again, finding bravery somewhere beneath his daunting words.

"Andrew, do you think I don't know what they've been through? What we've all been through? How about starting from the moment I lost my *virginity* to you, huh? How you swore to me everything was going to be nice and easy and romantic and instead it was forced on me in a mad fit of hormones! You want to talk about abuse and anger and frustration – then let's talk about the way you treat women!" She was finally saying the things that had been trapped for years, finally releasing the pent up emotions. Katherine took a step closer to him, inching him deeper into the front hallway. "And how would you have a clue as to what I ever wanted, huh? You don't know me, never did. You simply wanted a girl you could mold into a passive wife who would carry your babies and somehow, in a moment of absolute *stupidity*, I accepted your proposal!"

Andrew opened his mouth, but Katherine continued.

"And you know what that gave you? A *life*, Andrew – a chance to become a responsible father, which is the only thing you happen to be good at. And do you know what it gave me?" Katherine let the silence descend, let the tension mount between them. "It gave me nothing, Andrew – a vast, cold emptiness that I carry with me everywhere. To Chicago, I carried it, through boxing, through competitions, through the death of my only love and through fucking *brain surgery*. I'm the one who has it bad – not these children, who play all day long and are Daddy's little angels. It's *me*, who has nothing but scars and a reminder of what I could have been – me, that feels the rotting stench of my own decisions with every step I take."

Andrew let out a string of curses as Katherine continued, raking a hand across his face.

"All I've ever wanted was to get out of this town and make something of myself – to please my father, who never got to experience his own dreams. Well, you made me into something,

Andrew – someone I despise. And I will always hate you for that, even if I rot in Hell for what I've become. Though I can't imagine Hell being worse than living here with you."

She spat the last words, felt their power as Andrew dropped his head and sighed dramatically. She knew he'd probably start crying, trying to win her sympathy. That's how he worked. Spitting truths and cowering. Yelling then giving in. There was a pause between them as Andrew collected his thoughts, then released them quietly. "Katherine, you think I don't know all of this – that I don't know your feelings about me? I wanted to be with you because I thought I could change you. I thought if you had some sort of security in your own town you'd want to stop running and you'd realize there *can* be life where you were raised. You think I don't – "

"I'm not finished." Katherine silenced him with one look. "Because of my choices, four lives are ruined. Frankie and Lily's, though I truly think they'll be happier without me. My own existence, which has been proven almost worthless, and Brandon's." She said his name softly, still feeling the ripe pain at the two syllables, at the stifling memories. "My one true friend in this world is now dead and I never got to see him again. Live with that guilt, Andrew. Live with the knowledge that you killed your best friend." Katherine rubbed a hand over her scar and dropped her voice. "Because of my decisions, he's dead. And I know he was probably still mad at me when he died." Katherine let the tears fall freely, wanted Andrew to see how much she'd always cared for that boy. "And all because I married you."

"Katherine, it wasn't –"

"Andrew, I know what I did is the absolute worst thing a mother can do, but if I had stayed, you would have resented me even more than you do now – I am not a mother, I can't be at this age…I never had a mother and the only parental figure I had died when I was eight years old." Her voice caught, and she noticed Andrew reaching for her. She straightened up and crossed her arms. "I didn't come back here for your forgiveness, or the children's. So please don't patronize me and don't give me a hard time – just give me my divorce."

A Woman's Ring

Andrew turned away and stomped down the foyer, sitting on the leather couch that now faced the front windows. "Fine, Katherine, I'll call my lawyer on Monday. If that's what you really want, then fine."

Katherine walked up behind him, enraged. Was he not listening? Of course that's what she wanted! "Do you seriously suffer from some sort of personality disorder? One minute, you're blaming me for everything and the next you're a normal human being, asking if it's what I really *want*? Have you not been listening to me at all? Make up your – "

"Katherine, please."

Katherine stopped talking, a wave of fatigue suddenly hitting her. She heard the pain in his voice, the seriousness.

"What about the children, then? What do I tell them, Katherine?"

Katherine walked to the opposite side of the couch and sat with a groan. She leaned forward, placing her head in her hands. "Andrew..." She said his name in a gentle whisper, the kindest and softest he'd ever heard his name uttered. He leaned forward instinctively, reaching out and placing a hand on her back. She bristled at the contact, then let the feelings wash over her, the absolute confusion and surrender.

"Andrew, I just don't think I can do it. I don't want to be one of those mothers who gives a fake smile, who's divorced and only sees her children on the weekends. I can't live here with you in this house and pretend. We both know how bad I am at that."

Andrew sighed, falling back against the couch cushions. "Yeah, we do."

Katherine lifted up, her face red and tear-stained. "*Thanks*, Andrew. I appreciate that."

"Katherine, I know you don't think you can handle this. I know you've got unfinished business in Chicago, and that's fine. That's where your life is – that's where it should have always been, I guess. I know you think all this is a mistake, but Frankie and Lily are not. They're perfect. They're *ours*. Yours and mine. So however much you hate it, we will always be connected." He paused, licking his lips. "And I'm not asking much. Go, if you have to. Take a few months to calm down, to figure out what you want to do –" He stared at her head, grimacing - "to heal. But don't give up on all of us, yet. Please, Katherine. It's not just about you anymore."

Katherine let out a breath and nodded. "Andrew, it's never been about me, that's the problem. And I can't make any promises, but I can promise to think about it, to let go of all this resentment and to come back here… to see about things."

Andrew smiled, a genuine smile, and said all the things he wanted to through his eyes. Perhaps they'd all move to Chicago, perhaps she'd never come back, perhaps they'd all forget her. But in that moment, looking at her scarred head and obvious pain, he knew what she needed. He knew what she needed to finally let go.

"Katherine."

She looked at him, expectant, almost hopeful.

"You should go back to Chicago."

A Woman's Ring

Chapter Fifty

The bleachers rocked with spectators, men with draft beer in plastic cups, women with Golden Gloves T-shirts on, rooting for their child or girlfriend waiting in the wings for competition. The blue ring sat in the middle of the gymnasium, the basketball goals cranked up and secured with rope, so as not to block the view. Folding chairs dotted the area around the ring, six rows deep, where people had to pay fifteen dollars per ticket to sit, feeling as though they were V.I.P.s. Girls walked on the bleachers, dropping bottles of water into their gym bags, picking up hand wraps and flexing their muscles while looking at the onlookers admiring them. One of those competitors was Nora, smiling with her trainers, cool and lean. Would Katherine ever have her in that ring? Were all those nights spent analyzing her movements, mastering the skill of beating her deemed worthless now?

Katherine sat with her bandanna secured tightly around her head, dressed in black, inconspicuous in the very top row of bleachers, gazing down at the hard, blue box and the people surrounding it, her eyes searching quietly for Ethan. His face now haunted her memory as Brandon's did, the two of them merged into one, Ethan an older replica of the boy she once adored. Katherine watched the first three bouts, covering her face in embarrassment and frustration as these girls lumbered forward throwing windmill punches, showing less skill than beginners. Her hands balled into fists as they had on many occasions, her legs prepared to run down to the registration table and enter this competition, if just simply to prove that girls could fight.

The crowd, seeing the first three contests, began to boo, then cheer incrementally as someone's nose bloodied, a girl went down or fell into the ropes, covering her face with her forearms, trading punches into punches, attacks into unplanned attacks.

Beside Katherine, she felt the ghosts of her children, intrigued as she knew they someday would be when she would be the one fighting in Golden Gloves, and they would be watching with smiles of pride for their mother.

"I'll see you soon," she'd told them back in Ohio, clutching the twins to her waist, covering their ears so as not to hear her decision to leave yet again, toying with them in the worst way. She'd given them glimpses of a mother, only to walk away again, leaving their big eyes full of tearful hope, leaving them with Andrew's girlfriend, who smoked and laughed and dropped ashes on their skin. She'd already arranged for them to come stay with her next week, to show them the city and become reacquainted with them. It gave her a purpose, it gave her hope to be a better mother, to start over with them.

She knew that if she wanted to stay in Chicago, if she wanted the children to have a secure place to stay, she needed a substantial living, and with the help of Ethan she would soon have many interviews for positions in fitness or possibly even a boxing coach. He'd talked to her about starting his own gym, and though she did not know the first thing about running a business, she knew she could devote her life to it and be happy.

Outside the ring, Katherine spotted Ethan in a hooded sweatshirt, followed by Gretchen wearing a red Golden Gloves jersey. Her stomach curdled at the sight of Gretchen – trim but muscular, that mouth of hers set in a firm line, a winning line.

Ethan whispered words of encouragement in Gretchen's ear, as Katherine jumped up from her place on the bleachers, knocking someone's beer over in the process.

"Hey, watch it!"

"Sorry," she muttered, pulling her bandanna tighter as she stepped over small and large bodies, making her way down the steep rows of bleachers to the lip of the balcony, leaning over it to watch Ethan encouraging her enemy.

A Woman's Ring

On the blue side, a thick, dark girl parted the ropes, smacking her gloves together, raising her fists to the crowd. Not Nora. They roared all around, and Katherine stood, indignant, her head pulsing, wishing that she was in that ring, her limbs uncertain in the first round as she felt out her opponent, flicking out jabs, backing off, feinting then landing a big overhand, a body shot, a double right hook, her feet moving backward before the counter, Katherine so able to find the gaps in her opponent's game.

The bell rang and the two stepped forward, Gretchen anxious as she stuck out her jab and caught one, shaking it off and ramming into the other girl, as much as Katherine had in her first fight. She wanted to stay all evening, to wait quietly in the wings for Nora; that sweet ache in Katherine's belly as she'd witness Nora winning another title, when it should have been Katherine, when next year it would be Katherine, and only then – her head healed, her heart and mind, all of it pieced back together until she could dominate that woman, dominate boxer after boxer, round after round, rising to the professionals – where every last spectator would be impressed with her game.

Katherine found herself urging Gretchen on, willing her to slip, to fake, to counter. All that practice and she was blowing it, getting caught on the ropes, using muscle over finesse, missing uppercuts and body shots, always flailing. The girl that had tried to outdo Katherine was now outdoing herself, her shoulders too tense, her arms swinging mechanically, not dancing as Ethan had taught her, those quick feet that moved and twirled and lifted, those arms that swung and pummeled. All of it in Katherine's body as a stored memory, but to Gretchen it had never been so. She was still the same girl who caused trouble and spoke without thinking, wanting this game not for the beauty, but the brawn of it, for the toughness that she would never acquire because her intentions were not pure.

At the end of the second round, Ethan's eyes caught Katherine's, magically finding hers in that sea of anonymous people. Katherine leaned out over the balcony's edge, as if to touch him with her longing.

He stood from his crouched position outside the ropes, and Katherine saw him sigh; she saw his eyes fill from all those feet away, perhaps looking for her absent children somewhere behind her. Katherine felt the sudden pull in her chest to go to him, to let him hold her, to feel the thick, solid arms encircling her. The third round began and Gretchen stumbled forward, landing a jab, missing one, falling back into the ropes where uppercuts smacked her chin, then her jaws, grazing her nose enough to bust it up, where she would place ice packs every twenty minutes for the next three days. Katherine made her way down the remaining steps, past the tables with boxing gloves and jerseys for sale – past rows of people who looked at her gaunt frame covered in black pants and a long-sleeved shirt – past Nora who narrowed her eyes with an ounce of recognition, slapping her trainers' arms, whispering, "Isn't that one of the girls who got in that fight?" – but she kept walking, finally unafraid, finally a woman who'd owned up to her mistakes and was willing to make more if only to take this great chance on her dream. Assuredly, she walked – over to the side of the ring where Ethan stood, who yelled repetitively at Gretchen to throw a double hook.

In the last thirty seconds, Katherine took it all inside her – the goal she'd achieved of winning a fight, of coming to this city and making something of herself through trials, through doubts, through death and mourning; the unexplainable ache that pumped through every core nerve, every breath, as if Brandon was now living inside the tissues of her body, his spirit pumping her heart until she would one day vanish, condensed to bone, then ash, then nothingness.

Ten seconds left and Katherine slid up behind Ethan with her eyes closed, smelling him; the signature scent of a grown man who'd had much experience and had listened to her own tale with a slow, sad smile, who critiqued her and pushed her and held the faith of her talent like a mentor, a lover, a man. The bell sounded, and it was over – Gretchen was out of the finals, sitting on her stool, defeated and slick from her shunted minutes of fame. Ethan placed a hand on her shoulder as Katherine placed a hand on his. He turned, smiling softly with sentiments unsaid. They stood

A Woman's Ring

student to trainer, their eyes full of so much possibility in a crowd of many women, many men.

    Whatever happened now, Katherine knew that she had made it. Life was, she decided, a woman's ring, and she had lasted one more round. For today, that was victory enough.

REA FREY

Photo by Uchida Photography

Rea Frey currently lives in Chicago with her husband. She is a recent graduate of Columbia College where she obtained her B.A. in Fiction Writing and was Valedictorian of her graduating class. She is an amateur boxer as well. *A Woman's Ring* is her first novel.

Order These Great Books Directly From Limitless, Dare 2 Dream Publishing

Cat on the Couch by Cathy L. Parker	16.00	Hilarious
Kara: Lady Rogue by j. taylor Anderson	15.00	Adventure
The Amazon Nation by C. A. Osborne	15.00	Reference
A Woman's Ring by Rea Frey	16.00	NEW
Sweet Melody by Liana M. Scott	16.00	NEW
Deadly Rumors by Jeanne Foguth- OUT OF PRINT	15.00	VERY Limited
Walnut Hearts by Jackie Glover	17.00	NEW
Soldiers Now by Dean Krystek	16.00	November 2004
Home to Ohio by Deborah E. Warr	15.00	Mystery
The Mysterious Cave	12.00	Children's Adventure
Where Love is Not by Deborah E. Warr	16.00	NEW Ellen Richardson Mystery
		Total

South Carolina residents add 5% sales tax.
Domestic shipping is $3.50 per book

Visit our website at: http://limitlessd2d.net

Please mail orders with credit card info, check or money order to:

Limitless, Dare 2 Dream Publishing
100 Pin Oak Ct.
Lexington, SC 29073-7911

Please make checks or money orders payable to **Limitless**.

Printed in the United States
23432LVS00004BA/274-276